SUBURBAN SECRETS
A NEIGHBORHOOD OF NIGHTMARES

Edited by Amanda M. Lyons

and John Ledger

READ ORDER

29	7	31	67
	57		
161 (4)	141	125	89
153	165	189	205
19	177		
47	227 (12)		
115 (10)			

Edited by: Amanda M. Lyons and John Ledger
Cover Art by: David McGlumphy

http://jellingtonashton.com/
Copyright.

T.S. Woolard, Michael Kanuckel, Essel Pratt, Zoltan Komor, Kevin
Candela, Tina Piney, Jorge Palacios, Alice J. Black, C.S. Nelson, Amanda
M. Lyons, Michael Noe, Brian Barr, Dani Brown, Kent Hill, Dixie Pinoit,
Richard Ramsey, Jim Goforth, Justin Hunter

©2015, Authors

Table of Contents

Suburban Secrets (an acrostic)
By T. S. Woolard

S uburban nightmares, whispers of fear,
U sing legend to push darkness from underground.
B orrowing from murmurs of rape, murder and devastation,
U neasy feelings hold the community hostage,
R eleasing terror and destruction among residents.
B usy mouths and force fed hands wreak havoc
A nd are on the verge of destroying the streets.
N o one dares to put a toe across the line.

S ecrets evolve into monumental lies,
E roding a frail security in hearts and minds.
C razy neighbors, serial killers, and the supernatural
R eplace home makers, gardeners and chirping birds.
E verlasting demons overtake the jungle,
T hreatening to turn it into the gate of Hell.
S uburban Secrets—inner-city innuendos of horror—has begun!

About T. S. Woolard
    T.S. Woolard lives in North Carolina with his wife and five Jack Russell Terriers. For more of his work look for Indiana Horror Review 2014, and Ghosts: Revenge by jwkfiction, Floppy Shoes Apocalypse by J. Ellington Ashton Press, Siren's Call 'eZines #17 & 18, and his short story collection, Solo Circus. To connect with him, follow on Twitter @TSWoolard, or visit tswoolard.wordpress.com

The Town
By Michael Kanuckel

There was a package wrapped up in brown butcher's paper and twine leaning against Bryan's front door when he got home. Frowning, he picked it up and let himself in the front door. The rest of the regular mail was on the floor just inside the front hall, resting wherever it fell after coming through the brass mail slot. Bryan had never actually seen the postman--it was said around town that he kept odd hours and sometimes delivered the mail in the early morning or the middle of the night, depending on his whim. He was a peculiar old bird by all accounts, but the mail was always delivered in a timely fashion and so no one had any complaints.

Bryan took the long, thin package and leaned it against the wall, which was done in a leaves and sprites wallpaper that he had just finished hanging only a day before. Matched with the hardwood flooring, it made the front hall quite cozy. As always, he took a moment to look around his house and admire it; things were coming along quite nicely. He found some lovely pieces of furniture at the store and also from the peddler who came through once a week with various odds and ends (sometimes just junk, but Bryan had heard that occasionally the peddler brought very rare items indeed), and the place was really coming together.

It felt like home.

There was quite a bit of mail. Bryan knelt down and swept the envelopes into a pile, shuffling through them: a letter from the homeowner's association, congratulating him on his recent landscaping work (he had found some rose bushes and planted them along the side of the house in fresh, dark cedar mulch); a flyer from the store (special on apples tomorrow); two more letters from his new neighbors inviting him over to say hello; a post card from Dinah, his neighbor from two houses over, with a casserole recipe. Bryan saw a letter from his mother and set the others aside with a smile on his face. "Tried yoga for the very first time!" the letter said in his mother's huge, loopy cursive. "Your father says that my 'downward dog' looks more like a camel's foot, whatever *that's* supposed to mean…."

Bryan laughed out loud, shaking his head. "Oh, Mom," he said. Still grinning, he turned around to investigate the strange package leaning against the wall. There was a card attached to the twine; he plucked it off and read it. "Plenty of good fishing in the stream!" the card said. "We have a little competition going this month for the biggest bass caught- take the day off tomorrow and go try your hand at it."

The note was signed by Adeline Cook--his boss.

Bryan tore the paper away and revealed a thin, limber fishing rod with a silver reel. Still smiling, he pretended to cast it a few times in his front hall. The wrist action and weight of the rod felt good. It was a lovely instrument.

"Take the day off and go fishing," Bryan said to himself, walking into the living room with the rod slung over his shoulder. "Unreal."

Sometimes, he still couldn't believe how lucky he was. He had felt the need to leave home and start a life of his own, just one day out of the blue, but he had no real plan, no destination and no idea what to do when he got wherever he was going. He got off of the train here because he liked the name of the town--Jefferton. At the station, he stood and looked over the little village built on a series of little hills, lights glowing in the houses with a golden warmth, and fell in love. Then it had started to rain. A little fellow in a tidy vest came up, chided him for not having an umbrella, and then gave him one; and a job, and a house to rent. Just like that.

"Just like that," Bryan said, setting the fishing pole on his kitchen table and getting ready to make some tea. It was a good life: he spent his days running across the town making deliveries from Cook's store, chatting with his neighbors, and exploring the museum or the pocket parks and gardens sprinkled here and there, or just sitting by the fountain in the town square. He had even spoken to the mayor once or twice, a nice old fellow who liked chess and pocket watches.

He had a good life. He also had the day off to go fishing tomorrow, but as he went to his bedroom and got ready to lie down for the night, admiring his new book cases and the little lamp at his bedside that had a metronome built in the base, he thought that maybe he might do something else with his free day.

***

"Next stop is Springerton!" the conductor said in his big, booming voice. He looked as resplendent as he had on the day Bryan took the train to his new hometown, dressed in a blue wool tunic with gold piping on the sleeves and shining brass buttons closing it up from throat to waist. The conductor looked like he might be a real character when he wasn't on duty; something about his long side whiskers and the slightly crooked tilt of his hat seemed to indicate that he could be a bit of a rogue if you saw him in the pub and bought him a round.

"Springerton!"

Bryan sat back in the plush, red velvet upholstered bench seat and smiled. He was always smiling, it seemed. And why not? He turned his head to look out of the window as the green country rolled by then, and his smile started to fade. Away in the distance, seen through the heavy canopy of the forest, he caught glimpses and flashes of what looked like houses, and gardens, and the canopy of a gazebo not unlike the one on the edge of the cobbled town square at home. Closer to him, he could have sworn that he saw a shunting of the train tracks he rode on, curving away in that direction and covered over with reddish-purple vines and pale flowers.

Reaching out, Bryan caught the conductor by the sleeve as he passed by. "Pardon me, sir," he said, "but what about that town over there?"

The conductor looked out the window with a frown of concentration, and then his eyes widened slightly and his face went over pale. "There is no town over there, sir," he said, releasing his arm from Bryan's grasp. "You are quite mistaken." And then he went on down the center of the aisle of the long passenger car, shouting "Next stop is Springerton! Springerton!"

Bryan's frown deepened. He was most certainly not mistaken; he had seen the buildings through the trees, and the tracks in the earth. He had seen the face of the conductor as well; had seen a fear in his eyes. What could it possibly mean?

9

***

No one would talk about it.

His neighbors, whom he did indeed get to know and to like (for the most part) as time went on, would turn the conversation aside immediately if Bryan so much as brought up the town he had glimpsed through the trees that day on the train, overriding him with comments on the weather, or the new furniture they just put in their living room, or the big trout they had seen at the bend in the stream, where there was a small waterfall. Even Dinah, who Bryan was starting to think of as his "special" friend, with her sweet smiles and her big blue eyes and her penchant for carrying an umbrella even on sunny days to protect her very white skin, wouldn't talk to him about it. There was a map of the surrounding countryside outside the entrance to the train station, and another one at the police station in the middle of town, but neither of them showed a town between here and Springerton. They looked suspiciously new, in a town where everything felt very old.

Bryan was tasked by it. When he went to bed he would toss and turn, and then get up and turn on his lamp and go to his book cases to find something to read, but there was nothing there that he was interested in; the books had come with the furniture, quite a bargain he had thought at the time, but they were all dull. And the town had no library. When he *did* manage to get to sleep, he had fevered dreams of leaning, vine-covered houses with no lights to be seen in the broken windows, and something pursuing him through thick brush and clutching tree limbs until he woke, gasping and sweating and tangled in his blankets.

***

"You need to let this go," Mister Cook said to him one morning.

Bryan looked up from the wooden crate he was packing for a delivery run. "What?" he said.

Mister Cook smiled at him. It was a tired smile; fall was coming on, and it was a busy time of the year for him. With the changing seasons came the harvest, and new designs of furniture and fixtures that were all the rage in the big city that he would need to stock in the store and have installed, and he was also in charge of getting the town decorated for Halloween when it came.

"Don't be coy," he said. "You know what I'm talking about. It's a small town, and people talk. You've been seen, standing in your window at night and staring off into the woods. You've been asking questions that no one likes- and that no one will answer, anyway. You need to cry off, boy."

"Mister Cook--"

The small, tidy man waved a hand at him. "I like you, Bryan," he said. "I trust my gut when it comes to strangers, and I liked you as soon as I saw you there at the train station, standing in the rain without even a coat, let alone an umbrella. You came here without a single red penny to your name, a stranger, and what did I do? I gave you a place to work. I gave you a place to hang your hat, even though you couldn't pay until you started earning money here. You fit in here, like I knew you would. Your neighbors like you- except for this one thing that's bothering everybody and getting them riled up. Cry off. Let it go."

"Mister Cook," Bryan said, meeting his boss's tired, black-ringed eyes with a plea in his own. "What's out there? Why won't anyone talk about it?"

"It's *not town business*," Mister Cook said. He almost snarled the words, his lips lifting to reveal his little sharp teeth. "It's all fine and well to hop on the train and go visit other towns, son. We all do it from time to time, just to see what other folks are up to and take in the flowers and the trees and see how things are going there. Maybe we even bring something back for our own houses. But in the end, this is our home- Jefferton is *our* town, and our town is really all that matters. You belong here. It's up to you to keep the town well. Now, no more of this nonsense- and that's an order. Understand?"

"Yes, sir," Bryan said.

"Good! Now, let's shake our tails, eh? You get this order down to Mister Bloo's house in ten minutes, and he said he would have a tip for you. Hop to it!"

***

11

His breath came out in hot, jagged gasps. There was a dagger of pain in his side, and his left ankle was swollen from a bad turn on a rock and wouldn't support his weight as he ran blindly through the trees. A branch caught him in the cheek, just under the eye, ripping at his flesh and bringing hot blood. Up ahead, so close but impossibly far away, he could see the glow of the big glass-globed lamp that marked the edge of town- of home.

The brush rustled behind him. They were still coming, hopping and limping their crooked, misshapen way through the woods, and they were gaining. The ones who had stayed; the faithful, the ones who watched and kept the town well. They were closing in on him and he ran and ran, a low whine that was part pain and part despair coming from his throat, and the heat of his breath was scalding in his chest. He stumbled on the banks of the stream that was mild and peaceful in town but here was wider and deeper, dark and somehow ominous, and when he went to one knee in the mud they were on him, pawing at him and fawning and mewling-

Clawing at the air, a scream halfway up his throat, Bryan struggled with his bedclothes and rolled onto the floor. At his bedside, the lamp cast a buttery yellow light over the cozy room. The bedroom was cool, though; fall was almost here, and there was a chill in the air. He got up on shaky legs and went to shut the window that he had left open before going to bed because it had been such a crisp, pleasant evening. *No wonder you had a nightmare*, he thought as he pulled the window down and secured the latch. *Mom always said that being cold while you're asleep gives people bad dreams. It's freezing in here.*

Outside in the darkness, a few small lights twinkled in the windows of his neighbors and the wind sighed through the trees, whispering a lonely song of the winter that would soon be coming; no more fruit on the trees, no more flowers in the gardens, the hills made vague under blankets of snow. Bryan looked beyond the limits of his hometown, into the forest, and somewhere between the swaying branches of the old trees he swore that he saw a light-- a light from the town no one would talk about, the place everyone pretended didn't exist.

The voice of Mister Cook rose up unbidden in his mind. *Cry off*, his boss said. *It's not town business. Leave it be, son. Cry off.*

Bryan put on a new outfit from his wardrobe and rushed out

the door.

***

A strange sense of vertigo swept through Bryan as he stepped out of the woods, and he swayed on his feet. The town ahead of him looked just like the one he had left.

"That's impossible," Bryan said to himself as he stood there, a tremor in his voice.

When he took the train from Jefferton to Springerton and walked the streets there, he had been struck by some similarities in architecture and layout. He had passed this off as a regional thing; towns had a tendency to have commonalities when they were close together. This was something completely different than similarity, though: the streets; the burbling stream; the layout of the houses-- they were just like home. This was Jefferton, if some disaster had struck it and left it for dead.

What had once been neatly cobbled lanes were now humped and cracked pathways overgrown with lustrous green weeds and vines as thick around as Bryan's forearm. The small houses lining the streets were dilapidated shacks, dirty with neglect and leaning under the strain of standing untended in the elements. On some lots there was nothing to indicate that a house had stood there at all but for a muddy basement and ruined foundation; in the darkness of one such pit that he edged up to, Bryan saw a few articles of clothing and a chess table floating in three feet of foul water. Eyes wide with disbelief, he walked on toward the center of the town. *I'll come to the fountain and the gazebo soon*, he thought, and they were there. The fountain was choked with weeds and riotous flowers, the grass thigh high in the town common. The gazebo, that had once been painted a bright yellow, was stripped almost clean of paint and gleamed bone white in the moonlight. The delicate latticework walls were smashed and strewn over the ground.

A furtive step behind him made Bryan whirl around.

"Stranger in town, eh?" a voice said. The words came out uneasily, as if the speaker had not said anything for quite some time; the voice was rough as gravel, quavering and weak. "And with not so much as an umbrella." Shaking his head, the small figure in the gloom stepped forward and Bryan gasped.

13

It was Mister Cook.

Some terrible transformation had taken place in the kindly old man Bryan called his boss and friend, though. His tidy little vest was moth-eaten and faded, hanging from his wasted frame as if there was nothing to the man but skin and bones. His hands were bent, gnarled claws, the knuckles swollen and bunched and the fingernails gone black. His glittering eyes were sunk deep into black hollows, with a gleam as cheap as fake jewelry you could win at a fair game. "First time out in the world on your own, son?" this ghoulish transmogrification of Mister Cook said in his grating, phlegm-clogged voice. "What's that you say?" he went on, cocking his head. "Moving here? Why, do you even have any money for a house?"

Bryan heard a low whine building up in his throat; as close as he could come to speaking. He knew these words, because he had heard them before.

"Well, now," the shabby, tattered Mister Cook went on, shambling closer. "I could use a new worker down at the store. Very busy this time of year! And I might even have a house you could rent. It's small, but it should suit a young man of the world like you. Yes! That settles it, then! Let me show you to your place, and in the morning you can get to work!" The old man rubbed his hands together, producing a thin, whispery sound that made Bryan's skin crawl. He looked just like a rodent, wiping its paws over a morsel of cheese.

Bryan turned to run. Something struck him, and the world went black.

***

He came to at the train station--or what was left of it. In the wide plaza spreading out from the station's platform a huge bonfire blazed, flames crackling and licking at the night and giving off a sick, feverish heat. The flames illuminated a tremendous statue that stood there of a man in a pair of shorts and a flappy T-shirt with a stylish hat on his head. The statue beamed out at the town, arms raised up in victory. Bryan squinted against the light of the bright flames, his vision swimming as he tried to focus on the bit of profile he could see of the statue's face. He couldn't help but think that the golden sculpture looked a bit like him, and for some reason he didn't feel very surprised. *Its shock setting in,* he thought. *Or, maybe I fell back asleep after that first nightmare and none of this is happening.*

Several figures approached the station, shrinking back from the bright flames of the bonfire. They were dressed in rags and filthy, torn clothes, but underneath the grime and the stains Bryan thought he saw more than one pattern of clothing that Mister Cook sold in his store back home in Jefferton. He was sure of it. The people came on, and they were carrying something with them- some sort of wooden seat, supported by raw tree branches for handles. They set the chair down carefully, with something like reverence, and backed quickly away. Bryan looked on the pile of rags and trash in the seat, puzzled, and then with horror when the pile moved and the flames showed him the emaciated frame and blasted face of the mayor.

That it was the mayor was something that Bryan did not doubt. A tarnished pocket watch chain, silver going green, hung down from the pocket of the frayed, patched suit jacket. The scarecrow figure's shoes were worn away to nothing but flaps of leather, but dirty spats that had once been white still covered the tops of his feet. A top hat leaned jauntily on the old man's head, where a few wisps of hair blew about like dead straw and his skin was raw, and covered with weeping red sores. The mayor hobbled closer with the aid of a cane, and Bryan shrank away from him with fear and disgust; the old man looked like something beyond death, and he smelled of unwashed flesh and rotten meat.

"Did I not say it would be so?" the mayor said, peering into Bryan's face with milky, cataract covered eyes. Turning uncertainly, he wheeled to face the other gathered at the station and held his own arms up, mirroring the golden statue that towered over him. "Did I not say it would be so?" he said again, louder this time. His voice was haggard and hectoring, the voice of a done old man screaming at the children on his lawn. "Long ago it was, that our friend and benefactor Twink came to us here in Hoboton. He came without a bit of money or a place to live, but we took him in and befriended him. He planted flowers and trees, and caught the fish from the stream, and pulled the weeds along the paths. He wrote us letters and gave us gifts, and we all loved him."

"We all loved him!" someone in the crowd shouted, and others murmured agreement. Bryan peered at the speaker: knotted yellow hair, and pale white skin underneath the dirt and grime; she carried a lacy umbrella in her hand-- it was Dinah.

"And then there came the day when our beloved Twink got on the train and never came back," the mayor went on. Some of the people in the crowd wailed, shaking with their weeping. "Where did he go? No one knew. We thought only that he might have visited another town, and would soon return. But he did not. Weeds began to grow over the flowers. The fruit rotted on the branch. The fish swam away down the stream and perhaps into the distant sea. The cockroaches burrowed into the furniture and ate the stuffing from it. And our friends and neighbors, faithless and without courage, began to move away as well. They took the train and they never returned!

"But we few remained," the mayor went on. "Yes, we knew that this was our town and that one day, when we could not know, our beloved Twink would return to us and set right all that has gone so terribly wrong. Now, that day has come!"

The wasted people in the crowd let up a ragged cheer, waving their limbs in the air and looking on Bryan with a fever in their eyes.

"You're all mad!" Bryan said. "This isn't my town! I'm not this Twink, whoever that is! I don't belong here!"

"Oh, but you are mistaken," the mayor said, his eyes glittering in their sockets as he hobbled closer. "You've been away too long, your wits are addled. Everything will be put right, now that we have you back. You'll see."

"You're crazy if you think I'll stay here!" Bryan said.

"Calm yourself," the mayor said. "All in good time, my boy. Now, I'm sure that our Mister Cook can find a place for you to stay, and in the morning you can get to work. First, though, there is the matter of the new Law." Smiling, the mayor turned back to his people and raised his arms again. "What is the Law?" he said.

"Home is home and that's where you'll stay," the people said in one voice. "That is the law."

"Home is home," the mayor said, turning back to Bryan with the flames from the bonfire gleaming on his parchment thin skin. "Home is home and that's where you'll stay, Twink, my dear little lad."

A huge shape rose up from the shadows on the far side of the bonfire, and in his hand there was a saw, the steel glowing orange.

"No," Bryan said, the word falling from his mouth with no force. He didn't have the breath to scream, it seemed. When the mayor took hold of his right ankle and pulled it out straight in front of him though, he managed a scream well enough.

***

Lee set aside the novel he was reading and looked over at his son. "You know what I was just thinking of?" he said.

"What?" Robbie said, looking up from his PC game.

"*Friends and Neighbors*," Lee said. "We used to play that all the time. Collecting furniture for the house, and new fish for the museum, planting fruit trees...that was really fun. I even managed to pay off my house and get that statue in my honor at the train station, remember? Whaddya think? Wanna play?"

"We haven't played that in, like, three years," Robbie said. "Can you even imagine what our town would be like? Weeds everywhere, and bugs in all of the houses, and no friends or neighbors anywhere, that's for sure. Everyone would have moved away."

Lee chuckled, picking up his book. "Yeah, our town would be completely destroyed," he said. "Just imagine: the train goes by and someone asks the conductor 'What's that town over there?' And the conductor gets a scared look on his face and says 'There *is* no town over there, sir.'"

"Yeah," Robbie said. "Except, not everyone moved away, and they've all gone crazy, and they have some law-shouter like in that one book--and every once in a while someone riding the train at night can hear them out there, howling under the moon. 'What is the Law?'"

Father and son laughed.

On a dusty shelf beneath the TV in their entertainment center, the game lay silent.

17

About Michael Kanuckel

Michael Kanuckel lives in a small rural town in the middle of Ohio with his two sons. He has been writing since he was in kindergarten, and always knew that he wanted to be an author. Now he is.

Post Traumatic Return
By Essel Pratt

Upon my return, I didn't know what to expect. I knew the world would continue in my absence, without restriction of fates or destinies. I trusted my sacrifice would serve as the catalyst for the world to open its eyes and see the product of its sins and usher salvation. I went to war to save their futures. Now, as I walk the hollowed street, I weep before their displays of damnation.

My father set forth a prophecy, foretelling my second coming, like Jesus' did for him. He told me that my return would usher forth a new me, define my purpose in life, and purify my biased thoughts. He said I would return a hero, a leader, a deity in my small town. I anticipated a welcoming reunion, greeted by those that would praise my heroic deeds and celebrate me with pomp and circumstance.

None of that happened. I left the desert base on a Tuesday morning, to my Mishawaka home by Friday. The airport was nearly vacant, except a few older gentlemen that sat in front of a large window, sipping on coffee, and talking shop as planes returned and left. I noticed that each wore patches in their khaki shirts, signifying their sacrifice in Vietnam. I stopped to salute them, only to be ridiculed by their disgusting attitudes. I would have thought of all people, they would understand.

"You just get back from Afghanistan?" one asked. "What a damn shame you bloodied the sands for a war that wasn't ours."

"Disgusting, if you ask me," said the other as he took a drink of his coffee. "You probably sat on that damn beach filled country for the last year, or so, and drank margaritas and light beers. You wanna call yourself a soldier and wear our country's uniform, try fighting in a real war like Nam. When a hundred of your closest friends die, then you will be a soldier. Right now, you are only a pawn controlled by the government."

The words hit me like a ton of bricks. My head felt heavy as I stared at the floor, hunching my back I walked away. If a random guy on the street had said the same, I would have laughed it off and punched him in the face. Hearing it from a couple of Vietnam vets crushed my soul. Instead of pomp and circumstance, I got ridicule and berating. Maybe it made them feel better about getting the same treatment when they returned. Maybe.

No one was waiting for me, so I walked home with my bags slung over my shoulder. Maybe they didn't know what day I was to arrive. I tried to call, but the pay phone ate my quarter. So I walked, it was only thirty miles, I marched more than that in a day, in over 100 degree temperatures while I was overseas. The light drizzle outside was the only welcoming feeling I received upon my return thus far.

The walk home was met with indifference and blank stares. A couple people offered me their loose change and some dollars, mistaking me for a homeless man. One car that sped by threw a fountain pop at me, others yelled out hateful things like calling me a child killer and traitor. It seemed that the consensus believed we were sent over to Afghanistan to destroy a culture, rather than liberate it. I felt like shit for even being involved.

Before reaching my father's house, I decided to stop at the nearby park where I spent most of my childhood days playing with my friends and hanging out while trying to pick up girls. There were so many great memories there. I hoped to see some old friends and share some stories from our youth.

In place of the park, a series of bland condos were constructed, replacing the laughing children, and the undying memories. I found myself drawn to the old pond where cattails grew wild and the sticky algae that coated the surface was the perfect place for frogs to hang out. With the construction of the new homes, the pond also found new life with a border of manicured lawn and an artificial waterfall to help filter the water.

I stood in this same spot once, before I traveled the world to parts that were lesser known, where scared inhabitants lived out simplistic lives amongst the sandy flora and fauna. Now, in place, there are towering structures serving as tokens of status, where a simple abode would have sufficed if the park had to die. I felt a lump form in my gut as I think about the sacrifice I made to go to war, leaving my own land unprotected, only to be destroyed by my friends and family and those close to my own hometown.

Sadness overcomes me, as I am stricken with grief. I came back hoping my experiences in the Middle East would open my eyes to the beauty of my own little slice of the planet, only to find that my anticipations were just pipe dreams.

I hang my head as I sit upon a wrought iron bench staring at the fish filled pond, wondering where all the frogs had gone. A soft June breeze bushes across my face, sending a chill down my spine. It must have been eighty degrees out, but I was chilled in comparison to the triple digit heat I had become accustomed to. My mind was a whirlwind of thought; I realized I had no job, no formal education, and no sense of how the modern world worked after a three years of absence. I was a stranger in my own hometown and had no idea where I fit in.

While lost in thought and minding my own business, an older gentleman dressed in a fancy maintenance uniform approached me; his gruff voice causing me to jump in my seat.

"You can't be here," he said in a demanding tone. "No vagabonds allowed. If you don't live here, you don't belong. Now, get out before I call the police."

I stared at him blankly for a few seconds, wondering if he was serious or not. I couldn't believe it when I realized he was our old high school janitor, the one that used to tirelessly clean up after my friends and I spray painted graffiti on the walls or clogged the toilets with paper towels. He doesn't seem to remember me, and I don't make it a point to introduce myself. I did ask if he used to work at the school. He said yes, but that was before they tore it down and built a new on in the next town over that housed twice as many students.

I realized that a lot can change in such a short period of time. I realized that I have changed as well. I am not sure that I am a fan of change.

I didn't attempt to strike up a conversation with him, it would just draw out the uncomfortable feelings that I already have. Instead, I slung my duffle bag over my shoulder and walked toward home without saying goodbye.

Home was only a few blocks away, but it seemed so much

further. Nothing looked the same to me, it was all unfamiliar. Even old lady Dampney's house, which was bright blue for years, was painted white and her manicured yard was overgrown and littered with trash. A young black man was sitting on the front porch. I could only assume she had died, because her racist attitude would not let anyone without pure white flesh on her property. I waved to the young man and continued onward.

Home was just a few houses down. I could tell, as I approached, that nothing had changed there. The same wicker rocker was on the porch, an old coffee can ashtray sitting next to it, and the same flowery curtains hanging in the windows. My mom bought those curtains the same week she died. I always hated them, but they are the only welcoming thing I had encountered up to that point.

Dad's car wasn't home, so I decided to head downtown and see if he was at his office. My legs were tired, but the cool breeze and light drizzle felt good upon my body. It had been so long since I wasn't drenched in sweat and sand.

I walked for a few miles before reaching the edge of town. It was an old business district, not too large in size, about ten city blocks with towering buildings from the early 1850s. I grew up there, playing in the alleyways with my friends. I knew every nook and cranny that could be used to hide beer and cigarettes. They were a welcome sight in comparison to the canvas tents I stared at for the previous few years. Still, they seemed so unfamiliar to me.

I crossed at the corner of Main St. and Third St., near the library. As I stood waiting for the light to change, a man on the opposite corner held a sign that read, "The end is neer." I would have laughed at him in my youth, but I felt sorry for him. I wanted to point out the misspelling, but realized that he wouldn't have cared. Instead, I cross the street and smile at him.

There was a piece of paper stuck to his chest with a safety pin. It said that he had terminal cancer and only months to live. I wanted to stand with him, get to know him, learn about his pain. He knows that he is sick; he knows that he is dying. Yet he stands, each day, upon this corner spreading word of his love for God. I imagined that in his mind he hoped to save just one soul, as he yelled out, "repent, repent, and repent." I wished I had his bravery and clear view on the world.

A group of teenagers stopped to laugh, and ridicule his existence. I sat and watched, without a word, weeping at the scene. They soon grow bored and toss some coins into the old man's lap. He gathers them up and places them in his pocket, yelling out, "God bless you, I'll donate them in your name," ensuring they can hear him over the city's noise.

I couldn't handle it and walked away. After two steps, the man grabbed my hand tightly and asked me if I had been to hell. I simply replied with a yes and pulled my hand loose, walking away faster.

"Repent with me, we will rise to heaven together," he yelled after me. I raise my hand to wave thank you, knowing that the horrendous things I did overseas were not worthy of salvation.

Just around the corner, my Father's office windows were empty and the furniture was all gone. In the window sill sat the coffee cup I gave him when I was only seven. The black coffee that was within had long ago evaporated, leaving dark rings around the interior circumference. I stared at the cup for a long time; time ceased to exist until a car at the stop light honked its horn at another that was traveling too slow for his liking.

I stopped a man that was walking by and asked where my father's business had gone, without sharing that it was my father's. He looked inside, a mournful look spread across his face.

"Mr. Tinley's insurance office?" he said. "The papers said he died last week. Poor guy, he died alone. Rumor has it his son died in Afghanistan, so the landlord donated all his stuff to charity and cleared the office out. The last few years have been rough on him."

As the man spoke to me, I hung my head, but not before realizing that he and I used to play in the surrounding alleyways as kids. We were never close friends, but he did not recognize me. Maybe I had changed much more than I thought I did; maybe I was not longer the same person that I was in childhood. I knew I wasn't.

I was lost, with no idea where to go or what to do. I figured I could go home, sit in dad's favorite recliner, fester in sorrow for a few days, but what good would that do. My father lived a long and meaningful life. He earned the peace he achieved in death, with no need to repent. I, however, was full of sin and regret. My head began to ache with intense throbbing and my chest felt like my heart would burst. I had to find a place to be alone and gather myself. So, I rushed into the alley behind my dad's office.

Nothing had changed in the alley, the same old dumpster sat near dead end next to an old rusty blue door. I could still see the "f" word on the side; I had spray painted it there when I was only thirteen. It was quite faded, but still there.

I sat behind the dumpster; my legs pulled up to my chest, and cried. Images of Afghani children ran through my mind, each one with a face matching those that I killed. I didn't do it because I was a murderer; I did it because they had guns and grenades and wanted to see me dead. That didn't make it less traumatic. I hadn't had a chance to think about it while there and always looking over my shoulder.

The guilt and regret was too much, I had nothing left at home to celebrate, no one remembered who I was, and everything had changed. I ruffled through my bag and pulled out my survival knife. The two toned tan camouflage was quite noticeable against the gray surroundings. I wanted to end it all right there; I just needed to build the courage to do so.

I cried hard, my tears mixing with the rain. A few times I touched the blade to the flesh of my neck. Each time, I pulled it away and don't know why. Maybe I was a coward. I sobbed until I fell asleep, soaked in my clothes and cold. Still, I slept the best sleep I had in a long time; uninterrupted.

***

"Hey, are you alive?"

The poking of a stick on my face woke me from the dead sleep; I jumped in fright and grabbed the stick from the boy's hand.

"God damn it," I yelled at him. "What the hell are you doing?"

"Sorry," he said while the two boys at his side giggled.

I handed the stick back to him, apologizing for being so rude.

"Hey, is that your knife?" one of the other boys asked. "Are you in the army?"

I stared at him, seeing the excitement in his eyes. "I was, I just got home."

"Awesome," he replied. "I am going to join when I get older. How cool was it? Did you get to drive a tank?"

His naivete put a smile on my face. He didn't know me, didn't know the horrible things I had done overseas, but he felt comfortable enough to talk to me, unlike the old guys at the airport that had lived through my hell.

"I wasn't a tank guy, but I did drive a Hummer," I replied.

The third boy's face lit up. "My dad works at the Hummer plant, he installs the headlights. I bet you could see for miles at night with the ones he installed."

"I have never seen better at night. Maybe I'll have him install new headlights on my car; I know I can trust his work."

The boys began asking questions at a lightning pace. I answered each of them with an age appropriate response. It felt amazing that someone, regardless of age, was interested in me and the service I dedicated to the United States. All the horrible thoughts I endured throughout the day seemed to fade away amidst their innocence. Their youthful banter reminded me of my own at their age. It made me realize that I wasn't alive just for me, but for others as well.

The sun started to fade and the boys decided that they had to get home. Each said their good byes, and left one by one. The boy that poked me with the stick was the last to leave. He reached out his hand to me and I held mine out to his. As we shook, he said thank you, then walked away.

After a few steps, he turned and asked, "Are you going to get PTSD?"

I wasn't sure what to say, so I just stared at him.

"My uncle came back from the war and got it," he said while staring at his feet. "He cried a lot and stayed inside all the time. It made me us all sad. Then he killed himself and we weren't sad anymore. We were happy he was in a better place."

I couldn't believe what I was hearing.

"A better place," I asked, not believing my ears. "How can you just be happy that he is gone?"

The boy continued to hang his head, kicking his feet in the dust on the ground. I could not comprehend how he could be happy that his hero uncle had killed himself. I know he was young, but how could he be so disrespectful and crude.

"Are you not going to say anything?"

He started to weep, still looking down at the ground.

"God Dammit, do you even understand what your uncle did for you? He sacrificed his life so you can stand here in this alley and speak your mind, and all you do is weep while hiding your face, and tell tales of how happy you are that he is gone?"

I wanted him to run away, to leave me alone, but he stood there without saying a word. I began to think he wasn't there at all. Maybe he had already left and I was imagining him standing there. My own mind could have been mocking me. *God Dammit*, I said under my breath.

I tried to clear my head, but the sobbing youth was still there. I yelled for him to leave, but my words flowed through him. The disdain was driving me mad.

I grabbed the knife from my knapsack, hoping to scare the vision away. Looking at the ground, it did not see the blade in my hand. It proved to me that the child was in my head. I had to do something.

Clutching the knife tightly, turning my knuckles white, I stabbed at the air to erase the vision. I was startled when the cold steel met with resistance, but I kept slicing away amidst the confusion in my mind. I was blinded by rage for an amount of time that I could not intellectually measure.

When I came to my senses, my eyes met with a mangled mess of a disemboweled child before me. I fell to my knees in disbelief.

"What have I done?" I asked myself between sobs, while staring with eyes clouded in tears. "He was real, God damn it, he was real!"

I thrust my arms upon the ground, splattering the puddled blood upon my own clothing and flesh. It was warm and reminded me that the boy was real. I spent my entire tour of duty fighting to save boys like him from the Hell I endured; only to send him to God knows where.

I fought Satan's brood overseas, only to become the Devil himself. I needed to do something quick, so I acted on instinct. I rushed to the dumpster and emptied a large black bag, careful not to tear it open. I rushed back to the boy's remains and shoved them into the bag. Luckily, he was small in stature. One he was tied shut; I tossed him in with the other refuse, careful to pile more bags on top of him.

There was still a mess of blood and bits puddled on the ground. A water hose attached to a nearby spigot made clean up quick and easy. I was confident the alleyway rats would devour the pieces of skin and leave behind no trace at all.

The cleanup was quick and painless, yet I felt like shit. I wanted to end my own life, to do to myself what I did to that young boy. I was a piece of shit.

I held the knife to my throat, wanting so bad to end the nightmare. Yet, I could not do it. I was weak. Everything I fought for meant nothing anymore; my life no longer had meaning.

I sat on the ground, my back against the wall of the opposite building, and looked up toward the sky. The sun was high overhead, too bright to stare at, so I affixed my gaze at the building across from me.

The navy blue door directly across still had stickers that spelled my father's name. They were peeling and faded, but still there. I felt ashamed to have killed the young boy in the rear of my father's insurance agency. I had to make it right and killing myself was not the answer.

I searched my mind for an answer, not expecting to find anything but regret. Instead, I could only think of helping others in some way, to make my sin right.

Before joining the service, I became licensed to sell insurance, with a plan to become my father's partner one day. I never had the pleasure of sitting at a desk next to him. Yet, I thought, maybe the time had come to take his desk, and help those that might need some reassurance after a loved one is seriously injured or passed away. Just like the parents of the young boy that sleeps eternally in the garbage can at the end of the alley.

I grabbed my duffel and slung it over my shoulder, walking casually out of the alley and back toward my father's house, where I planned to rest for a few days before starting my new journey toward post-traumatic growth.

About Essel Pratt

Essel Pratt is from Mishawka, Indiana, a North Central town near the Michigan Border. His prolific writings have graced the pages of multiple anthologies, a couple self-published works, as well as his own creations.

As a husband, a father, and a pet owner, Essel's responsibilities never end. Other than a family man, he works a full time job an hour from his home, he is a writer for the Inquisitr, a full time student on his journey to a degree - while maintaining a 4.0 GPA, and is also the Chief of Acquisitions and Executive Assistant for J. Ellington Ashton Press. His means of relieving stress and relaxing equate to sitting in front of his dual screens and writing the tales within the recesses of his mind.

Inspired by C.S. Lewis, Clive Barker, Stephen King, Harper Lee, William Golding, and many more, Essel doesn't restrain his writings to straight horror. His first novel, Final Reverie, is more Fantasy/Adventure, but does include elements of Horror. His first zombie book, The ABC's of Zombie Friendship, attacks the zombie genre from an alternate perspective. Future books, that are in progress and yet to be imagined, will explore the blurred boundaries of horror within its competing genres, mixing the elements into a literary stew.

You can follow Essel at the following:
www.facebook.com/esselprattwriting
Esselpratt.blogspot.com

Secret Skull House
By Zoltan Komor

Some bratty boys from the neighborhood decide to make a secret clubhouse in my skull. They don't ask me about it, but I have no argument against the plan. So, every afternoon getting home from school, they occupy my head. The kids laugh loudly, and crack their chip bags. Sometimes smoke flies out of my ear. I suspect they are experimenting with their first cigarettes. Of course, I was just like them when I was their age, so I'm not going to tell on them, that's for sure. If only they wouldn't leave such a mess every time. It can be really awkward--when having a conversation with someone I begin to shake or nod my head and suddenly a crumpled porn magazine falls out of my ear.

Soon, the parents get wind of the secret clubhouse, and they step into my apartment swinging a bone saw. They insist on looking in my skull; telling me they have the right to know what their boys are up to behind their backs.

Now, the kids and I are both punished – they are grounded in their rooms, as for me, the parents won't give back my skullcap. It's quite embarrassing. Going to work in the mornings some cheeky brats on the bus are having a great time pushing spitballs and chewed bubble gum between my brain wrinkles when I'm not looking.

That's enough, I decide one morning, I have rights too. So I knock on the mother's door. She has my upper head.

She just stands there in the door, smoking, holding my skullcap in her hand, which looks like a half hairy coconut, and she flicks the ash into it. After I'm done with my speech about human rights, she slams the door in my face.

I have no time for a second round, I must leave to work. Scratching out a used ticket from my brain wrinkles, I catch the next bus. A young couple whispers and chuckles behind me. I quickly get off at the next stop, before they could plan a secret date in my occipital lobe.

About Zoltán Komor

Zoltán Komor was born in June 14, 1986. He lives in Hungary. He writes surreal short stories and published in several literary magazines (*Horror, Sleaze and Trash*; *Drabblecast*; *The Phantom Drift*; *Gone Lawn*; *Bizarro Central*; *Bizarrocast*; *Thrice Fiction Magazine*; *The Missing Slate*; *The Gap-Toothed Madness*; *Wilderness House Literary Review*; etc.) His first English book, titled *Flamingos in the Ashtray: 25 Bizarro Short Stories*, was released by Burning Bulb Publishing in 2014; his second English book, titled *Tumour-djinn*, was released by MorbidbookS in the same year.

Contact: komorzoltan@gmail.com

Drone
By Kevin Candela

Elisha May shrieked.

Wet and naked, she stood nearly paralyzed as the toy whirlybird bobbed a few feet beyond the second story window, its nose pointing right at her navel.

The sound of a door slamming downstairs shook her out of the trance to some degree; enough, at least, to enable her to quickly lower the slat blind. She took a step back, fear creeping into the mind space that shock was slowly ceding.

Anger tromped them both down. Moving forward again, she lifted a couple of the lint-coated slats and peeked through them.

It was gone.

Elisha threw a towel around herself and hurried downstairs.

"Annie?"

"Yeah, Mom?"

Annie's face appeared around a corner up ahead. Elisha stopped and stared.

"Which of your pervert little friends has a new drone?"

"Huh?"

"Come on. I'm sure it was one of them. Let me guess. Brett?"

"Mom, what are you...?"

"A drone? You know, buzzing little machine with a camera on it so I end up on the Internet for all the other sickos in the whole world to see?"

"You saw a drone?"

"I could hardly miss it now, could I? Stepped out of the shower, turned to the window and there it was! I just know it's Brett. I heard him snickering."

"Brett doesn't have the money for a drone, Mom. His mom has two part time jobs."

"He probably stole it."

"Do you want me to message him?"

Somehow the question cooled Elisha off a bit. "No," she said. "But I *do* want to know who's doing it. You know that video could already be posted?"

"Mom, I don't think…"

What Annie thought didn't matter. Elisha had already spun about and was heading back up the stairs. Annie set her sandwich makings down on the countertop and hustled upstairs too. She found her mom already at her bedroom desk, hammering away at the keypad. Annie moved up beside her.

Thirty seconds later her frustrated mom thrust up out of the squeaky chair and stepped aside.

"*You* search then!" she said.

Annie did, quite efficiently. Elisha's bare breasts and surprised stare weren't anywhere to be found.

Yet.

"See what your friends are doing," Elisha said. "Casually. But hurry."

Annie complied.

"Mom!"

"What?"

Old Lord Nicotine is a charmer. Elisha had dug a cigarette out of her sock drawer, lit it and taken a puff…all so distractedly that it was more of an involuntary reflex than anything else.

"Oh hell!" she said. Snatching it from her lips she snuffed the hot end on the dresser's glass top.

The search didn't reveal anything suspicious going on with Annie's half a dozen close friends.

"What if it's not one of my friends?" Annie said.

"What do you mean?" Elisha said, but she realized what her daughter meant before Annie could answer. "Oh god! You mean some sick shit in this neighborhood is …?" She looked pale. "I think I might…throw up…"

Annie ignored her mom's histrionics, rose from the chair and went over to peek out of the window blind.

"What did it look like?"

"What do you mean? It was a drone. Little sleek black metal thing hovering in the air."

"Like a helicopter?"

"I don't know. I guess. It sort of bobbed up and down a little."

"I'm gonna go outside and look around," Annie said, backing away from the window. "Maybe it's still out there."

"No!" Elisha spun from the desk to face her daughter. "What if it is?"

"You're being silly, Mom. It's not like it can shoot me."

It took a bit of talk, but Annie managed to calm her mother down and get her to see reason. Ten minutes later, Elisha was dressed and the pair stepped out into the steamy early evening gloom.

"I guess it's not going to be cooling off at night any more for a while," Elisha said, scanning her backyard from the patio.

"What?"

The crickets and cicadas were so loud that Elisha had to repeat her statement in a louder voice. Annie nodded. "I like early summer a lot better."

They circled the house slowly and cautiously, moving up to each subsequent corner and peering around it before exposing themselves to view from that next side. As they crept along they scanned the indigo sky around the neighboring houses as well.

"If it's still around we might be able to hear it," Annie said.

"Not over all these bugs," Elisha said. "Damn, that's loud!"

Their search yielded no results. The thing had apparently moved on. Elisha and Annie went back inside, tended a half dozen or so mosquito bites each and returned to monitoring their computers for "nude divorcees on parade."

To Elisha's great relief nothing embarrassing had showed up by sunset the next day. Feeling a bit better after an uneventful afternoon she headed out to the patio, settled into the lounger and snuck the rest of that smoke that had been sitting there all day on her dresser mocking her.

She hadn't been sitting there long when she saw it. She figured it was just an evening bird – a chimney swift – at first. Big one though. She caught sight of it purely by accident, as her idle gaze had become fixed on the white siding of the house beyond her back fence. The dark object shot across from left to right. No big deal. Just a bird.

But then it returned, moving much more slowly and deliberately and in a manner no swift could manage: it drifted up to one of the dark windows and hovered right in front of it.

"Son of a bitch!" Elisha hissed.

She snapped her cellphone up off the patio table and hit three easy digits.

"Yes," she told the emergency dispatcher at the other end, "I'd like to report someone using a drone to peep in windows." She verified her address and was given assurance that a patrol car would be sent to check it out. "Tell them to hurry or it'll get away!" she said.

The dispatcher's responses were too relaxed to calm her down. The drone was still there.

She got up as quietly as she could and advanced cautiously toward her back fence. She was about halfway there when the drone darted off to the right and disappeared.

"*No!*" she hollered. "Oh, you bastard!"

She gave Officer Mac Jenkins a full rundown when he finally arrived at her front door about half an hour later.

"It's been here two nights in a row," she said. "If you come back tomorrow around sunset, you might be able to catch it."

She could tell Mac was checking her out but he wasn't being obvious about it.

"I'll see what I can do about it," he said. "Thanks for helping with the paperwork."

The next day finally brought relief from the swelter in the form of a rain-heavy thunderstorm; this went on all day so what should have been dusk might as well have been midnight. Around the same time she'd seen the drone the previous two nights, Elisha went out in what had become a fine drizzle and spent a few minutes peering into the darkness. She gave up quickly. Mac didn't come by.

Two inches of rain made for a lot of steam the following day. This time of year breaks in the weather didn't last long. Elisha got home from a long day spent showing four local houses to prospective buyers and couldn't wait to ditch her sweat-drenched dress clothes. This she used to do in her bedroom with the blinds up, but no more. Once she was into shorts and a tee she headed downstairs and that was when she realized that Annie wasn't there.

She whipped out her cell and hit speed dial.

"Annie?"

"Hi, Mom."

"Where are you?"

"There's a note on the kitchen counter in plain sight."

"Save me a trip?"

The answer came after a distinct moment of hesitation. "I'm doing homework over at...a friend's ..."

"Which friend? Let me guess."

"It's me, Mrs. May," she heard Brett holler in the background. "I don't own any drones!"

"Dammit, Annie!"

"Sorry ..."

Elisha stewed silently for a few moments.

"Mom? Hello?"

"Get home before sunset," Elisha finally said. She clicked the phone off angrily. "Idiots."

Annie cut it close but made it home with the sun a blood red crescent behind the houses across the street. Her mom heard her coming in the front door and yelled to her from the kitchen.

"Take off your shoes!"

It sounded like an awful lot of shoes were hitting the floor.

Annie came padding around the corner in her socks. Brett was right behind her.

"What the hell?"

"Hi, Mrs. May!"

"It's Miss May, Brett. May is my maiden name."

"Oh wow. Hi, Miss May!"

His exuberance and cheerful smile didn't fool her. She knew he was eyeing her slightly-too-small t-shirt. But he was working the glances in cleverly between stints of eye contact.

"Hi, Brett. Why are you here?"

Brett's angular shoulders slumped and his grin faded.

"Mom!" Annie said. "I brought him over because he's got a great idea."

"I'm sure he's got a *lot* of great ideas, hon."

"No ma'am. Not at the moment. Just one."

The idea really was pretty good.

"Get online and see how cheap you can get one," Elisha told

Annie.

They did. Over the next couple of dusks, the drone was nowhere to be seen. The third evening found all three of them painting themselves from head to toe with insect repellant and taking group walks around the neighborhood with Maglites every hour on the hour until three a.m.

Nothing.

The camera drone arrived the next afternoon. By this point, Brett was part of it--whether Elisha liked it or not--so when Annie got home she had her daughter invite him over. Elisha herself had an early evening house showing across town so she reluctantly left the teens alone for what she hoped would be no more than ninety minutes.

She barely made it home before dark. Brett and Annie weren't up in Annie's room going at it, fortunately, and all the beds were still made. Fact was, they weren't there at all.

Elisha got tired of yelling for them and headed out, still in her agent's duds, to try to find them. She cruised around the neighborhood streets for fifteen minutes but saw no trace of them. Cursing under her breath, she pulled into the driveway and realized that there were more lights on than when she'd left. The front door was slightly ajar too. She almost panicked but as she was reaching into her purse for her cell she saw Brett coming out the front door.

Elisha hit the driver's window button but the car was already shut off so it didn't work. So she flung the door open.

"Where the hell have you guys been?"

Brett nearly fell off the porch. He spun around.

"Sorry Mrs...Miss May," he said. "But we saw it! We even managed to follow it a little."

"You what?"

Five minutes later Elisha was as wound up as Brett and Annie. But she was also still pissed.

"You guys could have at least left a note."

"There wasn't time, Mom. We saw the drone about two minutes after we finally got ours up off the ground. We had to follow it."

"You went after it with ours?"

Brett shook his head. "We didn't have the camera working yet," he said. "Went after it on foot."

"Where's ours?"

"In the shed," Annie said. "I locked it."

"Yeah," Brett said, "and if we hadn't spent time doing that, we might have seen where it went."

Elisha glared at him. "Do you know how much that thing costs?"

"I know," Brett said. "But you've got a fence. Nobody was gonna come over and steal it."

Elisha looked to Annie, her gaze softening. "Thanks," she said. "How far did you manage to follow it?"

"Far enough to know it's not from this neighborhood. We saw it go past the last houses on Hobbs' End and off into the field."

"Did it go into the woods past the field? Over them?"

She looked to Brett, who was shaking his head again.

"It was too dark," he said. "And we were out of breath."

"Well, I guess that's something. But I'm still really mad at you guys."

Her anger didn't last that long. By the next evening she was tagging along as Brett and Annie hauled the drone to Hobbs' Field. They set up along the strip of city-mowed grass that separated the soy from the patchy surface of Hobbs' End, one of the oldest streets in the county, beneath high tension electrical towers that made an eerie hum-hiss as loud as the crickets. Annie had figured out how to link the chopper camera feed to her cell phone, a feat her mom took for granted since she didn't realize that it took some considerable online maneuvering.

"Anybody need more Skin So Soft?"

Both Annie and Brett shook their heads.

"I'm all right," Annie said. "No bites. And it's almost dark."

"Well, I've got a couple," Elisha said.

Brett tried not to stare too obviously when one of the bites turned out to be cleavage adjacent.

Annie meanwhile was watching the canopy beyond the field, a couple hundred yards distant. More specifically she was watching for the Peeping Tom drone to appear in the quickly darkening sky just over the uneven treetop line.

All three were caught utterly off guard when the drone shot right past them not ten feet over their heads. Annie didn't even catch a glimpse of it, but the other two did.

"Oh my god!" Elisha said. "Was that it?"

"I think so!" Brett said.

He took off after it from sheer reflex, but it was already across the street and beyond several lines of chain link fencing.

"Watch out!"

Only Elisha's yell and a simultaneous shriek from Annie kept Brett from getting flattened by a pickup truck. He pulled up just in time. The driver swerved and let loose a horn blast.

Annie and Elisha came running up to him.

"I'm fine," he said. "Thanks to you guys."

He was still staring off the way the drone had gone.

"We'll wait for it," Elisha said. "Looks like it has routines."

They all agreed and decided to make themselves a little less conspicuous for its anticipated return. The sizzling towers were creepy to hide under, but the trusses and columns provided the only decent "drone blind" not on local private property. So the three set up behind one of the nearest column bases and waited.

"Hope we don't go sterile," Annie said at one point during the long vigil.

"Hope I do," Elisha said.

"*Mom!*"

That shut the conversation up a while. This was good because all three were focused on the task when the drone finally shot by on its "return trip." Brett had theirs after the marauder in seconds.

It couldn't match the speed, however. Not only that, but the camera feed wasn't giving them enough to even see what was ahead of their craft. As soon as this became apparent, frustration set in for Brett. He handed the controls over to Annie (Elisha was holding the cell) and took off into the field at a sprint, pulling out his Maglite and flicking it on.

About halfway across he realized that he was wasting his time – even his bouncing power beam couldn't pick out a dark drone against a dark background – but since he was already that far he decided to at least chase what he could no longer see up to the edge of the woods.

Elisha and Annie saw his figure shrinking into the gloom.

Then, most abruptly, the light went out and Brett dropped from sight.

When he didn't pop back up after a few seconds Annie turned worriedly to her mom.

"We'd better go see if he's okay," Elisha said.

They took off across the field, going as fast as they could while negotiating the rows of knee-high soy plants that were laid out exactly the wrong way for ease of passage. At last they reached the spot where Brett had vanished.

The reason was apparent. There was a deep crater here. Brett was down at the bottom, standing with his back to Annie and Elisha, head tilted oddly downward.

"Brett!" Annie yelled.

He didn't move.

The side of the crater was dry clay – rough, brittle, crumbling into large clods under their shoes and threatening to twist an ankle with every step. Fortunately, the slope was fairly gentle. Annie and Elisha made it down without incident and came up on either side of Brett.

He was staring down at a hole.

"Was this a pond?" he said as his companions joined him in studying the four foot wide circle of utter darkness.

"I don't know," Elisha said. "Probably. Looks like one."

"What happened to it?" Annie said.

"I'd say someone pulled the plug," Brett said.

"I bet it was all those quakes we've been having since they started fracking."

Elisha looked worriedly at her daughter. And even more worriedly at the hole.

"Wonder how deep it is?" Brett said. He moved right up to its crumbling edge and tilted his Maglite to point straight down into it.

"Oh shit."

Elisha and Annie crept cautiously up beside him again.

They both gasped. Elisha reflexively pulled her daughter back from the edge by her shoulders.

The Maglite's beam had an unimpeded path. As Brett turned it slightly this way and that, it struck a convex wall at least a hundred feet down. But it found nothing to reflect off in the center of the absolutely straight hole.

"I just had a totally weird thought," Brett said absently, still entranced by the hole. "What if this is where the drone came from?"

"Get away from the edge, Brett," Annie said. "You might fall!"

"Yeah," Elisha said, "she's right. Get back from there. You can't see anything more than what you see."

Brett went rigid. He spun about, his eyes bright.

"You're right!" he said, and he walked up to Annie and took the drone control from her hands. "I can't," he explained, nodding at the joystick, "but *this* can."

The drone was still intact and hovering since it was designed to idle when no flight instructions were being received. It was low on fuel, but they'd brought extra. Though it was already well past 10 p.m. Elisha's slate was clear for the next day until early afternoon, so she okayed the late night activity, albeit with some reluctance.

However, she was also scared: quite scared, in fact, such that, even though her curiosity was in every bit as much overdrive as Brett's and Annie's, she was still reluctant to do anything about their strange find right away.

"I still think we should call Mac. You know, in the morning, I mean. No need to bother him now about it. But seriously, that hole needs to be roped off or somebody will fall in."

"Mom, if we do that they'll never let us see what's down there."

"True, Miss May. That's how it works."

"Please, Mom?"

Elisha was only *mostly* a grown up herself at heart, so …

The chopper didn't have much lift to spare with a full tank and the smallest Maglite taped to it.

But it got up off the dark ground beside the hole, and that's all the encouragement Brett needed to send it down into the bizarre abyss.

Ten feet.

"You're doing really well keeping it straight," Annie said as she and her mom studied the circle of dry clay under the bright beam's horizontal glare.

"Thanks," Brett said.

The view swerved a little.

"Careful!" Elisha said. "Don't let it go to your head."

Twenty feet.

The circle was fading from tan to dark gray.

"Bedrock," Elisha said. "I guess it *is* a fissure."

Thirty feet. Forty.

Fifty.

"Too bad we can't tilt the light downward," Elisha said. "Don't go too fast in case we hit bottom."

"I think bottom is still a long ways off."

Sixty. Seventy. Eighty.

"I don't believe this," Elisha muttered under her breath. "I'm getting scared ..."

"Calm down, Mom."

Ninety.

One hundred.

More.

There wasn't really any way to gauge the depth. But at some point the circle of illuminated wall started getting smaller.

"You're drifting," Elisha said. "You're going to hit the wall behind the drone."

"No, I'm not," Brett said. "I'm only using the vertical control." They all looked on as the shrinking continued. Brett realized what they were seeing first. "The hole's getting wider."

"No. What?" Elisha was confused. "Hold it still for a minute. Stop the descent."

Brett let go of the joystick and the drone hovered.

"Can you rotate it?" Annie said.

"Sure," Brett said.

Dark wall moved beneath the still-bright beam. But it did not come closer.

"How are we on fuel?" Elisha said.

Brett checked it. "Still fine. Three quarters of a tank."

He stopped the rotation and resumed the descent.

"Wait!" Elisha said. But then she relented. "Oh, what the hell. Keep going."

Brett grinned at her. "I like you, Miss May. I really do."

Elisha reluctantly smiled. "It's Elisha, Brett."

"If you two are done flirting?"

They all watched the cell phone display.

The circle wasn't shrinking much now. The hole had to be a

hundred feet or so wide by this point, and with such a wide space there didn't seem much to worry about from…

IMPACT!

The light circle shuddered violently.

"You hit bottom!" Elisha gasped.

"No, I didn't!" Brett said. "I…I don't have control of it anymore!"

Annie was staring at the phone screen, where the spot of wall being illuminated by the Maglite had stabilized quickly but was now quite blurred by rapid relative motion.

"The camera's still working!" she said.

"What's wrong with the focus?" Elisha said, leaning in.

"Nothing," Annie said after a moment of study. "It's moving…fast."

"It's going down again," Brett said. "But shit…I mean, damn, look at that!"

Many feet of wall were going by with each passing second.

"I can't believe we haven't lost the signal," Annie said. "That's gotta be a mile down by now!"

Then, most abruptly, the white circle vanished.

"Did the flashlight go out?" Brett said.

"No," Annie said. "I think the wall's gone."

The screen was nearly dark, yet every second or two the flashlight beam would strike something shadowy for just long enough for all three of them to tell the camera and light were still on. What was going on besides inexplicable and out of control movement of the drone through a shadowy, semi-open vagueness was anyone's guess.

"Do you still not have control of it?" Elisha said.

Brett showed her the controller and demonstrated the futility of moving the joystick.

"It should be working," he said. "The controller says the signals are being received."

"Hey," Annie said, "it looks like the screen's getting lighter."

"What?" Elisha said. "How could it be light that far …?"

The answer came before she could finish, and the sight was so startling, so unexpected, that for a few long seconds the three just stood there staring at the cell phone display in abject disbelief.

"Oh… my …" Elisha said.

"God…" Annie said.

The illumination came from the sides of a cavern so vast that its incredibly ancient far wall had to be at least several miles distant. Between there and the high-flying drone three staggered stalactite-stalagmite columns stood like titanic sentinels overlooking a complex subterranean landscape comprised of many odd shapes and varying degrees of the same eerie blue-white luminescence that was coming off the mammoth cavern walls.

The drone was now descending.

Something rose up before it. A platform. With squiggling forms atop it.

The drone closed in on the platform's upper surface, bringing into closer view the bizarre semi-erect figures themselves. Bulbous, amorphous, like black oil in clear balloons, the shapes avoided the Maglite spot, parting as the horizontal light shaft descended toward their midst. They still couldn't be seen clearly, particularly in something as small as a cell phone view screen.

"What the hell are we looking at?" Brett said.

The drone moved into the midst of the shadowy blobs and came to a halt there. The Maglite beam went out, but somehow the ambient light actually seemed to improve visibility.

An utterly bizarre visage tilted in from the right side of the frame. Little streaks of pale blue-white light ran here and there across the roughly oval and human-shaped "head" of whatever was now peering right back at them from only inches in front of the camera lens.

It was probably for the best that the impossible visage shocked Annie into dropping the phone, which bounced off her ankle and went straight into the hole.

They'd all seen enough.

They'd seen that…well, there was no denying it…that *face*.

Elisha was crying. Bawling. Brett was still backing up while muttering "No fuckin' way" over and over under his breath. Annie was speechless and wide-eyed.

They finally got their collective act together after a few dazed minutes and walked home in silence. Not even the crickets felt like talking tonight, apparently. Their neighborhood was eerily, almost deathly, quiet. Something had sobered the frogs and crickets up. ALL of them.

And not one word was spoken until they were inside Elisha's house.

Then there were plenty.

Elisha handed Brett a beer. He was so out of it that he didn't realize she'd even done it. She set one down in front of Annie too and then pulled out another for herself. She chugged about half of it with one long draw.

"We're not old enough, Mom," Annie said.

"You are now," Elisha said, and she slammed the rest of the beer, burped loudly and then got out another one. "You just grew up."

"What are we gonna do about it?" Brett said, opening his. "Tell the police?"

"Of course," Elisha said. "We'll just explain that we sent a drone down into that hole and found a whole underground city full of big black lava lamp people who took our drone away and kept it."

"We should do *something*, Mom. What if that drone that's been invading our neighborhood really *is* theirs? What if they're checking us out?"

Elisha went for her third beer. She reluctantly let Brett have the last one in the twelve pack box.

"Can you believe how big that place was?" Brett said. "That cave must be wider than this ..."

He trailed off deliberately, his eyes growing wide.

"Yeah," Elisha said, looking as though the thought hadn't occurred to her yet either. "You're right. It's gotta be...a *lot* bigger ..."

"Hey, I've got an idea," Brett said. "What if we go out there tomorrow in broad daylight with some rabbit fencing, metal stakes and shovels and bury that hole under all that loose lake bed clay that's laying around it in clods? How strong could that drone of theirs be?"

Elisha thought about it.

"How long would that hold up?" she finally said. "You'd really need to pour concrete and I doubt a truck could make it through that field."

"I say we call the police about it," Annie said.

"Yeah," Brett said. "Let them call the Men in Black and scientists in unmarked coats."

"Brett!"

"Sorry, Annie. But that's what they'll do."

Elisha had slipped into even deeper thought. She came out of it in the next moment.

"I tell you what we're going to do," she said. "We're going to do what every normal person in 21st century America does when problems arise in their neighborhood. We're moving."

About Kevin Candela

"There is no such thing as a normal neighborhood," writer Kevin Candela says. "Look around. If you don't have a strange neighbor then it's probably you, and if no one is, in fact, truly weird then there's probably something you'd never accept as real creeping around in your backyard at night." Even his Dragon's Game Trilogy is inspired by (and in part about) neighborhood weirdness. Former aerospace engineer and university physics instructor Candela's lifelong fixation with 1950s-60s SF, fantasy and horror tends to keep him writing in that vein. Plus he is admittedly obsessed with all things supernatural. He and his remarkably patient and wise wife Jackie live in the mystical semi-reality of Godfrey, Illinois.

The Warp in Whittick Estates
By Tina Piney

It wasn't for the money, not at all, it was for the company, the noise, the life! She never had to think about money; there was always more, another bank account, another vault, another safety deposit box. She had hired Wayne to manage her finances when she became the last of The Whitticks and sole heir to the fortune that came with the title. It was now his granddaughter Elizabeth that looked after her money. It was Elizabeth that made the deal happen. After selling one hundred and twenty acres, her ancestral home was the "crowning jewel", a sprawling mansion on a five acre parcel, "the anchor of a prestigious executive community."

Before the sale and development of "The Whittick Estates" Mary Whittick had become lonesome. Now in her mid-eighties, it had been over sixty years since the last of her relations had perished. The handful of peers that had survived with her to reach their advanced age had neither the physical or mental prowess to interest her. They also had families of their own. So aside from the occasional tea party and the help (two fulltime maids Tara and Cheri, one part-timer Janelle, and a live in butler, David), no one really visited anymore.

While she never did make a conscious decision to become a spinster, that's exactly what happened. Sitting by herself, as her eyesight began to fail, she knew why. She had lived a great life. Her wealth and her love of the written word had set her on a lifelong learning adventure. She always had her nose in a book, but the love of her life was slipping away with every word she had to strain to see. She spent less time reading and more time thinking, reflecting.

Squinting at herself in the mirror, it seemed almost impossible that she was formerly known as a great beauty. She once had plenty of friends. Men, mostly scholars, were attracted by her obvious charms, but ultimately put off by her lack of involvement with them. Gone were her hourglass figure and her long soft hair. She could nearly put her pinkie finger inside the deep wrinkle that ran, angled to the right, between her eyebrows. She remembered one of her boyfriends, Charles, would kiss that exact spot back when it was only a tiny line. He called it her "thinking spot" because the more she was involved in a book, the more it would appear. She used to be so annoyed when he would interrupt her studies…now what a wonderful memory it was.

How long had Charles been dead now? Maybe twelve years? She hadn't seen him in much longer. He left her in her early thirties. He knew he would always be second to her books; he had said as much when he left. She barely took notice at first, but somehow the longer she went without him, the worse she felt. She didn't know how to tell him what he really meant to her. She never got the chance. He moved on, got a wife and had a son.

At least now she had a family of sorts in her neighbors. They looked up to her as the grand dame of the neighborhood. They took landscaping cues from her garden, invited her to all their neighborhood get-togethers. It was everything she wanted. She loved just about everyone but she adored the children. Most of them came to look upon her as a grandmotherly figure. Whenever she was outside, someone always came up to talk with her. For the first time in her life she began to regret choosing education over a family. Every baby she held, every child with sunshine playing off their upturned smiling faces, drove home the absence of children and grandchildren of her own.

She sat one night staring at the face of the clock she knew like the back of her hand, remembering the details but seeing only a blurred image. She thought of one of her favorite poems about death and flies. "And then the windows failed and I could not see to see" she whispered to herself. Here she was, a great thinker, a scholar with money at her disposal, accepting her fate. She could change this, but how? Her mind reviewed snippets of books still locked in her head and she hit upon an idea. It was farfetched, and she felt like a silly old woman for even considering the possibility.

Her library was, of course, extensive. Shortly after she inherited everything she had taken the original library of the house and expanded it to encompass the three rooms around it. In a move that her designer had called "bold," she also took out the ceilings, removing three bedrooms and a bath upstairs. Her two story wood paneled library had made it into a very influential magazine and launched an astounding career for her designer.

Her mind reviewed a passage that always stuck with her. "Time moves forward, never back again unless you find the warp within." The book that contained it was one that she had discovered on one of her many trips abroad. It was very old and handwritten, but finely bound and in nice condition. It was simply titled *Secrets Kept*. She hadn't paid it much attention, skimming through it when she was home again. She had placed it in her rare books section and not thought of it again. She remembered that the foreword said it was a copy of an ancient text. It read like a journal of an oral history that reached back further. Nothing about it at the time indicated to her that it was anything beyond traditional, herbal remedies and old wives tales. Still, what did she have to lose? She rose slowly and headed to the library her left leg, sore in the damp autumn weather, causing her to limp. This old age was for the birds!

She found the volume without too much hassle and eased into her favorite reading chair by the massive library fireplace. Using her glasses and squinting like hell, she dug into the section devoted to the warp within. She read it through, had a small nap, woke and read it again. She felt she could accomplish what the ceremony required, but she was concerned about the vagueness of the results. Following all the steps to find the "warp within", was one final line, "Be mindful of your friend and kin when traveling the warp within."

It was her Tara that finally interrupted Mary from her thoughts. She had a delicious smelling plate and a glass of cold milk with her. Mary smiled and thanked her. She ate here by herself so often that no one even asked if she wanted to anymore. After dinner she would start to collect what she needed. It was time to start on a new adventure.

A needle and a thimble to collect the blood, pieces that would give wing to her dreams, to take her to where she had once been, a window open for the winds of change, mud from the graves of those you loved, a candle of remembrance for the flame to unlock, a vessel of water to wash away your fears, she gathered it all. She lowered herself onto the floor carefully, by the window, with all of her tools for the warp around her.

Her bedroom was the safest place to accomplish the ceremony. Now that she had retired to her room for the evening, no one would be in until 8am, when they asked her where she would like to take her breakfast. She dipped her finger in the thimble and dropped a bit of blood on both of the pictures she had chosen as the pieces to give wings to her dreams. One was of her and the other one of Charles. Both were taken sixty years before. She spread the grave mud on her feet, splashed water on her face. She took a towel and dried herself. She lit a large candle and laid down on the pillow she put on the floor. She pulled her thick quilt up to her chin and breathed deep the cool autumn air through her nose. She smiled and closed her eyes. Despite her bones aching from lying on the floor, this adventure had made her tired. She fell asleep quickly and dreamed of flying.

She woke to sounds of confusion; yelling, shuffling and finally a key in the door. She looked around to assess the scene. Nothing had changed! What had she really expected? The looks on the faces of her staff that found her summed it up nicely. Tara and David figured she was just a rich old crazy lady lying on the floor, her feet caked with mud, surrounded with bloody pictures and a candle.

They seemed as embarrassed as she was when they helped her up. They apologized for disturbing her and expressed their concern when she didn't answer. She apologized right back, claimed a late night of reminiscing and that she would like her breakfast in the library today.

Sitting in the library, it seemed to be taking forever for her breakfast. Finally, Tara came in walking very slowly and spoke even slower, saying, "Will there be anything else for now?"

Oh terrific, Mary, she thought, *they are walking on eggshells, probably thinking you have lost your mind.* "No, thank you", she added carefully, "that will be all for now." Tara left, moving just as slowly as she had entered. *What?Are they afraid they'll startle me and I'll go crazy?* she thought, disgusted at herself.

She spent the day thinking, jotting down notes, pulling reference books. She must have really worked up an appetite because lunch seemed late. She was ferociously hungry when her clock chimed twelve noon just as Tara entered with lunch.

As usual, time spent in her library passed without her really noticing, however, her wristwatch indicated it was only 2:15 PM-- almost four hours until dinner--when she became so hungry she could barely stand it. She hit the intercom, asking Tara for a snack. She was so terribly slow in arriving, Mary was about to do something very out of the ordinary and verbally attack her. She squinted again at her watch when Tara came through the door, to quote the exact time it had taken and how it was unacceptable. Four minutes had passed and it was 2:19 PM. Her fiery words were extinguished before they crossed her lips. Tara moved at a snail's pace across the library with Mary's snack, set it down beside her and moved her head in a motion that appeared to be more of a scan than a nod. Mary thanked her. Instead of exiting, Tara stopped. Mary asked her if she was all right, but she did not respond. It was in her quiet amazement that Mary noticed the clock had stopped ticking. She held her watch to her ear.

Nothing.

Mary stood and walked around, more than any other reason, to see if she was still able. She assessed the scene again and she heard a tick as the clock started again. Gradually, Tara reached down, took the snack plate and backed out of the room.

***

As Halloween approached, the residents of Whittick Estates first started to notice things about Mary which the neighborhood referred to as her decline. Halloween was Mary's favorite holiday and her usual decorations were impressive. She started with a fall themed yard which progressed over a month into a spooky haunted house and realistic graveyard. Not only that, on Devil's Night she always held a pumpkin carving contested. The winners would be showcased in her spectacular graveyard for the whole neighborhood to see. It was midway through October when the decorations stopped advancing. Though she was unable to do the work, she had, in years past, always overseen every part of her Halloween display. No one saw Mary around much and whenever they tried to speak with her, confusion would flood her face; she would then smile, nod and back away. The children of the neighborhood still held out hope

51

that Mary would pull through on Halloween.

Kids and adults alike were always treated well at Mary's on Halloween night- as long as they wore a costume. Standard issue to everyone was a full sized Halloween loot bag containing six or seven chocolate bars, pop, chips, assorted candy (all Halloween themed, like eyeball gumballs) and a new homemade treat every year.

Halloween came and Tara, Cheri and David threw together some treats for everyone. Everyone was polite, but they were disappointed. Mary did not make an appearance. Some of the older children likened it to the day they found out about Santa. Some thought it was worse.

Strangely, the very next night Mary sat at the door with stacks of treats, looking forlorn that no one came to her door. The rumor of her senility began to spread like wild fire.

***

It took Mary awhile to adjust to time moving backwards. It was agonizingly slow at first, but when things sped up she took to heart the last line of the "Warp Within": "Be mindful of your friend and kin when traveling the warp within."

Because time was not passing, even in reverse, at the same rate as she was going, it was nearly impossible to gauge what day it was. Halloween was nearly upon her when she thought she still had two weeks left. At first people talked too slowly for her to understand. Once the reversal had quickened it sounded as though they were speaking in tongues.

One brighter and warmer day she had a bit of déjà vu. Her closest neighbor, a rather sweet mother of three by the name of Tania, backed across her lawn to where she was standing, smiled at Mary, looked up at her blossoming tree and said, "eert taht evol tsuj I." She went on to talk for a couple of minutes but Mary ignored her, remembering what Tania had said to her last spring. Tania, in the meantime finished what she was saying, smiled at Mary and backed away.

"I just love that tree!"

She remembered how Tania had smiled and the pride Mary had felt as she remembered planting it with her mother decades ago.

This was the key. She felt silly she hadn't thought of it earlier. Learning to talk backwards reminded her of Pig Latin and she picked it up easily enough. She tried to interact with her help and her neighbors again. It worked for three days, maybe, but the time reversal sped up again. To everyone else she was an unfortunate victim of dementia, acting strangely, disconnected. Within the warp, Mary was trying to communicate with their memories and much was lost in the translation.

She realized she was one day late for Halloween after sitting at the door feeling like the grandmother abandoned by her family at an old age home. After a short nap in her chair in the front foyer she realized a new day had donned and Tara and David were taking down Halloween decorations that weren't there the night before. They were moving so quickly, their edges blurred. Mary tried to assess the scene. It was Halloween; not this one, but Halloween last year--she recognized how she decorated the hall. In what she calculated was less than a month, she had lost more than a year.

Mary learned to be more self-sufficient grabbing handfuls of food and a drink whenever she came across them. She very quickly lost complete track of when she was. She attempted bathing a few times, but had been pulled from the bathtub, by whom she wasn't sure. To them it may look like she was in there for days before she had dipped one toe. Or maybe they couldn't see her either anymore and had pushed her aside to clean. Within her warp, she didn't know the rules.

When and where would it stop? She hoped the pictures from her life in her early twenties would halt the warp right there. What if it kept going? She would be born and then cease to exist. She decided that it was time to leave a note around the house somewhere that Tara, Cheri or David would find.

She knew she couldn't mention the warp within her, that would certainly ensure that no one would understand and follow her instructions. She had retained the same staff for twenty-five years, except for the part-timer. They were loyal because she treated and paid them well. Should she cease to exist, or as she carefully put it, pass on, she left instructions on what was to be done with her estate. She had done a will many years back and it did not include her staff or her neighbors. She wanted so badly to right the situation. She carefully recorded her instructions, dated it for the day before she entered the warp, and place it down on the large island in the middle of her kitchen.

It disappeared immediately.

***

People in The Whittick Estates openly mourned the loss of their dame. She began speaking in tongues. She would wander off backwards looking confused. A new will turned up in the kitchen. It was so caring and thoughtful, Tara cried when she read it. It was dated before all of her decline. Before that awful morning she and David found her on the floor with her feet caked in mud.

It was the neighbor, Tania, who called the authorities after Mary was found naked in the yard. This began a series of legends surrounding crazy Mary, passed throughout the neighborhood, children detailing where she would turn up and who she would kill if you spoke her name three times while walking backwards around her cherry tree.

By this time, Elizabeth had taken Mary's Power of Attorney and made sure that every request in her final will was carried to the letter. As they loaded Mary up to take her into the hospital, Cheri stood tearing up while Tara openly wept in David's arms. She had attempted to say good bye to Mary, to tell her how much she meant to her. It was too late. It was as though Mary couldn't see her at all.

As she had stated in her will, Mary was to have neither feeding tubes nor life support when her dementia robbed her of her abilities. After three weeks of hospital care, she slipped away.

***

Mary started to have more trouble knowing not just when, but where she was, and she guessed after she walked into a wall she was now in the time before her big library renovation. She had noticed other changes too. First, she quit limping. Her vision returned to normal. She noticed her hair lengthen and soften. Her body toned up and her waist shrank in.

She tried unsuccessfully to catch her reflection in the mirror. Everything in her face was in constant motion, it was impossible to focus on. And then she could.

A slowing had happened and her face finally came into focus - She gasped! It was exactly what she wanted! She was young, in her early twenties and in the library, not her library, the one original to the house. She needed to sit down.

As if on cue, Charles walked through the door. He took one look at Mary and burst out laughing.

"I never thought there would be a day where I would walk into the library and not only find your nose out of a book but looking directly at me -- *And* I can see your thinking spot from here!" He walked over to her and kissed the fine line that had once been a furrow. Mary smiled, stood up and kissed him right back. He laughed out loud, clutching at his heart in not quite pretend shock.

***

Mary Whittick was buried at the family cemetery that she started on the northwest side of her intact one hundred and twenty-five acre Whittick Estate. She was planted beside her husband Charles, who had pre-deceased her by a dozen years or so. Hundreds of family and friends gathered to send her off properly. A younger friend of hers, Tara, spoke of her generously putting her though school when they met by accident some twenty odd years before. About how she was a dedicated scholar and a lover of the written word. Tara received a laugh from the crowd when she mentioned Mary's work to prove that dementia was caused by time travel. Tara concluded that "Mary's main love in her life was her family, one that I was honored to be a part of."

About Tina Piney

After living her life with a head full of stories, Tina Piney began sending them out into the world. An avid reader, Tina especially adores Clive Barker. When not writing she spends her time with her twins Elizabeth and Erik and her pugs.

Girl In The Rain
By Jorge A. Palacios

As he kissed his beautiful wife, Diana, whom he called Webby out of love, memories of their life together rushed before Stephen Shusett's eyes. The first time the two met was while working at a coffee shop in Old San Juan, serving good coffee to boring housewives and pretentious wannabe writers (among others) to the tune of bad adult alternative rock over the recently-broken speakers.

He remembered their first date, when Stephen left his wallet at home, so she was forced to pay for the movie tickets. The day they married brought him the warmest thoughts, as it was a big affair with family from both sides. The arrivals of Cindy and Donna, who were already out of the car, giggling as they saw their parents kiss each other so deeply. Seventeen successful years together, and now their perfectly united marriage was taking a break. Diana was on her way to Prague to take a session of art seminars that would add a few substantial zeros to her art restoration salary, and she wanted to take the kids so that they would learn about art quickly and early. She worried about things like that: making them smart so that they could be intellectuals at an early age. Stephen agreed, but it hurt him in a way; being separated for two weeks seemed like twenty years. But it was for the best.

-"You will remember to feed the parakeet, won't you?" she asked, as soon as they unlocked their lips, staring at each other's eyes.

That damn parakeet, I really hate it, he thought to himself. *It bites.*

"Of course, honey, don't worry."

Diana smiled, and gave him another quick kiss. Stephen could see her eyes were getting watery as she walked out of the car, so he just smiled, pretending that he wasn't about to cry either. They waved goodbye as they walked towards the terminal, and he just saw them, getting smaller and smaller, with a smile on his face, until they weren't there to be seen anymore. He took a deep breath, sitting and reflecting on the long nights ahead for a couple of minutes, until the policeman's honking ordered him to move his car from the passenger drop-off area. He complied and went home.

The first couple of hours alone were pure boredom. The house seemed deserted, and it was clean too, so he didn't have the housework to distract him. He did one thing that he loved to do, but hadn't since the kids got here: smoke. He took a long drag out of one of the ash-sticks, which he hid under a shoebox in his bedroom closet, and it all seemed less stressful and boring for a couple of minutes. After that, he fed the damn parakeet, who, of course, tried to bite him again. Damn bird.

There were rumblings outside. Looked like a storm was coming.

He went back inside and made himself a ham sandwich and a glass of milk, then sat in the TV room, watching the channel that played old movies. Marx Brothers marathon, can't complain. He laughed all the way through *Night at the Opera* and *Duck Soup*, but by the time *Horse Feathers* came through, it was wearing thin. With his sandwich half-eaten, milk drained, and Groucho doing his shtick, he fell asleep.

CRASH!

The blast of thunder was so loud, it seemed to have landed right beside him. It woke him up like an electric shock. The loud falling rain was louder than the late-era Marx Brothers movie playing on TV, the one in the circus where Grouch was singing about some tattooed lady. He turned off the TV and went to the bathroom, as his hurting bladder needed release. He went back to the living room and kitchen area, deciding to look at what the storm was bringing. It was non-stop rain, crashing into the floor. His backyard looked more like a lake.

Then, with the flash of a thunderbolt, he saw her.

She stood in the rain under one of his backyard lamps, made to look like something out of a London streetlamp in the Victorian era. Her feet were under the water and couldn't be seen, but her wet white dress shone like a moth, clinging to the light.

Stephen gasped, and opened the window.

"Hey you! What are you doing out there? You're going to catch your death!"

He screamed over and over, but she didn't seem to budge, like she was anchored under the light post. Her head was the only thing that seemed to move, especially her eyes, which looked wide and confused.

Stephen took a deep breath, preparing himself to do something he really, really didn't want to do.

He was going to have to go outside.

Wearing a raincoat with an umbrella in his right hand, he walked up to the woman in white. She didn't seem to be bothered by the water hitting her, although her teeth were chattering. Her white dress was the only thing she was wearing, as Stephen could clearly see her nipples and every contour of her beautiful body, it seemed to fit like a glove thanks to the rain. From first impressions, Stephen could only think that she was beautiful, and very young, but also looked very sad and confused. Her makeup ran under the rain.

"Come with me," Stephen screamed, since the rain was so loud he doubted she could hear him in any other way, "Come inside, we'll get you dry and out of the cold!"

She didn't seem to respond, just looked at him with her wide, intense eyes, the only movement being her chattering mouth, which always seemed to be half-open.

"Come on, before you catch your death!"

Suddenly, she seemed to respond, and nodded her head. Stephen opened the umbrella and covered her with its shadow, although the gesture seemed pointless to him, considering how wet she was. They made it back to the house, the Woman following him as he held onto her andclosely guiding her, a splosh splosh with every step.

She stood in the bathroom, the floor covered in water as it dripped from her body. Looking at the curtains, not moving, just standing there, breathing and her teeth chattering. Stephen walked slowly towards her with some of his wife's clothes. She placed them on the sink.

She turned her head, looking at him. Her eyes looked cold.

"There are towels under the sink, Miss..."

He expected her to answer, but didn't, just kept looking at him. He grew nervous with each second.

She removed her white dress, revealing her beautiful body. It was small, but no doubt about it, she was a woman. It had scars and tattoos.

Bashful, like a teenager, Stephen laughed to himself, and closed the bathroom door.

The Woman emerged from the bathroom ten minutes later, and walked towards the living room. She was wearing a bra and hot pants, and a long red dress that covered them, all belonging to Stephen's wife. The rain continued, heavy outside. The living room/kitchen area held the distinct smell of coffee being brewed. And her suspicions were correct, as at the table sat Stephen, with two cups of coffee. He was already drinking his.

"I thought you might need this. Would you like some?"

She walked towards the table, and sat down slowly. She grabbed the cup and smelled it for a few seconds. Stephen watched her, not knowing what she was doing. Seconds went by, her smelling the contents of the cup carefully until she decided to drink it.

"It's good," the Woman said.

The Woman placed the cup on the table.

Stephen smiled, happy in the fact that he had finally been able to reach through the Woman's comatose-like state and get some sort of response from her. He drank from his cup, and decided to question her.

"Who are you, Miss?"

"My name doesn't matter, does it?"

Stephen paused for a second when he heard this. Seemed so philosophical.

"Well, you don't have to, Miss," he answered, "but I would like to know what possessed you to be out in this thunderstorm at this ungodly hour. You could have caught pneumonia."

She let out a small smile, and continued drinking from her coffee cup.

"Well," said Stephen, putting the cup on the table, "My name is Stephen, I am a teacher at Johnny Ramone Music High, I am married to an art restoration expert, we've been together for seventeen..."--he paused, smiling as he noticed something behind her—"well, look at the picture behind you!"

The Woman turned around slowly, almost like she was a wary cat, expecting something to happen, and saw what he was pointing to. It was a picture frame. She picked it up, and saw him, his face covered in a hippie beard that he'd shaved since the picture was taken, standing next to a beautiful blonde woman and two young daughters. They looked like the kind of perfect royal family pictures you saw in gossip and lifestyle magazines.

"Those two are Cindy and Donna, my two daughters. Two years difference, the oldest just turned seven."

She looked at the children, touching the picture with her fingers slowly over their heads.

"They are so beautiful at this age, aren't they?" she said, "so innocent."

She said this with a dead-blank stare. Stephen grinned, nodding proudly.

"Yeah. They were kind of a surprise. We spent a lot of time, just me and her, living our lives devoted to each other. When she got pregnant, we just said 'Fuck it', and decided to give parenthood a go. It was the best decision I've made in my life."

She put the picture back where it was. There was a bottle of laundry detergent next to it, recently bought since it was still wrapped in plastic.

"Do you need me to call someone, ma'am?" he asked, his smile turning into a serious look of concern.

The Woman sat still for a few seconds, seemingly taking everything in around her.

"Could I have some sugar for my coffee first?"

Stephen smiled nodding, grabbed her cup, and got up from the table. He walked to the kitchen and opened one of the cabinets, grabbing the sugar container. He opened it up, and was horrified to see that it was covered in ants.

"Aw, shit, looks like one of my daughters got into the sugar box on the weekend. This thing is full of ants!"

"Oh" said the Woman.

"Don't worry, ma'am, I'll open another one."

He threw the polluted contents of the container into the trash and washed it off. Leaving it to dry, he grabbed another bag from the cabinet and opened it, pouring a spoonful and a half of sugar into the coffee, spinning it softly until it looked just right.

He returned to the table, cup in hand, and gave the cup to the Woman.

"Should be all better now."

The Woman tasted her cup, and nodded approvingly.

"So," said Stephen, grabbing his cup, "is there someplace I can call?"

Stephen took a full swallow of what remained of his coffee. He stood there silently, waiting for her to answer. But she didn't say anything, just stared, her eyes dead-locked against his. Suddenly, his vision began getting blurry. The room seemed to be rocking back and forth.

"Wait... what the..." he said, in a groggy, shaky voice.

He tried getting up, but fell again on the chair. His vision wasn't well, but it was well enough that he could see her dead stare become a menacing grin. He also noticed the detergent had been opened, the plastic lying on the table. He tried to speak, but only nonsense and drool came out, and she decided, mercifully some might say, to knock him out into the black with the coffee cup, slamming it with all her strength until it smashed.

He could taste blood. It was warm and metallic, and from wherever it was coming from, he was swallowing it, his mouth full of it. He was regaining his consciousness, but he could see nothing. His eyes were covered with something; felt like a cloth, but he wasn't very sure. His hands were tied from behind, and he was definitely sitting on a chair. He tried to struggle, but he simply vomited all over his knees. Maybe he didn't see it, but he could smell it, and could also feel the warm liquid pouring onto his legs.

Outside, the rain continued.

As he finished, he took big breaths and tried to talk, but it all seemed to come out blurred. He would try to make sentences, to scream, to help, but it just didn't make sense. That was when he realized his tongue was missing. He let out a scream, but it all came out like he was biting down on a wet towel. His mouth dripped blood and vomit all over himself.

"Aw, shit!" a voice, a female voice, was heard from far away.

Steps made their way towards him quickly, crashing hard against the floor, seeming like they were full of hate, and the cloth that covered his eyes was removed. In front of him stood the Woman, still wearing the clothes he loaned her, only now they were stained with blood.

"I took such good care of cleaning your face up, and now you've covered yourself in this filth. You should have known better."

Stephen tried to scream, but it all again seemed muffled and wet, spitting the blood on her already stained dress. The Woman slapped him across the face, a slap so hard that one of his front teeth went flying across the living room, making him stop screaming, and start crying.

"Waf haf u dun tih mi?" he spoke, trying his best to create sentences and failing miserably.

She just looked at him.

"I have a lot to say, Mr. Shusett, and I don't want you interrupting me."

After she said this, she grabbed another chair, and was about to sit in front of him, but stopped. The two were now facing each other. She shook her head, looking down towards the floor in disgust, and grabbed a bag. Stephen didn't know where this bag came from, since she sure as hell didn't have it when he rescued her from the rain, but it was covered in mud and wet, so she must have kept it outside. She opened up the bag and grabbed a ball gag, its ball red with a black leather strap around it, and placed it over his mouth.

"I'm sorry, but your noises are disturbing me." she said over his muffled protests. She placed the leather straps behind his head, and tied them quickly, like a pro.

"There" she said, as she sat down in front of him again, "That's better."

Stephen protested, but all the muffled noise seemed pointless. Still, he seemed to be damned determined he'd make as much muffled protest as he could, thrashing about in his chair and making noises, looking at the Woman with intense hate. The Woman simply stared back, not smiling, not angry, not even breathing heavily, just staring, like a statue. Finally, after a couple of tries, Stephen began to tire himself out, and it even hurt to breathe.

"Are you done?"

Stephen didn't answer, just looked down at the floor, angrily.

The Woman placed her hand inside her small cleavage and took out a cell phone. She placed it in front of him. A picture of a young boy, aged five or six, with blonde hair and a smile, was on display.

"Do you recognize this boy, Mr. Shusett?"

Stephen looked at the picture, and shook his head in a negative fashion.

The Woman passed her finger across the screen, revealing another picture. A red-headed girl with freckles, about the same age.

"How about her?"

Stephen looked again, and shook his head negatively.

The Woman did the same as before, passing her finger across the screen, showing the picture of another child: a brunette little girl, the same age as the others.

"Do you recognize her?"

Stephen looked at the picture, and his eyes opened. She might be a small child, but there was no question: this was the Woman, about age five. She might have a killer body now, but the mouth, the eyes, the cheeks, they were the same.

He looked wide-eyed at the Woman. The Woman nodded.

"Yes, Mr. Shusett, that is me."

The Woman threw the cell phone in the bag, and returned to Stephen.

"You began teaching fifteen years ago, correct?"

Stephen nodded.

"And you remember none of the children except me?"

Stephen shook his head negatively, making noises, as if trying to explain himself.

"Oh... you don't remember me, you just recognize me?"

Stephen nodded.

"I guess I still look like a child..."

Stephen seemed to smile when he heard this, but the Woman seemed to get angrier as he smiled, so he stopped smiling as soon as he noticed. Something about her stare made him even more afraid.

"On August 15, 2000, my mother enrolled me in Johnny Ramone High School, where I was to learn to play the cello. I was one of your students."

64

Stephen listened on, trying to make a connection.

"On October 22nd, you asked me to stay over after school because you wanted to tutor me..."

At that moment, at that pause, Stephen's eyes widened in terror, and he remembered.

"Where you proceeded to tie me up, make me gag on your penis as I gave you a blow job, then raped me in my vagina and my anus for the next half hour."

Stephen began to cry and began to shake again, trying desperately to escape.

"You told me you'd hurt me if I told anyone. And until three years ago, I never did."

Stephen began to scream, his muffled noises heard all over the house and nowhere else.

During all this, The Woman seemed to stay completely quiet, simply looking at him, without any hints of emotion.

"I see you remember me now..." She took a cigarette box from her bag and lit one of them.

Stephen continued to struggle with all his strength until he gave out again and collapsed on himself, too tired, crying hysterically.

"I think you remember the rest of the kids, too."

Stephen cried as memories flash in front of his eyes. He was a sick man, hiding under the mask of wholesomeness, having gotten away with the sexual abuse of fifteen children, boys and girls, in his years as a music teacher.

"Three years ago, we began to get in touch with each other, Mr. Shusett, thinking about how we could get over our nightmares, our traumas, and our pain. We all have the scars of your work, Mr. Shusett. Some of us were able to deal with it, some of us didn't. Jessica Rogers killed herself two years ago, as did August Mercedes and Joseph Greenstone."

The Woman took the cigarette from her mouth and blew smoke towards Stephen's face. Stephen coughed, drawing more tears from his eyes.

"I was picked as the tool of our vengeance, Mr. Shusett.

Time to pay the piper."

Saying this, The Woman stuck her cigarette into Stephen's left eyeball. The pain soared, it seemed to turn everything into white and black. He let out a muffled scream of pain and felt the high-heeled kick crashing into his stomach, followed by the sensation of falling back onto the floor. But nothing compared to the pain of the fire in his eyeball.

He could hear the Woman's footsteps, and the noises of her taking something out of the bag. But the pain. It was just too much to bear.

The neighbors heard the screams throughout the following hour, screams so horrifying that they could have easily been heard two or three counties away by the Devil himself. They all listened, they all wondered. Some didn't do anything, and thought it was probably a horror film; after all, Mr. Shusett was a big fan of horror movies and had a couple in his collection. Others thought it might have been some sort of kinky sex game. His front door neighbor, Ms. Withers, a woman in her 80's who read fortunes on her spare time, figured he was simply practicing the act of primal screaming, since she had recently read a book on the subject.

Oh, how wrong they were.

Finally, angry over the fact that he wasn't getting any sleep, Mr. Worshone, who lived at the end of the street (yes, the screams could be heard all the way down there) called the police. It took ten minutes, and by then the screams had stopped, but they reached the house. With their raingear on, they walked under the pounding water that had been falling all night towards the house. Sergeant Richards and Deputy Orloff, one a seasoned veteran and the other a rookie in his third month on the force, answered the call. Richards was the one who knocked on the door.

"Now stay alert, kid," he said towards Orloff, giving him the stern and grilling look of a man ready for anything, "you never know how crazy these house calls can be."

With nobody responding, Richards called his supervisor for permission to knock the door down and grinned when he received the OK. This was one of his favorite parts of the job, and every time he had the opportunity to do it, he took it, even if it meant pushing the other officers out of his way to do so. So, with all the strength his forty-five year old body could gather and concentrate towards his foot, he kicked the door in, breaking it off his hinges and making it crash towards the floor. Deputy Orloff looked on, impressed as the Sergeant walked in towards the dark house.

"Look for a light switch, Orloff!"

Hearing his order, Orloff began to touch the walls. He had left his flashlight in the car, and was hoping to God that he could find a switch before the Sarge realized his mistake. Thankfully, and in less than a couple of seconds, he found them, and turned on the lights.

What they saw would never leave their minds. They both screamed at the same time, and the Sarge, who thought had seen everything, puked the contents of his stomach onto the floor, a thick mixture of fast food and bourbon.

It was the music room from Hell.

A Cello had its strings removed -replaced with the intestines of Mr. Shusett. The torso had been severed, and an arm had been attached to the hole where the head used to be to make it look like some kind of deformed guitar. His feet were stitched together and had holes drilled into them, making them look like a flute. And his head, most macabre of all, had his skin completely peeled off, the top of his head scalped and cut to look like a drum. Two bones sat on top of it, like drumsticks.

The walls and the floor were covered in all his organs, bones, and blood.

A parakeet happily picked at the birdseed that had been dropped on top of the liver.

The window had Mr. Shusett's penis and testicles taped to it, and in blood, the murderer had written "He made me cry, and cry, and cry, but now I made him cry..."

The Sarge lay on the floor, writhing in his own vomit, crying in despair like a child that had received his first bruise. Orloff just looked on, stunned, as his hair turned white.

She had walked for five minutes, letting the rain clean the blood from her body as it fell on her. She heard the police screaming from down the ditch behind Mr. Shusett's house, and walked towards a small man-made river that resided there. Its waters had risen almost to the house itself. She removed her dress and threw it into the river, followed by the bag containing everything she had brought. She sat down on the muddy grass and thought that perhaps she would die from drowning when the river's water rose enough to engulf her completely.

Maybe she'd die from pneumonia. Or, more probably, more

cops would arrive, and one of them would eventually notice her and she'll die resisting arrest, getting shot by men and women with the macabre artwork, the Bosch-like images of her creation burned into their brains, never able to be shaken. It didn't matter; she was smiling, not just any smile, a smile of true happiness, something she hadn't done in many years. She would die knowing that she avenged herself, and her family, and her friends. She just wished there was more time to enjoy it...

About Jorge Palacios

Jorge Palacios is a failed exploitation filmmaker turned horror writer. He lives and writes in Puerto Rico, where he watches extreme horror, exploitation and porn movies, reads fucked up books and publishes zines full of his own writing. He also goes to punk shows and hits on chicks with weird hair.

The Otterman Place
By Alice J. Black

Their new house was huge, colossal even. It stretched over a plot of land that extended right onto the woods bordering the whole street. As Callie stared out of the back kitchen window into the trees beyond, a cold shiver snaked across her shoulders, despite the fact that it was daytime. She didn't like it. Not one bit.

"Callie, can I get some help?" her husband called. His voice was strained though, whether it was through lifting or some mitigated anger, she wasn't sure.

Husband. Funny word, she thought. Sure, he was her husband legally, for just over a year now, but in all other senses of the word, he failed to live up to expectation. He was the breadwinner—had insisted she quit her job—and that meant Callie became the dutiful housewife; cleaning day in-day out, cooking his meals for when he returned no matter what the hour, and becoming a yes woman. Everything about Callie and her life had changed since she met Jason and it seemed there was no finding her old self again. Even now she realized how stupid she had been to agree with moving to the country—she was isolated now.

She was nothing but a waif, a woman who nodded absently and agreed with the man she was to spend the rest of her life with. Life was a mirage and she was living in the reflection.

"Coming," she called back, pulling herself from the window and the naked trees beyond. Autumn was passing and with winter coming on strong, the cold winds were picking up and the colors that she so loved were fading into dull black and grey hues.

Making her way through the huge house, she went to the front porch. Jason was struggling with a huge box, face red as he heaved it up into his arms and waddled towards the house. He shooed her away with an angry grunt.

"You think you can actually *do* something today?" He pointed at her face, eyes bulging out of their sockets.

Callie dropped her head, where she found herself staring into the half-open cardboard box on the floor. Dust motes floated in the air and in that moment she felt the last of her fight leave. She was done. She was a housewife, meek and demure, and that's all she would ever be. She had been assigned her lot in life; it was time to live up to it. "Sorry," she murmured.

As he turned to leave she noticed the sweat patch on his back and stifled a smile. One thing Jason hated was anything being dirty or unclean. She supposed that's why the house had to be cleaned top to bottom on a regular basis and anything worn even just for five minutes was thrown in the wash. No wonder her laundry pile was as big as it was.

As Jason heaved boxes and furniture back and forth, Callie began to sort and unpack. She pushed boxes into their rightfully located rooms and stacked and organized. Organization was her strong point and it was at times like this she revealed it. But any time she made her way into the kitchen, those dark barren trees caught her eye, and as the day drew on, the shadows beneath the trunks deepened.

It was way after nine when they finally stopped. The night had drawn in completely with a damp chill that seemed to permeate everything. The van was empty and locked, their new house was stacked and cluttered everywhere with boxes and hastily placed furniture. As Jason paused to drink a coffee Callie had prepared for them, he gazed about the kitchen.

"This place is a tip. What have you been doing all day?"

"I was sorting the boxes into rooms." She took a sip of her own coffee. The liquid was strong and bitter with a slight sweet aftertaste, the consequence of not finding their cutlery yet.

"We've been at this all day. I've emptied that entire van myself." He drained his coffee. A drop of the liquid dripped down his chin and he swiped at it with a dusty paw.

Callie shrugged. There was no point in arguing.

Something caught her eye from outside, a swirl of darkness amongst the shadows. Squinting, she peered closer. All she could make out were the sentinel of trees and the darkest blackness she could ever imagine. "Did you see that?"

70

"What?"

"I saw something move outside."

Jason stepped closer to the window and leaned on the sink to get a better view. He gazed outside for a second, letting his eyes adjust before he pulled back.

"There's nothing out there, Callie." A huge sigh followed his statement and it said everything he intended it to. He was wondering why he'd brought a city girl to live out in the country. It was a huge adjustment to her life. But like a dutiful wife would, she followed him blindly when he asked and so here they were in their new neighborhood in the country, where it got pitch black by sun down. There would be a lot of adjusting indeed.

***

It took a few days, but finally Callie managed to get their house in some order while Jason did manly things like organize the garage and his study.

Slowly, she began to get used to the place with all of the noises that came with night and the loneliness that seemed to close in around them, yet she could never settle. Whenever she was alone, she felt the hairs rise on the back of her neck as if she was being watched constantly.

Their street was a ghost town. There were ten houses in total, each with huge gardens and driveways identical to theirs and not once over those few days did she spot a neighbor. She craved human contact—other than her husband—and as Friday rolled around with Jason off to work in his habitual routine, she made her way into the small village.

It was a short walk and as she strolled into the town centre, she found she was glad to see other people going at their daily routines and minding their own business. Something close to relief folded over her in that moment and she came to a stark realization that she was lonely.

The road was lined with small shops, stores, antique places and, of course, the obligatory café. It was there she made her first stop.

A bell tinkled over the door as she entered. The door creaked and, with her first footstep on the hardwood floor, it seemed that all eyes in the café were on her. To her right there was a little counter with a glass display full of tasty treats and to her left, an array of tables covered with lace tablecloths with fresh flowers in the centre of each. *Quaint.*

"Can I help you?" asked an older woman from beyond the counter. She was rotund and homely. Her grey hair was set in a perm and the apron she wore was dusted with remnants of flour. As the woman smiled, Callie felt herself relaxing.

"I'm Callie, I just moved in up the road."

"Ah." The woman smiled. "We've been wondering."

"We?"

The woman nodded in the direction of the tables, where it seemed all of the customers were monitoring their conversation.

"We don't get many new folks around here," she added in way of explanation. "I'm Martha."

"Nice to meet you."

"How are you finding it so far?"

"Different. I'm a city girl."

"Oh it's not as bad as you think. We have all the modern things now. Card machines and Internet." Martha patted the reader beside the till with doughy hands.

"Oh, it's not that." Callie shook her head. Sure, she was a city girl, but she wasn't high maintenance.

"Then what?" Martha asked, a frown forming on her brow.

Callie paused for a moment. How could she explain it? There was nothing, and everything. The place was eerily quiet, she had no friends and the woods behind her house always seemed to beckon. More than once she found herself on the back porch just staring at the trees beyond without being able to recall how long she had been out there. "It's… just quiet is all."

"Well don't you worry. Us girls are always in here ready for a gossip if you ever get lonely."

"Thanks."

"Can I get you anything?"

"Just a coffee, thanks."

Cup in hand, Callie made her way to a seat beside the window. Outside, the world was blowing a gale. The sky was soft and grey; winter was coming.

Sipping at her coffee, the bubbles of the latte caught on her tongue, fizzling. She had been trying to convince Jason to get her a coffee machine for the house but it had been six months of asking with no result. Jason controlled everything financial and anything she spent she had to justify. *Is married life really supposed to be like this?*

"Hello, dear." A voice caught her off guard. Callie shook herself and looked up to see two elderly people, a couple, looking down at her with kindly smiles.

"Hi, I'm Callie," she introduced herself again.

The old woman pulled out a seat and made herself comfortable while her husband stood behind her, hands resting on the back of the chair. A gentleman. *Jason could take some lessons from him.*

"I'm Olive, and this is Jack. Did you move into the old Otterman house?"

"Yeah, we did. Me and my husband." Callie nodded.

Something flashed across Olive's face in that moment. A spark of fear lilted in her eyes.

"Is... is there something wrong with the house?" Callie ventured. The question rolled from her tongue too readily. Ever since they moved into that place something weighed on her. Lethargy played on her body and her mood was dropping. She had known it was too good to be true. A house that had stood empty for so long had to have a story behind it. Jason had assured her there was none, but then she had known him to lie to her on occasion.

Jack took a seat beside his wife. He clasped his fingers together and as he watched her, his eyebrows knitted together. His face was stern, lips turned down at the corners. Something passed between the couple in that second the almost imperceptible shake of the head.

"She deserves to know, Olive," Jack argued against the silent point made. He took a deep breath and Callie leaned in, eager to hear what he had to say. "That house has been empty for coming up ten years now. The Ottermans lived there. The parents, Zack and Julie, and their three kids. They moved into the place when Jenn was just a baby and were there until... well, until it happened." His voice quieted and he leaned forward, a connoisseur of gossip.

"What happened?" Callie's voice was quiet as she controlled the shake within her vocal chords. Her heart pumped faster and her stomach knotted. She had known from the moment she set foot in that place. There was something wrong with the house. A bargain like that wouldn't be had for any other reason, but Jason and his damn stubbornness wouldn't listen. Anger boiled in her veins.

"Most of what happened that night is still a mystery, but us neighbourhood watch folks put our heads together and we've come up with a theory. Blair was the middle kid and he had always been the troubled one. He was shadowed by Jenn, his big sister, and then there was... oh, what was her name, dear?"

"Emily."

"Yes, Emily, the little one. The girls were always so pleasant. We would always see them playing out in the yard, in the street- but it was rare to see Blair. When he hit his teens—we live right opposite, you see—the arguments started. It became a daily thing."

"Those poor parents were at their wits end," Olive added with a definitive nod.

"Then one night," Jack leaned further in, his voice softening. Callie was enraptured, listening hard. The knot in her stomach tightened. "The arguments stopped abruptly. Just like that. There was silence for a short time. And then came the screams."

"It was terrible to hear." Olive shuddered.

"We called the police, but by the time they got here it was too late."

Callie's lips were parted, jaw dropped as she hung on the words. "Too late?" Her voice was a whisper.

"They were all of them dead. Murdered."

The word rang through her mind. *Murdered*. The family was murdered in their house—her house. Sharp fingers traced their way down her spine and goose bumps popped on her flesh.

"All except for Blair," Jack went on. "He was never found."

"What?" Callie gasped.

"Jack!" Olive remonstrated with a sharp slap to his hand. "You're scaring her."

Cradling his hand, his wife rubbed it softly. Callie saw bulbous veins popping out of his flesh, blue worms beneath translucent skin. "She lives in the damn house, Olive. It's her right. Am I scaring you?" He turned his attention back to Callie.

"No... I... it's just... I had no idea. I mean, I knew the price

74

was too good to be true, but I didn't expect *this*."

"Surely the estates agent told your husband?" Olive questioned.

"He didn't mention anything."

"I'm sorry, Callie," Jack finally spoke. "It's the local story around here, everyone knows it. I thought you would have heard something before moving in."

"Don't worry about it. I'm fine."

"Come on, Jack," Olive ordered. "I think we should go before we do any more damage. Can we give you a lift home?"

"No, I'm fine. thanks. I'm going to the shop."

Olive nodded and stood, her chair scraping across the linoleum floor. Jack followed suit, but before he turned to leave, he paused and looked over his shoulder. He shuffled back to the table, his hands coming to rest on the back of the chair once again. As he looked down at Callie there was something in his eyes. She couldn't tell whether it was concern or fear. "If you need anything, or you have any trouble—at all— just call across the road. We're mostly always in at night." With that he walked away, leaving the café. The bell tingled in his wake.

***

By the time Jason rolled through the door it had long since been dark and he stunk of booze. It wasn't the kind of smell that told her he'd had a couple of pints after work with his colleagues. No, he was roaring, stinking drunk, which wasn't like him at all. And the worst thing was that after the smell of vodka faded away, she was hit with a sickly sweet candy-shop smell. Another woman's perfume.

Callie wasn't the sort to jump to conclusions. After all, he probably had some female colleagues. All the same, she didn't like it.

"Where's ma tea?" he demanded as he strode into the kitchen.

"I didn't know when you were coming home."

"Tha' shouldn' matter. I'm hungry," he slurred his words as he dropped into a seat at the kitchen table. He looked up at her expectantly.

With a deep sigh, Callie busied herself in the kitchen making him something to eat while having to listen to his drunk babbling about his work day and how tough it was and how he wasn't sure he would fit in but that he would make it work. For them. He emphasised the last point. Them. It was a dig. He wanted a family, craved having children, but in the last year she hadn't managed to conceive and it was grating on him. A lot. *Maybe that's why he's drunk.*

Callie set down the sandwich on the table in front of him and as Jason tucked in with the ferocity of a big cat, she slide into the seat opposite. "Jason," she started. She tried to keep her voice neutral.

"Wha?" he answered between chews.

"I went into the village today to do a bit of shopping and I met some of the neighbours."

"Oh yeah? We should have a party or something,' don' you think?" He sprayed a hunk of chewed bread on the table.

"Yeah, if you like," she agreed to keep him on side. "But listen, I was talking to Olive and Jack and they were telling me about this house."

"This one?" He pointed to the table, pressing his finger into the wood as if that very spot was the heart of the house.

Callie nodded. "Yes. They told me something about it, a story."

"An' you believed 'em?"

"Did something happen in the house, Jason?" she pressed, ignoring his question.

He sighed audibly and dropped his fists to the table top. He stared at her with deadpan eyes. "The estate agent might have said something about why the place was so cheap." He was beginning to sober up.

"A family was murdered here, Jason. *Murdered.* " Her voice broke.

Gesturing with his hand, he waved it off. "Don't be silly. Even if that's true, it's in the past."

"If that's your way of reassuring me, you're wrong. They never found the kid that did it. He could still be out there."

Suddenly his eyes were thunderous, his mouth turned down in an ugly grimace. It was like he was changing, a different person almost. Dropping the rest of his sandwich on his plate he stared her down. "I am the breadwinner in this family. I am the one who chooses where we live. We are staying here."

"But—"

"Stop it, Callie," he growled. "This is none of your concern. I'm going to bed. Make me some dinner for work tomorrow."

Their conversation was over. He had made that clear. His feet thumped up the stairs and he was muttering to himself as he went. Callie got herself up and, like the good wife, prepared some sandwiches for him for the next day. She pushed them into the fridge in his lunch box and flicked off the light.

Just about to follow her husband to bed, something caught her eye. Some movement out in the garden. Or was it the woods? Her heart slammed against her chest and her breathing sped up. Peering closer, she saw a shadow dashing across the boundary of the trees. It moved so quick that she could have blinked and missed it but yet, there it was. It was tall and broad. She couldn't help but recall the story of their house, the Ottermans, their son. He was still out there, still at large, as the news would tell her. *Would he have moved on by now?*

Finally shaking herself, Callie went to bed but sleep evaded her that night for fear of the shadows outside.

***

Jason rolled beside her with a deep grumble as the alarm shrilled from his side of the bed. It started Callie, and as she shook the fog of semi-consciousness from her mind, the shadows slowly disintegrated, melting into the background of her subconscious.

Reaching out, Jason slapped his hand on the clock and, smacking his lips together, settled back down onto his pillow.

"Jason, get up." Callie shook him. "You have work."

With an incoherent mumble, he shook her off and closed his eyes. "Make me coffee."

Callie forced herself from the cocoon of the bed. The outside world was cold and as she headed down to the kitchen, she pulled on a robe. Frost covered the lawn outside and as she filled the kettle, setting it to boil, she could see the tiny drops of ice sparkling in the morning sun. It was beautiful, serene. In that moment she realised it was the first time she had seen beauty in their new home, their new life. *Perhaps I can make this work after all.*

Minutes later, Jason appeared at the foot of the stairs. His hair was truly bed-ridden and his day-old stubble was gruff. He looked—and sounded—like a caveman as he trudged to the kitchen and snatched the cup from Callie's hand. He gulped the liquid, chugging it down quick. Callie knew he was looking for a hit of wake-me-up. Inside she chuckled at his stupidity. Drinking on a school night. That used to be a big no-no for Jason. Something had obviously changed and she didn't like it.

After Jason left for work, Callie was restless. The house was clean and tidy and there was nothing for her to do. From where she stood beside the sink with her second coffee of the day, she couldn't help but stare out of that kitchen window. There was something out there that she didn't understand. Something that scared her.

It was noon before she knew it, the sun reaching a nestling place above the woods. Beams of light filtered through the naked branches falling to the last of the icicles clinging to the ground.

Compulsion took over. She wanted to—no, *had* to— go into the woods. She had to know what was out there.

Moving as if her life depended on it, Callie rushed around the house grabbing her coat, pulling on her winter boots, locating a scarf. Within minutes, she was ready for her expedition and was stepping out of the back door and onto the porch where frost crunched under her boots. Zipping up her coat, Callie wrapped the scarf tight and with an air of determination, strode into the morning.

The air hit her chest and plumes of white breath escaped her lungs. The journey down the garden was her first exploration and she took in the shrubs on either side, still lush in evergreen immortality. A lone tree stood in the centre of the garden—as barren as the trees beyond—and not far from that a concrete bird bath stood, the water frozen in a crystalline pool.

Then she reached the border of the woods. Shadow loomed across the length of the tree line, a chill emanating from the heart of the trees. Brown leaves settled on the floor, dry and untouched but for the sparkling frost webbed across them. Trunk followed trunk, and though a shadow hung overarched, frail light filtered through.

Callie stepped into the trees and was immediately swept up into the atmosphere. Darkness blanketed the area along with a chill that not only caused her hairs to stand up on end but hit her right in the gut and sent spasms of ice spiralling out into her stomach.

Yet still she didn't stop. On she wandered, her feet crunching across dead leaves, all the while her eyes darting this way and that. Everything else was silent. There were no birds, no crickets chirping in the undergrowth. She was alone in the dull void of the trees.

A chill trickled down her spine. The air around her got thicker, colder. Her heart pummelled in her chest, beating against her ribcage in a frantic metre. She had to move. Everything in her body, in her mind told her to move. She listened. She had to get out of there. Callie spun, about to make her way back through the trees to the house.

A figure blocked her way. This was no tree trunk. It was a man, his face partially covered by the tree trunk he crouched behind. His hands cradled the bark lovingly. They were red, raw and were full of sores, his knuckles were blistered.

The face behind the trunk was something to behold. A shaggy beard upon a young face—or a face that should have been young but for the wrinkles set deep into the pale skin. He watched her with wide eyes, not moving, lips pressed together.

Everything halted. Time itself stood still as Callie was frozen to the spot, the heel of her right foot lifting from the ground, ready to stride forward. Her arms hung at her sides, hands dangling loosely. Breath poured from her chest as her anxiety rocketed.

It seemed they stood there for an age, each of them staring, neither of them moving. Callie knew that this man was not a neighbour. He was someone else. Fear gnawed at her gut.

"Hello," the man spoke. The word was an exploratory one.

She was dumbfounded, unsure. Then finally, she responded, "Hello." She heard the quiver in her voice. He eyed her once more, dark eyes looking up and down her tall form and then, as if satisfied by her appearance, he stepped from behind the tree trunk.

The man who emerged had weathered too many storms, seen too many things. He was a young man, but had the aura of someone who had travelled the world twice over and did not want to think about the traumas he had seen.

"I'm Blair."

The words hit her like a punch to the stomach. The wind

flew from her chest as she sputtered over words, her mouth opening and closing like a fish out of water. He was the boy from the story—the man—the one who murdered his family.

Everything went black.

***

When she woke, Callie could only stare at the man before her. He leaned over her, concern knitting his brow. He was young yet old, his eyes holding the depths of the unknown. She knew it was crazy, yet in that instant she wanted to know his story.

"What happened?" The words fell from her mouth.

"You fainted."

"I mean your family." Silence ensued. Tension filled the air as Callie held her breath. Recognition sparked in his eye and his lower lip twitched. Then finally, he opened his mouth.

"You must think I'm a monster," he stated quite simply. "I wouldn't blame you if you do. The rest of the town does." He was well-spoken.

Callie could only listen. Her mind was racing, his words flying through at a rate of knots going over and over in cycles across her brain.

"I murdered my family, it's true," he disclosed. His shoulders heaved and sagged in a sob, and in the thicket of trees Callie glimpsed the silvery trail of a tear as it tracked down his weather-beaten face.

Callie felt two things in that moment. A fear so intense she almost backed up and ran right there. Here was a man standing in front of her, telling her he murdered his family. The skin prickled on her flesh beneath the layers she wore and her thighs twitched with adrenaline. She was alone in the woods with a killer—a murderer. Yet something made her stay. Something in the pitiful way he looked at her with eyes so wide and full of sadness that kept her there. This man— Blair —had more to his story than most believed.

"Why?" she finally asked.

"They made me do it." His words were quiet, yet firm. They filtered into her mind and she went through a series of frowns as she contemplated their meaning.

"*They* made you do it? As in your family?"

He nodded. Callie's eyes widened. It seemed madness, what he was telling her, but if it was true then it meant there was so much more to this than the town knew about.

"There's something in that house. Something evil."

A cold trickle raced up Callie's spine. His words resonated within her as she realised that evil is exactly what she felt in that house. There was something that pulled at her, nipped at her skin and caused her stomach to clench when she was left alone in that house. Something dark.

"What... what do you mean?" she stammered. It seemed absurd to be talking about some unknown force of evil residing in her abode, yet at the same time, as she looked into Blair's eyes, she knew it was true. And she felt it, deep within her soul.

"I don't know what it is. It was there when we moved in and it never left. Do you feel it?"

Callie nodded. "It haunts me. It's like there's something standing watch whenever I'm there."

"That's how it started for us. Feeling uncomfortable for a while, then it escalated."

"Escalated how?" She dreaded the words he might say next.

"It became malevolent. Started moving things, doing things. At first it was small stuff, confusing us. Then it got worse. I woke up one night to find my dad standing over my bed with a knife in his hands."

Callie gasped, hand flying to her mouth.

"I managed to wake him out of his trance but it was then that I knew how far it had gone. He was possessed with... something."

"The evil."

Brian nodded. "It started affecting my mum next, then my sisters. My family would fly off the handle for no reason, every one of them overreacting to things- and they changed. My family was not my family anymore. I was living in a nuthouse, too scared to sleep."

"It didn't get you?"

"I didn't let it." He shook his head. "Then one night my dad came into my room. He was lucid and he was terrified. I could see it in his face. He asked me then to kill them all. He knew with the last ounce of normalcy he had left that I was the only one who could end it."

"So you murdered your family."

"Yes."

A huge gust of wind whipped around them, sending leaves scattering about. It reminded Callie where they were and she crossed her arms over her chest, huddling close.

"You feel it, don't you?" Brian startled her from her thoughts with his quiet voice.

Callie nodded.

"And has it affected anything else yet?"

Pausing to think, Jason was the first thing that came to mind. They were the only two people in that house and as far as she was aware, she hadn't changed. But Jason had. His temper had thickened, become an oozing rage that took over everything. He was doing things he never would, despite not being a great husband and, she realised with a dull finality, she was scared of him. She was scared of how he had changed and the possibility that he could continue to change, to get angrier. To absorb the evil of the house.

"Yes."

Callie finally realised that she wasn't going crazy, that everything she was experiencing was real and to be fearful of it was the smartest thing she could do.

"Your husband?" he asked.

Callie nodded.

"You need to do it, before it's too late." The words burned a pit of dread in her stomach. Bile rose up her oesophagus and burned her chest as she heaved. It spurted from her mouth in a hot stream to the ground.

"Callie!" Her name was shouted, loud and bristled. It was Jason. Fear wrenched her heart and her hands trembled. Callie checked her watch. She had been out there for hours.

"I have to go." She stumbled backwards.

"Wait!" Blair shouted.

"Callie!" Jason's voice again. This time it seemed to echo around her, bouncing around the trees, in her head. There was something in it, in his voice. She swallowed hard.

Callie ran through the trees back to the house. Her chest burned as she moved, her legs working harder than they had in a long time. She hurried on and finally reached the boundary to her garden just minutes later.

There she stopped. Jason was standing on the porch. His arms hung down at his sides and his right foot was thrust forward. Everything about him, his stance, the furrow on his brow and the darkness in his eyes, told her he was furious.

"Where the fuck have you been?" He marched across the lawn to meet her.

"I went for a walk." Callie motioned to the woods.

He stopped just inches from her face. Veins throbbed in his temple, pulsating. "I go to work all day and you think it's okay to go take a stroll?" She could smell whiskey on his breath, hot and sour.

"I didn't mean to be out there that long." She dropped her head, one quick way to dissipate his anger.

"I'm starving."

"I'll make you something now."

Callie scooted past him, rushing up the few steps and into the house where she shed her coat, dropping it on the back of a kitchen chair and busied herself in the kitchen preparing something for dinner. Jason took a little longer to come into the house and as she watched him out of the window, all she could barely see was the hint of her husband. Jason was different, angry. Possessed? Maybe—but she had no idea in hell what to do.

Dinner was a sombre affair. Jason's anger had somewhat dissipated but the air was thick and the sound of cutlery scraping across the plates was the only thing that could be heard. They sat across from each other at the kitchen table. The lights were on, giving the room a warm glow and the heat from the oven kept the temperature up. Outside, dusk had drawn on and the sky was dark grey. The silhouettes of the trees stood tall and wide, branches swaying side to side in the now rocketing wind. It howled around the house and shot down the chimney breast where it released mournful wails.

"Why you so quiet?" Jason shot across the table. When Callie glanced at him she saw a scowl on his face and something hiding there, just behind his visage. She wondered whether he knew it was there. *Hell, he probably invited it in.*

"Just enjoying dinner." She forced a smile.

"Why? It's shit." Picking up his plate, he flung it across the kitchen, where it smashed on the wall sending shards of china and tangled pieces of spaghetti to the floor in a slop. Callie squealed and jumped in her seat.

"I was just trying to make something quick. I knew how hungry you were."

"If you were a good wife it would have been ready for me coming home."

"Sorry." The head drop again.

His chair scraped across the floor and fell backwards. Fear sliced Callie's heart. He was on his feet. Then something on the table, a slight scraping noise. Biting her lip, she worked up the courage to glance up. He held a knife in his right hand, knuckles white.

Callie swallowed. "Jason?"

When he looked at her, his eyes were black pits of tar that had soaked up all of the evil in the house. She could see it in his scowl, in the way he stalked forward. She was his prey.

Slowly, Callie pushed her chair backwards and stood, putting the table between Jason and herself.

Jason cocked his head to the side and paused, staring at her. "Why are you running, dear?" The smile he gave her in that moment sent shivers coursing through her body.

"Jason, you're not yourself."

He took a step. She took a step.

"Let me get you some help."

"Help? Help is it?" He took another step, this time his foot fall so heavy it sent vibrations through the table. "You think I need help? You want to lock me up, more like. Stupid bitch."

He had hit the nail right on the head, but she wasn't going to agree. "No, I mean a doctor. You might be coming down with something."

"Oh no, dear." He grinned again, displaying too many teeth. "That's you."

Her legs ached. She wanted to run, to get away. But everything in her mind told her that to move now would be her death.

"What do you mean?" she whispered.

"You're coming down with a case of being dead." With a

roar he rushed forward and with his free hand, threw the table aside. It landed with a heavy crack on the floor and spilled its contents across the kitchen floor.

Callie skipped past him and rushed down the passageway into the bedroom. Jason's steps were close behind, his breaths heavy. She thrust the door shut and seconds later his bulky form crashed against it. It jarred the door, but Callie kept her weight there. Once he moved she locked it, but she knew it wouldn't last long.

Backing away from the door, she watched as it rattled in the frame when Jason barged it once more. Again and again he pounded against the door, grunting and growling in frustration. No longer a human, he was a monster.

Callie cast her gaze across the bedroom, looking for something, anything she could use as a weapon. Then it hit her. Jason kept a bat under his side of the bed. *Perfect.*

Rushing across to the bed she dived onto the floor, stretching her hand under the bed frame as behind her, the door splintered. When she whirled, crouching on her haunches, Jason's face was peering through the door. His eyes were blacker than night and the grin that broke on his face in that moment settled ice in her heart. She was going to die.

He moved back and continued beating the door, bit by bit the wood chipped away, splintering and cracking and falling to the floor. He crashed through the remaining door, taking the rest of the wood out with him. His bare arms were bleeding from numerous cuts and scratches yet he didn't seem to care—to even notice.

Callie gripped the bat with both hands. "Jason, don't do this. You don't want to do this."

"Oh, I do." He grinned. "I want to plunge this knife right into your stomach and slice you all the way up to your neck until you spill your guts."

Callie's stomach lurched. She bit back the bile. Lifting herself, she rose from her crouch and poised the bat. Her hands shook.

Jason stalked forward, knife held in front of him with a death grip. His black eyes never left her—he watched her, took in her fear, and revelled in it.

"Jason, please." A tear spilled from her eye.

It made him pause, just for a moment. He looked at her, cocked his head once more. In that second she saw her husband, saw the anguish in his face. Then he was gone.

With a roar he lifted the knife above his head and made to charge. Callie tightened her grip and focused her mind. She had to time this just right. He was running, almost on her. His face was a mask of loathing that reached right down into his soul. Her husband was gone.

Just before he reached her, Callie swung as hard as she could, twisting her whole body. The bat connected with his temple with a dull crack and he instantly dropped to the floor, the knife falling from his hand. A small whimper escaped Callie's mouth as she stared down at him. Blood oozed from the cut on his head and he lay motionless, eyes closed.

Slowly, she lowered her weapon. The bat came to touch the floor and it fell from her grasp, hitting it with a hollow echo.

But she knew it wasn't over. Jason was still alive and so was the monster that possessed him. He was no longer her husband, but the idea of finishing him was almost too much to bear. Her chest heaved in sobs as she dropped to her knees beside him. His breaths were short and shallow but they were there.

Before she had a chance to make a decision, his eyes flicked open and with it he bore the full ferocity of his anger. Flipping himself over, he knocked Callie to the ground, where the wind flew from her chest. He picked up the knife once more and stomped across the room to her with robotic feet.

Jason looked down on her and Callie realised she had never seen anything so ugly, so malicious in her life.

"Goodbye, dear." His words—so banal—were so final. Grasping the knife with both of his hands, he lifted it high into the air. Callie could only watch as the blade came rushing towards her. Squeezing her eyes she prayed like she never had before. Prayed for divine intervention.

Her prayers were heard. The knife didn't pierce her gut as her husband intended. Instead, she heard another dull clunk and then his weight dropped on her and she was winded for a second time.

It was at that moment she opened her eyes. Standing behind her husband was Blair. He stood tall and defiant. Reaching down, he grabbed Jason by the scruff of the neck and dragged him off Callie. Jason was motionless once more, a puppet.

Blair picked up the knife intended for her and knelt close to Jason. Raising it, he was about to drop when Callie called out, "No!"

It stopped Blair in his tracks and he looked at her with quizzical eyes.

"I have to do it."

Callie crawled across the room and snatched the knife from Blair's hands. She straddled her husband and in that moment she took everything in. The blood seeping from two wounds in his head, the monster he was, and the monster he had become.

Just as he opened his eyes, those black discs screaming a fury of ages they had not known, Callie plunged the knife into his heart. His mouth opened in a silent scream as he stared at her, hands clawing for purchase.

The life faded from his eyes, all hatred dissipating along with her fear, and then he was gone.

Callie had murdered her husband.

"What now?" she asked Brian. Her life was in tatters.

"Now we leave."

About Alice J. Black

Alice lives and works in the North East of England where she lives with her partner and slightly ferocious cats! She writes all manner of fiction with a tendency to lean towards the dark side, but she also likes to challenge herself and write out of her genre too. Dreams and sleep-talking are currently a big source of inspiration and her debut novel, The Doors, is a young adult novel which originally sprouted from a dream several years ago and grew from there.

Markets
by C.S. Nelson

"Wow. This one will eat us alive for sure, but still… four bedrooms, two and a half baths, 2,900 square feet, and—that can't be right…"

The apartment thrummed with the quiet *whumba-whumba-whumba* of thin-walled coitus from next door. The kids were probably listening, too. Jarell had no doubt Bethany worried over such, though she feigned ignorance.

"What can't be?" Jarell reached for his glasses from the nightstand and hovered over his wife's shoulder. He kissed her neck, winning a distracted smile.

"This."

He inhaled deep through his nostrils and sat up straight, taking over the newspaper.

"Four beds, two plus baths…" he tapered off until he hit the mark and Bethany's eyes glowed. "Holy crap, baby girl."

"What do you think?"

"That's it. But 'contact for price?' That just don't sound legit to me." He caught himself mid-screw-up, his lawyer's brain about to pop her dream bubble, and asked over his glasses, "You?"

Her eyes slow-rolled up to him, a confounded swirl of hope and helplessness peeking through platinum bangs.

Whumba-whumba-whumba-whumba…

Jarell looked away and stared at the print without seeing words. Inside, his head told him to listen to his heart. His common sense told his heart to shut the fuck up, while his eyes watched the excitement building in his beautiful bride.

"Babygirl," Jarell said, Bethany snuggling deep against his chest, "we *need* two kitchens. One for you to do your wedding cake magic, and one for me to nuke Spaghettios for the kids."

"Ugh! You will *not* feed our children that garbage!" Bethany said, pushing her perfect breasts up and away, entwining *la creme* white legs with his, her vaginal heat warming his dark chocolate thigh. Her knee worked his groin.

Whumph! A spent moan filtered from next door.

"Okay." Jarell's voice wheezed submission and Bethany laughed before diving into him. Tomorrow they would start the process of buying their first home.

What the fuck kind of name is Serenity Hills anyway, Jarell thought before he came.

***

"And sign here… and here—nono! Oops. My mistake." Selena Lopez flashed Jarell and Bethany her laser whites. "Just needed initials." She ducked her head in a tinkle of tin jewelry, and muttered, "You'd think as a real estate agent I would have this down by now, right?"

Jarell gave her a tight smile before scribbling his monogram and cocking his wrist for his wife to take the pen.

Bethany wiggled forward in her seat. Her perfect *BFG* swirled and flowed into bodacious loops. Selena watched with raptor's eyes. "Aaannd… there we go. All done save for HMO and escrow."

Jarell turned to Bethany, then back to Selena, "You mean that's it?"

"Yep. Bank's in. Congratulations, new homeowners."

"Wow." Bethany's tears brimmed, her mascara damming the flow.

Jarell stared at the hefty stack of paperwork, behind them now and thank God. So many papers. A crushing weight of sign-heres and initial-theres. But in truth? "It seems so… so—"

"Easy?"

"Yeah." *Empty.*

"Well, Jarell, you're an up and coming attorney with a beautiful family, and Serenity Hills is an exclusive neighborhood." Selena laughed again as she shuffled and blocked pages. "Let's just say the Greenes sit *mucho* top shelf-o for the Serenity Hills menu. This Home Owner's Association goes to great lengths to ensure positive balance and beauty for your new neighborhood."

Jarell sat back. Was this the early fruit of his law school labor? If so, it tasted good. Bethany squeezed his fingers in hers and leaned into him. After so many false starts, struggle after broke-ass struggle, low-bid jobs, slum-lord apartments, night school, unexpected family additions, sacrifice after unscrupulous sacrifice, more unexpected additions and things neither one of them would ever admit to doing just to feed their unexpecteds; now they stood witness to this budding sign of success.

Their first house.

A gorgeous house.

A Greene Family legacy house secured in an elite neighborhood.

With two kitchens and enough room to dream—

"One last thing."

They both blinked at Selena.

"As part of the HOA clause, you have to interview with the Serenity Hills Home Owners' president."

"What?" He wasn't ready to make an impression right *now.*

"Plus, it closes the temporary escrow and rolls over into your new," she paused and squealed a tight, "*homeowners'* escrow."

Jarell felt stupid. Why couldn't this be a compromised evidence case or a weighted litigation issue? Something he understood. Property law was as far left to him as "motherfucking marbles to magnolias," as his grandmother, Mama Greene, used to say. It made mud for sense to him.

"What's that mean, exactly? And why do we have to meet them? I'd rather be prepared, you know—" he spread his hands over his casual Dockers and baby blue, Target-wear button down, eyebrows scrunched. The HOA comprised the folks he had to impress, right? The one entity other than the bank that could rip his and Bethany's beautiful new legacy out from under their kids? The invisible jury with the power to force a foreclosure if the new, interracial, Greene bunch and their heathen brood failed to keep the bustle out the hedgerow? Hell, Debo the damned hedgerow. Shit, this was going to be awkward.

Selena rolled her eyes over a huge, knowing smile. "Oh, formalities. They just want to get to *know* you, Jarell. I'm telling you," ear bangles jangling with flashes of sunlight, she leaned in close enough to taste the saccharine reek of Wrigley's Spearmint and Juicy Couture, "this community is to *die* for. You'll see. Trust me."

The door opened to the whisper of its felt sweeper licking ceramic tile. Bethany turned first, rays of sunlight casting across her cheeks to ignite glitter in the salts of her flesh.

"Selena." The voice rolled with cool confidence and a banker's smile. The sound money makes when it slips from a widow's hand. Jarell swallowed and followed his wife's doe-eyed gaze to the entrance.

"Oh, hey, Glenn—and Lynda! Come on in and meet your new neighbors." Selena scuttled to the door with the clatter of centipede heels and bracelet charms, ushering a perfect and swarthy, god-sculpted couple. The man stood at nearly his own 5'10" in a Nautica sweater and khakis; the woman a perfect hourglass brunette with hazel eyes, wrapped tight in a dress of black velvet showcasing sensual curves.

"Hello," the woman said sultry. "I'm Lynda." She took Jarell's hand in both of hers. "Welcome."

She looked to Bethany and her eyes upturned to crescents as she motioned wide for an embrace. Bethany smiled to match Lynda's warmth and stepped into her arms. Sexual heat rolled off the stunning woman.

"Looking forward to having you in our community," Glenn said, pumping Jarell's hand. His voice didn't exactly boom, but his confidence carried the weight of power. "Please, let us get to know one another."

"Now that wasn't so bad, was it?" Selena pushed her cleavage and Maybelline foundation center stage. The ladies parted and took seats. "So, now, Glenn and Lynda, this is Jarell and Bethany, glad we've all made nice, but," she riffled through her accordion file and came up with another stack of documents, "we need to finish the package."

Jarell shifted in his chair. "What's that? I thought we were complete."

"Oh, you cute lawyers," Selena said, patting his thigh and bending over to spill more of herself from her strained buttons. "It's just another formality. I *told* you, the HMO and escrow have to cross some T's and I's. Formalities, Jarell. Formalities. Won't take long." She ended on her pearly row of chiclets. Jarell's bowels filled with ice water. "So sign here... and here."

Bethany grabbed the pen all happy-frazzle and sunbeams, signing away before he had a chance to squint through the finer print.

"Wait a minute, can I have a moment to at least look over these?" He didn't bother to hide his frustration.

Selena's party-girl facade gave way to a cold and monotone, "Go ahead, Jarell."

"Thank you."

He ignored her, and the godlings, and even Bethany, and placed his maxed credit card beneath the first sentence of the new page. Line-by-line, Jarell absorbed the addendum. It took time, and time made for uncomfortable, especially when the only one making noise was Selena's wardrobe. Sweat beaded his brow. Bethany scowled and cleared her throat.

He sat upright and ripped his glasses away, directing his incredulity toward Glenn. "You mean to tell me we have to take a physical just to close? *And* our children?" He looked back at the micro-verbiage, hovering over his seat. "What the hell is this Familial Financial Responsibility Clause—?"

"Oh for crying out loud, babe! Just sign it so we can stop listening-in while other people fuck next door!"

Glenn gave Jarell an amused, cockeyed grin. Lynda's lips curled ever so slightly, her black gloved fingertips covering her mouth beneath glimmering eyes. Jarell turned to Bethany, flushing, and just like that, all of his fire petered out.

He watched from a million miles away while his inkball rolled across paper, scratching and bleeding his signature, agreeing to take physicals, indenture his wife and children to the estate in his incapacitation, and stay current with the PITI payment by keeping the Principal & Interest rolled up with a Taxes & Insurance escrow.

And to ensure the escrow never dipped below a ten percent surplus margin.

And escrow also came with its own additional annex of teensy lines packed tightly within legal paper.

And it even had a medical insurance rider somehow, legally tied to the home coverage, and which he purposely skipped over without anyone's notice. But the addendum *really* liked the escrow model.

There was too much to take in under pressure. Jarell closed his eyes and leaned his head against his wrist, glasses dangling by the stem.

"Okay." His voice rang hollow.

"Yay," Selena said, thumbs up and shaking her hips.

Bethany gripped Jarell's hand and glowed at their new HOA.

"When do we meet the escrow people?" His voice sank with defeat. *I'm so damned lost right now. Way to go, new partner.*

Glenn laughed and gave Jarell's shoulders a sporting squeeze. "Jarell, we *are* the escrow. Serenity Hills is a very tight community and we like to ensure both matters of neighborhood upkeep, as well as the financial guarantee of your home. We're all about the house staying with you and not coming open to the free market where," he looked at Bethany with evangelical foreboding, "*anyone* could move next door to your blossoming teenage daughter."

Bethany held his gaze while Jarell clenched his fists. Was this ass-hat really going there—?

"Not to mention," Lynda said, "the dangers of having your little boy exposed to pedophiles, bullies, or worse- plague. We keep Serenity Hills safe from the filth, Bethany."

Bethany followed the meter of Lynda's voice with tight little bobs of her head.

"And it's obviously not just for you, but all of our families. That's why we're so protective. So," Glenn stood and threw his arms wide, "welcome to the family."

Jarell had no words.

"Oh, thank you so *much*," Bethany said, rising for more body hugs.

***

"Oh." It was a clipped *oh* of disbelief encroaching on indignation. Jarell watched the woman swirl her lemonade and blink in flutters. Her smile crazed her face to a near mania he knew all too well from living without: Envy. "You have a water feature."

"Don't you just love it? I've always had this fascination with

94

fairies, and I think children are our most precious gift from God."
Bethany to the rescue—"Jarell bought it for me after we moved in
and he even put it in himself"—and without a filter. His mind
calculated jealous neighbors and the possibility of fines for building
without a permit. They already pushed the budget to bust with the
escrow on the mortgage. The pond-sized water garden qualified as a
recreational pool at three feet deep and ten in diameter, with
Bethany's host of nude little girls frozen in a blossom of pouring
streams and butterfly wings over the center. *Oh, babygirl. Why
didn't I just buy you some damned bling instead?*

The woman and their new neighbor, Mrs. Deborah Pandry,
met his wife's innocent enthusiasm and melted to nice. She held
herself with an air of nobility, and Jarell thought she was attractive
in her own way, but flawed. Perhaps it explained her aloofness, her
pride bordering on arrogance, but Deborah Pandry had no right ear
and the collapsed blouse over the vacancy of her left breast left him
with a sense of compassion overlooking her attitude toward
Bethany. If he had to guess, he would put bank on cancer. The two
women moved to the kitchen and the conversation shifted onto the
kids.

"Hey, boss." Jarell turned to Bill Pandry, an automotive
design engineer built like a Cummings diesel, and relaxed. "Don't
sweat that regs bullshit. Hell. Myself, I added a whole damned
machine shop last winter."

Jarell jolted at Bill's uncanny ability to read him, but relaxed
at the larger man's easy demeanor. He liked Bill.

"The county didn't say anything when they assessed?"

"Of course they did." Bill kept a straight face over his
lemonade. "Glenn and Lynda said don't worry."

"Really?"

"Yep. The assessor wrote me an apology and asked if I
wanted a recommendation should I ever need to get on with the
Harden County Motor Pool."

"No shit."

"No shit, boss."

"Damn."

"Yep."

"I guess Glenn and Lynda are good to be in tight with."

"Yep." But Bill's voice lost its champ and Jarell squirreled his eyebrows. "Just make sure you keep good on your escrow and you'll be fine," Bill muttered.

"Yeah. That escrow thing, man—"

Bill jerked and raised his finger over his glass, eyes shifting. He leaned in and spoke low, saying, "Not here, boss. Where are you working now?"

"Carnegie, Carnegie, Halfax and Greene. Why?" He suddenly felt as if a pack of wolverines swirled behind him.

"Yeah yeah. On East Main and 10th. You'll be there Monday? I like to do lunch at one, you know: miss the crowd."

"Of course."

"If you want, I'll pick you up. We can go grab some grinders and a pitcher over at Penalty Box. Catch a game and talk more relaxed."

"I'm down with that."

Bill grinned big and showed a mouth full of hockey gaps. Jarell must've dropped his guard, because Bill explained, "I used to play league till a few years back."

"As goalie?"

"Ha! Nah. Too much of Penalty Box grinders for that. Plus, I got less than half the reflexes needed to be goal tender. No, I's always a wing." He winked and added, "And enforcer."

Jarell cracked a smile, the first in a long time.

"Monday at one it is, my man."

"You got it, boss. And we don't talk about it."

Jarell's face slacked and he nodded.

"Jare?" Bethany hollered from the kitchen basement door. "Baby? Can you come look at this?"

Bill raised his glass and gave a nod of curiosity. They moved to the kitchen, toward Bethany's voice, following her down to the basement where Jarell's next renovation included a pool table, jukebox, wet bar, flatscreen, and more decorative girls, only these hardly wearing their Chicago Bulls cheerleader outfits. At the bottom of the stairs, he and Bill stopped, following their wives' gazes to the ceiling.

"Holy shit, boss."

"What the fuck?"

"Jarell!" Bethany hissed.

"Sorry." But he was more concerned with the three-foot

bloom of dark mold spreading from the northeast corner of the ceiling. He said more to himself, "We just passed the damned closing inspection."

"That's some fast growing stuff, then." Bill took a cigarette lighter from his pocket and poked the end at the bloom. It mushed in, black water dripping down the plastic. Bill held the lighter to his nose, curled his lip, and shook it to the floor. "Sorry about that, but yeah. You got black mold. Don't let it go too long, now. Shit'll eat your house, then your lungs."

It also ate Jarell's spirit. How the hell did he get rid of black mold? What *was* black mold?

"Maybe we can just pick up a spray or something from Costco, babe." Bethany guided Deborah to the corner, continuing her tour. "Jare's putting the 60-inch here, and then our youngest, Kalel, has got the coolest video game seats—"

"I'm sorry. Kalel's your boy, right?"

"It's fine, we get it all the time. But yes. Our ten-year-old."

"Oh? Starting middle school this year, huh?"

Bethany made huge eyes. "He hasn't stopped talking about it, poor thing's so nervous. He's made himself sick the last two days. I'm scared to death he's going to miss the first day over his nervous tummy."

"He'll be fine, trust me. But I have to ask, such a remarkable name. After a family member, I take it?"

"Superman," Jarell said over his shoulder. He and Bill stood at matching stances, arms crossed and heads tilted to the bloom.

"I think that shit's growing right in front of us, boss."

"Yeah." *Mother. Fucker.*

"Pardon?" Deborah asked.

Bethany laughed. "Jarell is a huge DC Comics nut. He's got oodles of boxes down here in the closet."

"I still don't..." Deborah looked from Bethany to Jarell, then to her husband and back again.

Jarell explained, "Kalel is Superman's real name. His Krypton name."

"And Kara is his cousin, Supergirl," Bethany said.

Deborah's face went back to that crazed smile again.

"Their daughter, hon," Bill said, taking his place beside her.

"Huh? Oh... Oh! Okay." She relaxed and nodded her head

in big circles. "Your children are named after Superman and Supergirl. I get it."

"Right," Jarell said.

"Neat!"

"Yeah," Bill agreed. "That is pretty cool." His eyes darkened and the diesel-steady demeanor sank with them. "Wish we had—"

"Children. We wish," Deborah said, cutting him off, "we could have children."

"Aww. Well you haven't stopped trying, I hope," Bethany said.

"Oh jeez. Look at the time." Bill's expression flatlined and he thumb-swiped his phone before dropping it down his pocket. "Hey, hon. Time to get this pumpkin home. Got wrenches to turn and grease to sling."

Deborah thanked them and pulled her husband up the stairs, Bethany trailing.

"Babe? You going to tell them goodnight?"

Jarell stared into the growing fingers, falling into the fuzzy black forest of spores stretching from the corner.

"Yeah, babygirl. I'm coming." He shook his head and killed the lights on the way up.

Maybe he'd call Glenn tomorrow. There had to be other houses in Serenity Hills with this issue. The HOA probably had a list of reliable maintenance contractors. Glenn would know.

"Penalty Box tomorrow, boss," Bill called. Jarell reached the landing as the front door sealed his family in with their new house and its mold.

The next evening, they lay next to one another, comforter pressed down into a valley between them. Bethany watched TV with the sound muted. Jarell stared at his client's deposition, lost in the spaces between words. This wasn't working.

"Do you want to talk about it?" she asked.

He let the folder collapse to his chest and pulled his glasses away. No. He didn't. Because it made no sense.

"Was it lunch today, babe? Did something happen with Bill?" He caught the trepidation in her voice. Bethany thrived on friends and appearances. It wasn't a superficial thing; she cared about his career as much as the kids' social comfort. In her perfect world, everyone loved the Greenes and no matter where they went, they were surrounded by friends. Never alone.

Two months into the perfect house with two kitchens and a neighborhood "to die for," Jarell found his sense of security for his family fleeting with the flora in his basement, bloated credit card balances, and a conversation with Bill that had left him shaken.

"Jare?" Bethany rolled over to prop on her elbow and hold him with her soft eyes. He felt like crying, but that would never happen. Fuck no.

"I'm sorry. Lunch was fine. Bill just told me some things about this neighborhood and the HOA that's been bothering me some. It's probably just me stressin'. You know how I get."

She purred and snuggled against him. "Silly. Everything's going to be fine." She nuzzled into his chest and he kissed her crown, her fingers walking down to slip beneath his boxers. "Mmm, what's this big guy doing all alone down here."

"I know," he said, purposefully ignoring her to stoke the flame. "I'll call the home warranty company tomorrow and see if we have coverage. I think we'll be able to at least keep from going out of pocket too much to kill the mold and repaint."

She nibbled his ear and ran her fingers across his waist band. "I already fixed it, baby."

He held his breath a beat before speaking. "Say what?"

"I called Lynda, and Glenn is going to take care of it."

He sat ramrod and yanked her hand from his flaccid penis. "Why? No!"

Bethany's eyes watered and she matched his posture, pulling away to her side of the valley. "Baby, don't look at me like that, please."

"Bethany, what did they say? How are we going to pay for the repairs?"

She sucked in a shallow breath, then another, speaking around her revving hyperventilation. "Lynda said it would be fine. They just take it out of escrow and we can repay the difference before next month's mortgage payment—"

"No." Jarell ran his hands through his tight curls and leaned between his knees, scattering the forgotten deposition. His voice fell to a whisper. "Bill said don't do that."

"But why?"

"He said don't ever borrow against escrow."

Bethany's breathing calmed and she rubbed her hands up the coils of his back.

"He said to avoid help from Glenn, and most of all," he tilted his head to the ceiling and spotted a patch of spongy black in the corner, "never, *ever*, let you go to Lynda."

"I don't understand, baby. She's really sweet and even invited me to her Delightfully You party next week."

"Her what?" He furrowed his brow and tilted up to stare at her without understanding.

Bethany straightened her back and said with shame-sullied dignity. "They're just for women. She has her own line of romantic accessories for us girls."

Jarell shook his head. This was stupid. He eyed the manila folder and his left brain ran the numbers. They were still living paycheck-to-paycheck, but he should be able to close this new case in a week and have enough to fill-in the escrow ding. Plus, Bethany's cake business should be kicking off soon and that would hopefully put them in the clear. This would be the only time. He turned to her and sagged, letting his lips pucker into his doghouse smile. It usually worked *after* he screwed things up to the point of sloppy tears and his woman scorned, but he hoped it worked preemptively as well.

"I'm sorry, babygirl."

"Good." She melted against him. "You can do all the work tonight."

He kissed his way around her Venus neckline, stopping at the niche of her throat, and traced his lips between her perfect breasts to her pink areola. From the airside of the sheets, he heard her say, "Glenn ordered the adjusters for tomorrow and Lynda said we'd talk later, but not to worry for now."

Adjusters? Whatever.

"Mmhm. Did she say anything else?" He rooted into the blond down of her pubic triangle.

"And she said to make sure you—hhww—keep me well oiled... oh, baby..."

The night disappeared beneath sweat and passion and the potpourri of their juices.

***

"Mom! Dad!" Kalel yelled from downstairs. "Someone's at the door!"

"Who is it, honey?" Bethany groaned and cinched her robe while Jarell chased his glasses across the nightstand and dug for his boxers.

"Some freaky dudes!"

"Coming."

Jarell followed the heavy sway of her ass beneath pink chiffon. He pushed to the bathroom for a cold rinse, pulling at his stuck scrotum.

Voices floated up through the shower spray, garbled, two monotone males and Bethany.

"Jare? Baby? Can you come down here?"

He leaned his head into the cool tile and watched his mighty, Super Babymaker wilt. So much for morning services.

"I'll be right down," he yelled.

A pair of sweats and Bulls hoodie later, Jarell stood in the living room between two men in white paper suits and masks, and his wife and son. Kalel was still in his pajamas; Bethany stood arms crossed, dressed for an afterhours Showtime special.

"This is my husband, Jarell. Baby, these gentlemen are here to take care of the mold."

The two men moved around him without speaking.

"Hey! Wait, don't we need to sign something?" Then to Bethany, he mouthed, "What the fuck?"

She shrugged.

"Mr. Greene," one of the house surgeons said from the basement stairs, "your escrow covers everything."

"So that's it?" he yelled. "I mean, we got more mold upstairs now, too."

No answer.

A half hour later, one man moved up to the bedrooms wearing a backpack-tank and wand set, covering walls and ceiling in a mist of clear herbicide. Behind him, the second followed with a paint sprayer to hit the compromised areas of the infestation. Eventually, they rallied in the living room, leaving behind wet walls

101

and the sharp smell of acrylic-latex.

"Mr. and Mrs. Greene," Herbicide said, mask still in place. "We arrested it and your house is clear. Keep an eye out for respiratory issues and call Glenn if anything comes up."

"Sure. But don't we need a copy of the bill? After-treatment instructions? Something?"

Herbicide packed his kit and moved out the door to their boxy white truck without answering. Painter answered on his way to the curb, "Your escrow'll cover it, sir." He walked to the passenger side of the odd vehicle, again, mask still on, and said, "Just don't let it fall behind."

The engine cranked and the unmarked truck crept down the street to the stop sign, making a left deeper into the neighborhood.

"That's some weird shit, babygirl."

Bethany leaned against the doorjamb. "It was so easy, though." Then to Jarell, "See? We're all fixed up."

"What's fixed up?" Kara called from behind.

Their seventeen-year-old Harvard hopeful stood in a Maroon 5 jersey and panties, pouring a bowl of Fruit Loops at the kitchen bar—the family kitchen, Bethany's cake room was a much bigger add-on to the back of the house with patio and driveway access for loading. He really wished she'd start using it soon, too.

"Sweetheart, get some clothes on," Jarell scolded.

Bethany nudged him. "You're fine, Kara. And Mr. Glenn and Ms. Lynda sent some weird guys over to fix the mold in the ceiling."

"Oh." He doubted she even heard. A pair of Bose by Dre ear buds trailed red flatwire down to an iPod clipped to her panties.

Jarell shook his head and plopped down on the couch with Kalel.

"Hey, Dad."

"Hey, killer. What we watchin'?"

"Tom and Jerry.'

"Say, *what?* That was my show when I was your age."

Kalel spooned another lump of Fruit Loops into his mouth, a drop of milk clinging to his lip. His eyes stayed riveted to the tv. Jarell tousled his hair and got up for his own bowl. In the background, Jerry ran through Tom's mouth and blew out his tail.

"Dad?" Kalel coughed once.

"Easy, kiddo. Yeah?"

"I still feel sick."

"Uh-oh." Bethany padded around the couch to put a mother's touch to his forehead. "Where's it hurt? Just in your tummy?" she asked.

Kalel nodded. "And my throat's all scratchy—"

Blergh.

Kalel bent over the side of the couch, crying as half-digested loops and rainbow swill splattered the beige carpet. Smells of stomach acid and fructose effervesced in a miasma, choking Jarell and tickling his own gag reflex.

"Ohgod," Kara said, running to the bathroom.

"Shh, it's okay, baby," Bethany cooed. "Jare, will you grab me a—"

Ssblorghhh...

"Mom—" Kalel heaved again, twin snot trails twisting into the puddle.

Bethany escalated, "Jarell! Bring me a damned towel!" and quieter but with the same intensity, "My God, what is this stuff?"

Jarell ran back with a wet rag and stopped just over the back of his son, brow stitched tight at the dark puddle of vomit. It *moved.*

"Come on. We're taking him in," Bethany said. "Kara! Get some clothes for Kalel and meet me out front. We're going to the clinic."

Five minutes later, Bethany and Jarell pulled from their drive, her changing into jeans and a jacket to cover her bra-less tee while Kalel puked more black wigglers into a lawn bag in the backseat.

Kara met them at the Serenity Hills Clinic with clean clothes and room deodorizer less than three minutes behind. A second full trash bag later, the on-call doctor followed. Triage went messy, but a half hour after intake, Kalel passed out from exhaustion on the exam table and Dr. Brandt finally sat back to wipe his forehead.

"What is it?" Jarell asked.

"Gastrointestinal fungal infection. A tenacious one." The doctor was old, his white hair and wild eyebrows nearly connected at the brow.

Jarell and Bethany shared a lost look.

"But it looks like worms moving in the vomit," Jarell said.

"A reaction to the air and bile, my friend. The fungus is just a plant, and what you're seeing is an accelerated wilting process. Nothing more. He'll be fine."

"How do we get rid of it?" Jarell asked.

Dr. Brandt offered a tired smile. "It's tough. Fluids feed it, but he needs to hydrate. It acts like a parasite, though unlike hook worms and others, this type of flare-up doesn't want his food."

They hung on the white haired doctor's words.

"It wants his real estate."

Jarell froze. "Our son's a garden?"

"More or less."

Bethany cried against his shoulder.

"How?"

"Probably something in the air. Usually mildew or mold spores. Kids inhale them through their noses. They line the mucous membrane, take seed and whatnot. You're parents—you know how kids tend to sniff and swallow." Dr. Brandt demonstrated, then ducked his shoulders and finished with, "It is what it is."

They got the mold too late. *Son of a bitch.*

"But Mr. and Mrs. Greene, don't fret. I'm giving him one concentrated dose of glyphosin steroid now intravenously, so it'll hit the main infection, and a month's worth of the pill form should keep us from a relapse. Superman ought to be back on his feet in time for school to start." He gave a weak smile and Bethany's lips palsied to return it.

Jarell felt the tension drain and a sense of trust settle, leaving him weak but reassured: Dr. Brandt was the first white person to recognize Kalel's namesake.

"I'll have your meds up at the front desk along with home-care instructions. Okay?"

"Thank you so much, Doctor."

"No problem." He started for the door, but took a step back with a concerned snarl of his eyebrows. "You're one of the new Serenity Hills bunch, aren't you? Do you have your own health insurance, or did you take the, um… that escrow rider deal?"

Jarell swallowed. He remembered specifically skipping the rider's initialing block on the escrow packet. And, no. They hadn't picked up medical insurance yet.

"Oh, we have the rider," Bethany said. Jarell turned to her,

104

signaling his confusion. "You forgot to initial, but when I talked to Lynda, she said to go ahead because it's so ridiculously cheap. And it covers just about everything."

Dr. Brandt's shoulders sank, but he said, "It does, Mrs. Greene. I don't always recommend the rider if you live in Serenity Hills, but it will cover those who can't afford medical insurance upfront, at least. Especially with the cost of the medication."

"How much?" Jarell didn't want to know. *And what's he got against the rider?*

"Just for the IV and injection, you would've been looking at $5,000 out of pocket. Now each pill goes for upwards of $20, and this round I prescribed him ninety to keep him on a constant cycle. So that, combined with cost of a Saturday call, you would have been looking at a good $8,000 visit just to weed out some bad plants in your son's belly."

Jarell couldn't find the strength to talk. Kalel was going to make it. Their next mortgage payment was not.

***

"Hello, Glenn? It's Jarell Greene...yes, he's doing fine. A little scary there, but we're kryptonite-proof once again. And thank you, sir. It means so much to us...Oh no-no! I can meet you, no problem...tomorrow sounds fantastic... lunch. I'll be there, sir... oh, okay, 'Glenn' it is. And thank you again."

Jarell closed his eyes and tapped his cell against his forehead.

"Baby? What did he say? Did you tell him?"

They missed last month's payment, but caught back up thanks to Jarell's big win from a false testimony. Now they were not only in the red again, Kalel's cough had returned. And the HOA sent a letter letting them know the water garden would have to be removed in order to meet the new Serenity Hills water conservation standards.

Removed professionally.

"I didn't get to. He told me to meet him at the Serenity Club House for lunch tomorrow." He turned to Bethany, steeling for a presentation of confidence he wasn't feeling, hoping she couldn't tell.

"Oh, baby," she cooed, rubbing his back. So much for hiding it.

"Yeah. I'll take care of it, babygirl."

"We'll be fine. Plus," she waggled her eyebrows and shook her hips in a way that used to turn him on. She bit the side of her lip and said, "I got my first customer."

"That *is* good news."

She nodded. "Yep, and ready for this? It's *monthly.*"

"Oh wow, babygirl. Good for you. Who's it for?"

"Lynda."

Jarell's throat closed.

"Lynda's scheduling Delightfully You parties once a month and she needs cupcakes to match her erotic motif. So I showed her the spread I did for the bachelorette party last year and she loved it. You remember? The scarlet silk icing on dark chocolate? Crème filling?"

He pulled her into his arms by way of an answer, more to hide the fear he felt.

***

The next evening Jarell stepped into his house somber and sober. Bethany met him at the door wearing an apron smeared in sparkling red icing. Her sunbeam eyes dropped at the sight of him.

"What?"

He shook his head and shuffled to the family kitchen and the E&J calling his name from the liquor cabinet.

"Jare?" she said, following him. "What happened, babe? Did Glenn say he would help us keep the house?"

He nodded, arms splayed across the counter and snifter center mass beneath him. He swiped the glass and downed it, poured a second and dropped an ice cube to melt while the first slug warmed him.

"Yeah. He's got a way for me to catch up on the mortgage and meet escrow."

"Well, that's good." But he couldn't make his face talk in sync with his words and Bethany picked up on it, asking, "Isn't it?"

He found a nowhere spot above her shoulder and swallowed hard before taking a drink, then laid out Glenn's method of

106

repayment. When he was done, Bethany flew from the room for her cell phone. Jarell limped back to the door, where he'd dropped his briefcase and set it on the kitchen counter. He thumbed the locks and pulled the new stack of forms. Pages of sign-heres and initial theres. Medical releases. A special power of attorney naming Glenn. The cut sheet reflecting his balance, past due, handling fees, and post-op total.

"No," she said, stomping back into the kitchen. "You are *not* doing this, Jarell Matthew Greene. Do you hear me?"

The fire in her eyes meant a lot to him, but it lacked the one thing they needed more than love. Money.

"It's just a kidney, babygirl. I've got two and they're both made of Krypton steel."

"No." Her voice wavered and choked. She tried again, weaker. "No."

He kissed her on the forehead and swiped her tears with his thumb, whispering, "We'll be okay, babygirl. I promise."

***

"How is he?" Bill asked.

Jarell watched half-doped from his bed. His own bed. Glenn and his "adjusters" performed the procedure in the house, down in the basement after turning his man-cave into a clean-room. Glenn's surgical staff were much like the two mold adjusters. That's what Bill called them at lunch so many weeks ago. Adjusters.

"You see those white trucks that look kind of like ambulances? Yeah. Because that's what they are. Trust me, boss. Once you start dipping into escrow, the HOA has the power to balance the ledger however they see fit. And Glenn's a surgeon. Did he tell you that? Yeah. The kind that specializes in transplants."

Bill had drained the whole pitcher by himself that day. Jarell remembered wondering if he would bother going back to work.

"Guess there's quite a market for iced organs, boss. Just keep your family away from those two. Please."

Jarell hadn't said a word, but Bill insisted on divulging. It was as if he needed to get it out, to spill their messy secret. "Adjusters been to our house a few times, you know." He poured the last of the pitcher and downed it. "Teeth are good for small

107

change. Maybe a couple hundert to catch up because you have to pay the landscapers to pull the crabgrass when it gets out of hand and HOA pins a note to the door."

"Oh man."

Bill continued nonplussed, "But when the pipes burst in the winter because your old lady forgot to set the spickets to drip, well that one's probably gonna cost an eye. Or an ear assembly."

"Bill, man. It's okay."

But he was already buzzing down a dark place. "And when the zoning laws change and you have taken over the next door lot by three feet... and it's a sinkhole abscessing out to the goddamned street...yeah, one tit oughta cover it. At least get you caught back up, anyways."

"Jesus, Bill."

"Guess there's all kinds of girls out there needing a replacement boob to fill the mastectomy crater. It's all just sink holes in the end, really."

Bill had sobered enough to shake it off, but he left Jarell with a haunting message: "But whatever you do, don't let that Lynda bitch touch your Bethany," he whispered. "She won't bounce back, boss."

Now he lay beneath heavy clouds of morphine, following Bill and Bethany as best he could.

"Is Dad gonna be okay, Mom?" Kalel peeked behind her leg. His curiosity gave way to visible fear. "Dad? What happened?"

"Honey, Daddy had to have surgery, but he's okay now."

Kalel coughed once, then broke down into a fit, pulling Bethany away and leaving Bill at Jarell's side.

"You got to get them out of here, boss. This is only the beginning. Please."

He licked dry lips. Bill pressed a straw to his tongue and let the warm water soothe his throat. Speaking was not much different than surviving a bad hangover once he got through the cobwebs in his mouth. "We can't. Glenn said we're locked in. If we try and sell, he can use his power of attorney."

Bill closed his eyes and shook his head.

"Then you just leave, boss. Take your family and get as far the hell away from here as you can before the next big hit."

"The kids' school—"

"For chrissake, Jarell! The goddamned HOA took our boy right *out* of that fucking school!" Bill stopped short, panting, tears tracing his ruddy cheeks. "Yeah, there's a market for that, too."

Minutes passed in silence. Bill took a deep breath and patted Jarell on the shoulder before turning to see himself out.

Jarell lay alone, staring at a tiny patch of black bleeding out from the same ceiling corner as before. He slept.

***

Pressure weighed heavy near his feet. Someone sat on his bed.

His abdomen hurt, not the sharp pain of gas or lactic acid from a new gym membership, but the deep tissue bruise of his body trying to fill the void where a vital organ once pulsed.

"Jarell? You in there, buddy?"

Glenn. Jarell groaned. He fluttered the godling into a sideways view.

"Hey there, sport. Looking good. Have some water. I would offer you coffee, but we need to keep that last little guy in tiptop shape. Dialysis gets expensive and we don't want to wipe out your escrow after you just broke even, right?" He laughed, a healthy, happy sound and void of life.

Broke even.

Jarell winced and pushed up to his elbows. His body wouldn't let him go any farther as his ribs threatened to bust free from his abdomen.

He spoke in a hoarse whisper, "I thought you said this would cover it?"

"Of course it did, buddy. One hundred percent up on mortgage and escrow. You're doing great and I talked to the senior Carnegie. They're giving you thirty day's convalescent leave with pay. See? We're good."

"But," he coughed and it hurt. "But just even?"

"Well, you've got to figure in the cost of the surgery, the transport, then of course there's the ankle biters such as all this." He passed his arm around the sterilized basement cum operating room. "It adds up. But now you have a clean slate and we can get back to living. Say, Lynda's having one of her Delightfully You parties and

I understand Beth's been quite the master pastry chef, heh?" He gave Jarell rows of too many tiny shark teeth.

Fear radiated from Jarell's core, raising the hair on his back, crawling up his scalp. He flared his nostrils. "It's Bethany. She's never gone by 'Beth,' and you leave her the fuck alone."

Glenn's smile shattered, revealing a face predatory and calculating.

"No, Jarell. She goes by Beth when she's with Lynda. Perhaps you should get to know your wife the way we have."

A silence filled the space between them until it seeped into Jarell's spirit, sucking him down to a darker place than he'd ever experienced. A lonely abyss without hope.

Glenn stood and paced the perimeter of the room, running his finger along the walls. "Looks like the mold's back. Oh," he said, snapping his fingers, "that reminds me. The HOA did a safety inspection on your property while you were under—hope you don't mind—but the HVAC in this home was compromised, my friend."

Jarell closed his eyes, willing the monster to leave him.

"Yeah, looks like the mold did more than just wall damage. You're going to need to purge the system, then install all new ductwork. But think about it, Jarell. Once you're within HOA standards, your boy'll be healthy and, more importantly, your neighbors won't have to live in fear of your filth spreading out to touch *their* kids."

He laughed again, a cold and malevolent sound.

Jarell kept his eyes closed.

"It's only going to cost you, let's see, I have that estimate here somewhere—oh, there it is." Jarell heard the rustle of papers. "Oh boy. Yeah, buddy. Looks like you're going to need at least $80,000 by the time the adjusters get through with de-install, licensing, permits, install, and of course, final scrub down. Disgusting."

Moist, warm breath pregnant with raw meat smells painted his cheeks. Glenn leaned down close enough to kiss him, whispering, "Do you have it, Jarell? Can we count on you to fix the filth you've injected into Serenity Hills? Can we?"

He kept his silence and his darkness. The void was kinder than the HOA president.

"If not, do you want to go ahead and draw against escrow?

We can have it done next week."

He spoke, eyes still shut. "Motherfucker, you know we ain't got it." But the bite in his words sounded like the desperate plea just before an emotional breakdown. Jarell bit his cheek hard enough to taste the metallic tang of blood. He would not cry. Not for this white demon.

"Of course. I'll see what I can do. I'm leaving a packet for you to sign. It will cover twice the cost of the repairs, putting you two months ahead and also allowing for penalty-free foreclosure if your family needs to relocate after the operation."

Jarell opened his eyes. Glenn remained passive and professional once more.

"What operation?"

"It's just a transplant. I have a heart patient in San Antonio and I ran the labs from your escrow physical. You're a perfect match, Jarell."

"Get out."

***

Black amoeba- and ghost-shapes spread corner-to-corner in the basement. Jarell let his eyes wander the gooey plane of popcorn coating. It pulsed with millions of microfiber tendrils feeding from the surface, farting out spores in unseen clouds to drift up through the HVAC intake. Where they colonized the rest of the house and Kalel's body.

Bethany screamed from upstairs over their son's cries. He retched again and sounds of vomit splattered against the floor above Jarell's head.

Kara flew down the steps three at a time and ran to his bedside.

"Daddy! Please do something!"

More wetworks up top. The threadbare cohesion inside him finally uncoupled and he turned from his daughter. "Get me Mom's fondant knife," he croaked. "It's the little stainless steel one she uses for detail. I think she keeps it in the main kitchen, though."

Kara stared at him though tears and fogging glasses. "Why, Daddy?"

"I have an idea."

"What's going on?" Bethany moved down the stairs, striking each in a deliberate cadence. Her voice was no longer sweet. "Kara, what did he say?"

"Mom, he's asking for your *decorating* knife?"

Bethany leaned over him, her angst and desperation melting long enough to reveal the angel he fell in love with. She put her hand to his cheek.

"Oh, baby. No. I know what you're going to do. We will get through this."

"How?"

Kalel screamed and gagged from upstairs. Bethany ignored him.

"It's my turn, baby. I'm going to get us out of here."

Again, "How?" His voice broke. Still, he did not cry.

"I talked to Lynda. She's already made arrangements with Glenn. No more asinine operations, Jare. I'm going to help her design her products, starting this evening. She said she will compensate us enough to fix the house, then talk about getting us out from under it."

He inhaled through his nose and let the cold take him back to the place inside where he could be alone.

"Kara, honey, I'm going to get Kalel to sleep. His stomach is empty, but listen for him in case he wakes up and has to upchuck again, okay?"

"Why?"

"Just do it. I have to go with Ms. Lynda in a few minutes and I won't be back until the morning."

Kara cried beside Jarell, both of them watching Bethany disappear up the stairs with more grace than before. Kara bayed and buried her face in her hands, sobbing next to Jarell's bed. He couldn't find his way back from the dark to comfort her.

***

"Mom?"

Jarell opened his eyes. He lay on the couch. Memory came in cottony wisps, Kara crying and bracing him as he climbed the stairs, Kalel crumpled on the living room floor in stained pajamas. They had settled together, the three of them breathing the bile-steeped spores of Kalel's rotten gut, falling into a quiet sleep while waiting for Bethany's return.

The door opened and two faceless adjustors escorted her through the foyer. Jarell sat up despite his burning insides. She wore a white satin dinner gown and carried her heels. Her hair spilled hapless from a broken French twist.

Bethany's eyes stared wide and unblinking through too thick eyeliner. Her feet carried her in shambling half steps across the room. She stopped, facing the wall.

Blood stained the crease of her buttocks and flowed in tiny runnels down her bare legs.

"Mom?" Kara escalated.

"Babygirl?" Jarell pushed to his feet. He lurched forward, arms outstretched to his broken wife. Before his hand could touch her, extend what warmth his heart still held, she screamed. Bethany collapsed at his feet and shook with whole body tremors.

"Mom!"

Kalel woke and called for Jarell.

"No!"

The door opened and Glenn stepped through with his attaché case.

"Hey there, Jarell. She did fantastic. I'm going to leave your copies here on the counter if that works."

Jarell's head swiveled to follow the HOA president.

"You would've been proud. Beth's a real trooper."

"What did you do?" His voice rolled out in a broken growl.

"She volunteered to test Lynda's new Gladiator line. I think we're going to have a winner with this one, too. Now, Beth's going to need surgeries, but nothing I can't take care of—heck, right here in your basement, since it's already prepped." He smiled.

Jarell launched for him and stumbled short, sprawling across the kitchen floor. His chin slammed, bouncing his head and conjuring sparks around his field of view.

"Easy, sport. Bad form." Glenn hiked his slacks to kneel down into Jarell's face. "But we're squared up on the books and escrow is looking good, buddy."

Kalel shuffled in a crouch for Jarell. "Daddy—"

He *hic*-ed once and vomited a thin stream of black fuzz and mucous.

Glenn curled his nose in disgust. "Still with the filth." He turned back to Jarell and sighed. "Looks like we may need to dip back into that escrow after all. Well, let's see. You're not up for the transplant offer, so what to do."

Glenn stood and crossed his arms in thought, tapping his finger against his lips. His eyes rested on Kara. Jarell's dilated.

"You know, Lynda's also working on a teen product and I bet if I ask her, she may just be willing to cover Superman's medical for another test run. What do you say, Jarell?"

"And send my daughter to your slaughter, you sick fuck?" He spat the words through roiling emotion.

"Oh-ho!" Glenn laughed. "That's rich buddy! Don't be so dramatic. It's just a bunch of girl toys. Hell, Supergirl'll probably love it." He grinned at Kara. "Want to give it a whirl, Kara? This new Rávagè by Delightfully You line could be a cool thing."

Kara screamed and fell across her mother's shaking body.

"Well, I'll let you kids figure it out, but I wouldn't wait too long. Little man here needs to get to Dr. Brandt quick."

Kalel gagged, but held it in.

"Or maybe not."

Glenn left.

Jarell pulled himself up to the counter and scanned across the wreckage. He glanced down at the forms. One for Kara's release of liability; one for his heart transplant.

Wiping a tear, he opened the kitchen drawer and pulled out Bethany's fondant knife.

SOLD

About C.S. Nelson

CS Nelson holds a BA of English and has appeared in US and Canadian ezines and anthologies. When not writing, he spends time with family, performs acupuncture therapy on puffer fish, and serves as a US Army Cav Scout out of Fort Irwin in the Mojave Desert. By the time you read this, he will already have been exiled to the Arctic paradise of Fort Wainright, Alaska. And for this, the puffer fish are happy. www.nelsoncs.com.

School's Out
By Amanda M. Lyons

Kyle Myers was a friend. I mean we'd known each other since first grade and besides Gary and Brad he was the only guy I could talk to. Well, really, I guess you could say he was my best friend. I'm writing this to get it all down, to make some sense out of everything that happened now that it's over.

My name's John, I'm a teen, this would have been my last year of school, but well, I doubt if they'll let us finish now. I was one of those quiet kids. You know, the guy that does his homework, reads and talks to maybe three other guys? That was me. My friends and I were picked on, singled out for hazing and that sort of thing since we were the 'losers' in my class. We put up with a lot of crap, a lot of pain at home and almost everywhere else too. Kyle had it the worst. He had Coach Troyer to deal with until he had a stroke over the summer (the Coach that is) and then there was his brother Jim.

Jim killed himself, he had a hard time of things too, only he dealt with it a lot worse. The problem was that Kyle looked up to him, he was his big brother and Coach Troyer's bullshit started with Jim and ended up being carried over. It was one of those things where a teacher just assumes you're the same as your brother and it gets twice as bad for you. Well, after Jim died Kyle got angry, real angry, at everything and everyone. And all the crap we took before, suddenly got a lot more unjustified for him, and then for all of us. That's when Kyle came up with his plan.

At first it was just talk, you know how it goes, when you get tired of all the stuff going on and you say all those "I oughtta" "we shoulda" kind of things? At first it was "I oughtta beat his ass!" or "we shoulda tackled them!" but after it got to be things like "You know what? We should make 'em pay." After a while Kyle had it all

115

planned out, he said we owed it to Jim and all the kids like us that took crap from older kids and jocks, the hip-hop and redneck guys plus the serious bitches. He said that it was time to hold a trial, to make them see what they'd done and kept doing to guys like us.

His plan was solid. They built a whole new school a few years back, trying to accommodate all the kids (about 1000) and also to make the school easier to lock down if a school shooting ever happened. It was about 2001 when they finally got it done and let me tell you, it looks like the prison kids have seen it as for decades. Each hallway is designed to be able to be cut off and the office looks more like the guard room when you enter and have to present your ID in a prison. It's a lot to work around just to feel like a student and not a prisoner. The biggest differences between here and a prison? We don't have metal detectors, real guards, or IDs. So it looks like a prison, it can be cut off like a prison, but it's still a metaphor when you get down to it.

They kept a couple boxes with keys on hooks in them in the office, Kyle knew about it because he was an office helper and handled some of them from time to time. Kyle also had access to guns through his Nam vet Grandfather, who was a serious gun-nut with connections. Yeah, I think you can see where I'm going. The main difference between an all-out school shooting and what Kyle had planned was that he wanted to put them on trial first, to try to make them see what they'd done and give them a chance to make up for it before anything more serious went on. None of us were happy with our lives, I want to make that clear; but we weren't going to be conducting mass homicide, we weren't planning to kill them because all of them were responsible for our lives. None of that fit what we were trying to say at all.

But in the end none of that mattered. It all got out of hand and...Well, it was a bloodbath.

At first, it was all about doing trials. All of the rest of us walked into that scenario thinking that was what was going to happen. Kyle got us the keys to the lockdown controls and we turned them into lockdown mode. It didn't take long for the secretaries, a couple teachers, and the principal to come charging into the room after us. Kyle raised his gun and walked them back out into the office. He had me and Gary take them out to the storage shed behind the building and lock them inside. We put a snow chain

116

and padlocks over the normal lock too. While we were out there, we cut the communication lines.

After that, we got to business.

We took the kids in groups to the gym and interviewed them individually. We had a few additions to our group before too long and Kyle had a room full of kids that were supposed to be facing whatever punishment he decided on in another room. The kids that joined up got a gun and helped the rest of us. Things were running smooth.

And then Kyle started punishing the prisoners.

At first, I didn't know what was going on. I'd been interviewing kids for an hour and a half and was starting to get a little tired. I stepped out of the gym and toward a water fountain to get a drink. What I saw made it clear that Kyle wasn't as interested in justice as he was in punishment. Joe Stutzman walked with his arms tied behind his back between two guards, his face was red and he was bleary-eyed from crying. Joe was one of the football jocks, a dick with a real hard-on for torturing guys like me.

"John, you got to tell 'em! Tell 'em I ain't that bad, man! I don't wanna die!" His eyes and his face were an open plea, looking to me for rescue after all these years of being his punching bag. I knew something was wrong before he even mentioned death.

"What's he talking about?" I was talking to the guards.

They looked back at me with wry amusement before they said anything. "Kyle's orders. He's started turning out punishment and Joe's headed to the showers."

"What's his punishment?"

"They're gonna kill me!"

"He's right. We are."

Bald shock and horror made my jaw drop and before I could say anything else, they carried him off. I could guess what it was they meant to do. The showers were in a room that was pretty easily shut off, I could hear him screaming as they locked the doors shut and sealed them after him, the steam rising out of the room making it clear that the water was as hot as it would go. With eight showerheads going at once it wouldn't take long to fill the room and what happened next...I stood helpless as I watched the water rise on the other side, his body carried aloft as he screamed, boiling alive as he fought the drowning waters.

I ran to the office to confront Kyle, hoping that maybe I could stop the bloodshed before it had gotten worse. I had no idea how far it'd already gone.

There were bodies on the floor by the office wall; they'd been shot execution style, twenty kids in all. It was only the first sight I'd see before the day went much further, much less the way it would end.

There was a row of chairs outside the office, lined up underneath the open gatehouse windows, the kids that had been through judgment sat here and against another wall sat the kids who were going to be judged next. In that row were two girls I knew well. Sarah Markman and April Conner, April was a friend gone rival from elementary; Sarah was a years long crush I still clung to the hope of pursuing. They were best friends, April held her as Sarah wept. I hadn't thought about the two of them going through this, I hadn't thought much at all about any of this, I guess.

Maybe it was a test, some way to prove I was loyal to his cause. I walked over to her and crouched on my haunches.

"Sarah, listen, I want to tell you a few things before you go into that gym. You should really be told what-"

"What do you want?" Her voice was a hiss, resentment coloring her words. "What did Joe ever do to you?"

"Sarah, listen, I didn't know any of this was going to be so bad. I can help if things go right and you're in the gym when I'm interviewing you, but right now I have to get in there and see what Kyle's plans are. Where all this is going. I have to try to stop it before it gets worse, all right? The trials are supposed to be about being fair, about righting wrongs. It's gone bad, but maybe there's something I can do to stop it."

"Will they let me live?" Her eyes were an open question, pleading for a positive answer. What else could I do but give it to her?

"Yes, I think everything's going to be all right."

April looked at me, a cold look in her eyes as she studied my face, knowing that I couldn't promise them anything. "Then go. Make him stop, John; Sarah's had enough of this shit."

I walked away from them with a weight on my heart. I didn't know what I was going to find out, much less what I could do to stop it.

I walked to the door and opened it, stepping into the cooler area of the office and over to the desk that Kyle had made his center of operations. He looked up at me with a cold smile on his face, it was almost contempt. He held the PA in his hand, the button pressed down as he spoke into it.

"Mrs. Thomas send Robert Fillmore, Holly White, Scott Weiman, Teri Keane, Brian Milner, Maria Adkins, Kurt Morton and Sarah and Sam Harvey to the door."

He let the button go, a derisive laugh coming from him as he set it down. "I'm not going to put those ones on trial. Their lists are too long for that. They're going straight to their punishments. They deserve it."

"Kyle, I--"

"Shh, come with me. We're going to see what happens." I followed him out of the office and down a hallway, it was the one that led toward the front of the school and the shop labs. The line of kids, Hilmont High's most popular, were led into the open breezeway in front of the school doors and lined up. Beyond them, I could see the parking lot and, on its other side, a long row of cars and kids that blocked anyone from coming into the drive.

Closer to the doors was a row of kids, their angry glares directed at the prisoners in from of the doors. Two groups of guards split the prisoners into separate groups. Sam and Sarah Harvey were led off toward the back of the room and the others were led outside. Kyle gestured for me and the guards to follow him, we did, the twins in tow. Their friends looked after us, their faces confused and frightened. I couldn't overlook the feeling of this moment. It was as if I were in the middle of a slasher film, only instead of being a victim, I was one of those responsible.

The guards switched on one of the saws and one of Sam's legs was placed on the platform in front of it. They couldn't possibly mean to do what I thought, could they? Dark red blood and chips of skin flew away from her as she screamed, and then her other leg was slid up onto the plate and it fell off within a few minutes, joining the other on the ground. I rushed forward to try and stop them, but Kyle motioned with a finger and I was pushed to the ground by another guard and held there, helpless to do anything but watch. Her arms soon followed and then she was laid against the wall, where she howled, blood gouting from her stumps until her eyes began to flutter and soon, go dead. She was gone just like that. It was horrible, a revolting and awful thing to have seen, but Kyle smiled with yellow teeth and stretched red gums- he'd enjoyed it.

Sarah stood in numb shock, her eyes wide, and her mouth gaping as she wept. Brad grabbed her arm and led her over to the table by the saw. She squealed, an almost inhuman keening sound, as her eyes latched onto the saw and what it might mean for her. He shoved one of her struggling arms into the blade and lopped it off at the elbow, the blade grinding on her bones for a moment before snapping through and into the leg he brought toward it. Her other arm and other leg soon followed.

They laughed, all of them. They'd become monsters.

As I watched, helpless to do anything but whimper to myself, Kyle ripped away what was left of her clothes and rammed himself into her, raping her as she bled out on to the floor and finally going limp as he finished with a grunt of satisfaction. I wept, knowing that it had all been a game, a way to let loose his monsters on the school and get others to help him do it.

They drug me to my feet and I limped along, the girls' blood smeared onto me from their bodies. As we walked back to the breezeway, I saw what they'd done to the others, and I folded over, vomiting on the floor. They'd been torn apart by vehicles, drawn and quartered, and now scattered across the ground as the others hooted and shouted with unrepentant glee. It was like a call to horror, the school going mad with sounds of torture and pain while others called out their pleasure, taking their pain out on those who had hurt them before and those who were unlucky enough to be in their path.

Caught up in the glee of it, the guards left me where I was, too weak to get up for a few moments, sickened by what Kyle had wrought. A line of cars had begun to climb the hill to the school; they were slaughtered by those at the gate, sweeping down with knives, guns, and any other weapons they had on hand. With a terrible sense of grief and loss, I started to stumble back against a wall. It would come to an end, it had to really. They would only be able to hold the rest of the world at bay for so long before it got through. We were at the edge of town, but surely the police would sense something amiss. I had to get to Sarah and April, to get them out of there before the battle began. I threw all of my strength into getting up and started to walk back toward the office, where I'd seen them last.

There were people walking around with trophies from their victims, necklaces of ears and peeled faces worn like masks. How could I ever have helped this happen?

The line of chairs where they'd been were bloody and scattered across the floor. I ran down the hall, looking into rooms, trying to find them, hoping against the odds that they'd escaped.

I knew the battle had started when I heard it. Wandering through the halls, I found them at the back of the cafeteria kitchen, hiding in the pantry. They were scared, the blood on my clothes making them scurry away from me. Gunfire and screams carried through the walls and into the little space, a counterpoint to the pace of my heart. I walked closer to them, my hands wide and my voice soft as I moved. April held a gun and I didn't want to set her off.

"Are you all right? We have to get out of here. It's going to be hard. I think the people in town figured out that things went crazy. I-I just want to get out of here, I want to try and make it right somehow, to save who I can."

"Can we trust you?" April's eyes were feral, watching my every move.

"I'm probably about the only person in this place you *can* trust. You saw what happened. You saw...I'm sorry...I'm so fucking sorry I didn't know. I didn't. I didn't want anything like this!"

She nodded, satisfied.

We slid down the halls, April firing on anyone who tried to stop us as we ran for the nearest exit. The sounds of battle became a roar as we got out of the doors. Concerned parents, police, and curious pedestrians who had joined the battle were being slaughtered in their cars, taken down by teenagers.

We crawled through the teacher's parking lot, staying low to avoid being shot. April acted as backup, firing on anyone who tried to approach us for attack. The bus garage was nearby and clear of combatants, so we ran in short bursts, trying to reach it without being hurt.

"Okay," I said. "We'll go through that narrow area and then get a bus. I locked the principal and some secretaries in that building, I have to get them and meet you at the bus.

I ran across the yard as April and Sarah continued on their

path to the bus garage. I took the keys from my pocket and pulled the chain free of the door.

"What's going on? What is all of this?" The principal's eyes were wide with shock as he took in the scene over my shoulder.

"I can't explain right now. We have to get out of here before we die too. Just follow me and I'll take you where the others are. I ran across the yard, toward the bus garage, not waiting to see if they followed, but soon I heard them moving behind me.

When I reached the garage I found Sarah and April trying a handful of keys in the door of the nearest bus. It didn't take long to find it and we climbed inside, rushing to get free of the nightmare around us.

I pushed the gas pedal and charged out of the garage, out over the bodies, and through the battlefield toward the only exit that lay open. Gunfire broke out, shattering a few of the widows, making Sarah and the others duck and cover their heads. A ricochet hit April in the arm, but otherwise we were safe. Driving away from the school and out of town.

That's everything that happened, that's why we fled. Now I don't know what will happen, it's all up in the air. Wish us luck, wish us peace. Hope to hear from us again.

About Amanda M. Lyons

A longtime fan of horror and fantasy, Ms. Lyons writes character driven novels that, while influenced by her darker interests, can also be heavily laced with fantasy, romance, history and magic. Amanda M. Lyons has lived her whole life in rural Ohio where she lives with her fiancée and two children. *Wendy Won't Go: Collector's Edition*, *Eyes Like Blue Fire*, and *Water Like Crimson Sorrow* came out from J. Ellington Ashton Press in 2014 and she's currently at work on *Apocrypha*, a short horror collection. She is also the author of *Feral Hearts* with authors Catt Dahman, Mark Woods, Jim Goforth, Edward P. Cardillo, and Michael Fisher, a contributing author to the extreme horror anthology *Rejected for Content: Splattergore*, and co-edited *Autumn Burning: Dreadtime Stories for the Wicked Soul* with Samatha Gregory. Look for *Under the Bridge*, *Inanna Rising :Women Forged by Fire*, *Fata Arcana*,

Cool Green Waters and shorts in several other anthos in the coming months.

Amanda is also Lead Editor, US Division with J Ellington Ashton Press and a freelance novel editor.

Guilt
By Michael Noe

Sometimes he wakes up the middle of the night bathed in sweat, a scream locked in his throat. The darkness is thick like pea soup. Beside him he can feel his wife huddled under the sheet.

"You okay?" she murmurs softly.

"Yeah, another damn nightmare." Robert grabbed his pack of cigarettes off the night stand. His hands shook as he tried to the light the damn thing. At least his heart no longer sounded like Lars Ulrich had taken up residence inside his chest.

"I thought you stopped having them?" Sophie sat up and placed a reassuring hand on his knee. In the darkness she was an unidentifiable lump.

"I guess they came back." The clock on the night stand read four thirty, which meant he wouldn't be sleeping any more that night. Robert stubbed out his cigarette and swung his legs out of bed. His bladder throbbed achingly as he walked to the bathroom. He flipped on the light and got a glimpse of himself in the mirror.

His face looked haggard. Dark circles had formed under his eyes. He hadn't been sleeping well lately and the nightmare didn't help at all. Just thinking about it made his blood turn cold. He tried to rub away the goose egg sized bumps that exploded on his exposed arms.

It had been months since his last nightmare, which was about the time he had thought about not seeing the psychologist. At the time he didn't really think he was helping and the Xanax made him feel like a zombie. The sessions were always the same. He was forty years old and still afraid of the dark, and nothing the psychologist did seemed to help. What he had seen all of those years ago couldn't be erased. Robert wanted to put it all behind him, but that was easier said than done. The nightmares were always the

125

same and it was all because of that damned house. That was where everything went wrong in his life. The bad dreams, the feeling that he was being watched. The worst were the nights when the closet door would swing open and he heard laughter.

He finished urinating and walked downstairs to the kitchen to start his morning. It was the second time this week that the nightmare had kept him from sleeping through the night. There had to be something he could do. There had to be a way to confront his fear and prove that this was all a product of guilt. What had happened to Nate wasn't anyone's fault.

You didn't have to go into to the house. This was true, but he and his friends had, and because of that, Nate had died. It was an accident. *You know it's more than that.* Did he? Monsters weren't real. It was just an empty house. Nothing more. What he thought he had seen was just a product of his fear. *Now you sound like your shrink.* When the nightmares were that bad the shrink's advice was usually a meaningless drone.

"You need to face your fear, Robert. Until you do that the nightmares will keep coming back." It was the same horseshit he was always telling him. If he were smart, he would tell him to piss off, but the shrink had been right. That was the part that *really* made him angry.

The nightmares were always the same. They never changed. When Robert was thirteen, he and a couple of friends decided to go into the abandoned house on McAllister Road. It was harmless kids' stuff—in every neighborhood in America there was always that one house that never stayed occupied for long. There were rumors that it was haunted, and that there was once a man who killed his family— so many rumors it was almost laughable—but the kids were *afraid* of the damn thing and swore that if you ventured onto the lawn late at night you could hear screams. There were reports of a woman who stared out of the living room window as if she were waiting for someone. Robert was thirteen at the time and had just discovered Freddy Krueger. The idea that a house could actually have real ghosts in it was too good to pass up.

"We should go in there," he said as they walked home from a pick up baseball game. That was the summer that he had finally begun growing into himself. His two best friends were Timothy Hamilton and Nate Kessler, and that summer they were as tight as friends could be. They practically lived together at that point, but the thing was that they never got into trouble. They were good kids who loved horror films and the Cleveland Indians. At that age, all they cared about was making the most of their summer; and so far they had.

Nate shook his head and began walking again. They had all stopped to stare at the house. They had talked about it for a couple of weeks, and they all were thinking the same exact thing. Going inside. It would make them the talk of the neighborhood for months--no one else had the guts to go in there.

"I ain't going in there." Nate replied.

Timothy playfully punched him on the arm and laughed nervously. "You scared? Afraid the boogeyman's gonna getcha? Are you packing a vag in your shorts?"

"No, it's just I heard things. Bad things. I don't want to go in there."

"They're just stories." Robert began. It was just a house. It looked *normal*. The lawn had been recently mowed and the smell of fresh cut grass reminded them that, despite the abandoned appearance, the house looked just like every other house on the block. In horror movies houses like this had peeling paint and broken windows. This one had a fresh coat of light beige paint and the windows sparkled in the dying rays of the setting sun. "Does it look haunted?" He finished with as much bravado as he could muster. The more he stood there gazing at it the more uneasy he felt. He wondered if they felt it too.

"Where's your sense of adventure? It's not like we're going to spend the night. We go in, look around and leave. Easy breezy lemon squeezey," Timothy offered. He was the kind of kid who was easily led, and never had any ideas of his own. He may not have ever thought about going in, but now that it was presented to him he wanted to do it and prove just how brave he was.

Nate shrugged his shoulders as if his body had already given up the protest, even if his mind was still deciding. "Fine, but we can't do it now. We'll come back later on this evening. We're still sleeping in your backyard?"

"Yeah, all we would have to do is cut through Mrs. Jenkins' yard. We'll be in and out before anyone even notices that we're gone," Robert replied. They were always sleeping in someone's backyard that summer. In those days it was safe to do things like that. There was no stranger danger back then, because in those days everyone knew one another and kids didn't come up missing, or get targeted for being kids.

The rest of the day had gone slowly. Looking back on it, Robert could say with certainty that nothing *seemed* out of the ordinary. They had set up their tents and then later his dad made them all hamburgers on the grill. After dinner they swam and seemed to just waste time until the darkness had settled over Milford like a warm blanket. Years later, he would hear about the killer who had lived there and the unease that everyone felt, but this was nineteen eight six, the year he had discovered Iron Maiden and Ratt. It was the one time in his life where all the pieces fit and he felt alive and ready to take on whatever challenges came his way. That summer was the one that allowed him to discover himself. Everything was possible. It was right before the awkwardness set in and he became unsure of himself and who he truly was.

***

At the time, he had thought that the house was some sort of rite of passage. Every kid has to do a few things that defy any real logic. This was just a house. It wasn't haunted. Ghosts weren't real. But as they began to sneak their way toward the house, he wondered for just a moment if he had been wrong. Robert was smiling on the outside, but inside he was full of fear. The hairs on the back of his neck stood up like the quills on a porcupine. He looked back and saw his friends close by and knew that there was no turning back. This had been his idea, after all. Did he really want to pussy out in front of his best friends? Of course not. Failure wasn't an option.

Over the years he thought about that night and how *surreal* everything appeared. It was a still night with just a hint of a breeze. His heart thudded inside his chest, and he couldn't shake the fear that something was off. The house stood there bathed in moonlight. In their neighborhood this was the closest thing they would get to a haunted house. How long had it been sitting there empty? Three months at the most. Yet for some reason Robert felt as if it had been longer. There was always someone moving in and out. The longest anyone ever stayed was a year. He had seen the horror movies and knew that houses like these were supposed to be rundown with peeling paint and broken windows. There should have been some sort of history, but as far as he knew there wasn't one.

"Come on, you guys, hurry up!" Robert hissed. He could see the kitchen windows from where he crouched in the bushes. There was an inky blackness inside that seemed to end just at the back front door. In a bigger city they might have heard the sounds of passing cars, but at this hour it was silent. So silent it felt *alive*.

***

"How are we going to get in?" Nate asked. He was slightly out of breath. That was a good question and one that Robert ignored. He hadn't planned that far. They were in luck though. The back door was unlocked, which seemed a little odd, but Robert dismissed it. There had been people in and out to work on the house and people looking to buy the place, so it made sense that someone had overlooked it.

They stood in the kitchen looking around as if they were waiting for someone to introduce themselves. Even in the gloom they could make out the shapes of cupboards. The kitchen sink faced the window, and if Robert squinted hard enough, he could almost make out his own house. The air was thick with Pine-Sol and a slight musty odor, the smell of a house that hadn't been occupied for awhile. A short hallway branched off to the living room, and to the right were the stairs. The houses in the neighborhood all had the same layout except some had a larger basement or an extra bedroom.

"We should've brought a flashlight. It's dark as fuck in here." Timothy whispered. He was too close. He looked around, but didn't see Nate anywhere.

"Someone would see it. Let's go find Nate before he falls and breaks something."

"He was just beside me. Damn it! I bet he ran out." Timothy was moving toward the living room. Robert could hear his footsteps moving toward the front of the house. The hallway was so dark that he couldn't see anything in front of him. He placed his hand in front of his face but couldn't see them. He moved past the kitchen doorway with his hands placed out in front of him and then, once he got near the living room, the shadows cleared and he could see the streetlights bathing the living room in weak light. Nate wasn't in the living room. There were only a few cans of paint and a couple of empty boxes that had been placed near the front door.

***

Robert could hear the stairs creak as Timothy walked upstairs. He stayed put and felt his skin shrivel on his back. There was someone standing in the back corner. He blinked and they were gone only to materialize a moment later. He wasn't sure how long he had been standing there or how long it had been watching them, but it frightened him. Whoever it was had made no movement toward them. He wanted to run up the stairs but walked as calmly as he could. What scared him the most was that he had to turn his back to it. He stopped breathing until he was at the top of the stairs and once again he felt the oppressive weight of *wrongness.* It didn't matter if that wasn't even a word. That was the only word that fit.

"Tim? What's wrong?" He reached out to touch him, and heard something he would never forget. It was the soft whining a toddler would make when it was uncomfortable or hungry. The pungent odor of urine filled the narrow hallway. There were no words, no movement at all. All he could do was point. Mixed in with the pungent odor of urine was the coppery odor of blood. Nate was half in and half out of a doorway. Even in the dark he could see that he was dead. There were dark spots which looked like ketchup around his battered body. Robert tried to call his name but his voice was frozen shut. His legs were shaking so hard he swore he could hear the hollow knock of them clacking together.

Without a word, they just ran until they were at Richard's house, panting and gesturing like madmen, trying to tell Robert's frightened parents what had happened. It no longer mattered that they were in the house. All that mattered was that Nate was dead. It would be weeks later, when his parents told Richard what the police thought had happened. Nate had startled a vagrant that was staying in the house and in a fit of either rage or fear he had killed him. No one blamed them, of course, but it didn't stop either of them from feeling *responsible.* It was Richard who had shouldered the most guilt. It was his fault that they had gone in and it was *his* fault that

130

Nate was dead. He may as well have been the one who murdered him.

Over the years that one event had triggered panic attacks and of course the nightmares. The guilt seemed to lessen, but sometimes, when he was alone, he would feel it gripping his heart in a vice like grip that made it impossible to breath. Nate should be alive, with a wife and kids, or at the very least, doing something besides being dead. Life was full of twists and turns that you never see coming. The therapist had repeatedly told him that the guilt was natural and it would eventually fade, but that was a crock of shit.

Robert sipped from his coffee and tried to keep his thoughts from overwhelming him like they always did after a nightmare. It was always the same nightmare as well. It was that *fucking* house! He would see shapes like wisps of smoke chasing after him and no matter fast or how far he ran they would always be right behind him, nipping at his heels, whispering his name. He would often see Nate lying on the floor covered with a sheet and as he got closer, the soft rustling of the sheet would be even worse than whatever was chasing him. Nate would reach out and grab his ankles and the feel of his cold dead skin was like a thousand knives ripping into his flesh. "Your fault! It's all.....your...fault!!!"

Robert would wake up with a scream locked in his throat and sweat pouring from his naked body. In the dark he would search for Nate, fearing that he had followed him out of his dream. The smell of blood and rotting flesh filled the room with a pungent odor that he could taste. Robert had never felt a fear so real that it paralyzed him and filled him with dread. He couldn't tell his wife just how badly it frightened him, but his therapist knew how scared he was, and just how much guilt he felt. Maybe if he was able to stop feeling guilty then maybe the nightmares would stop.

He set his cup on the counter and went for a quick jog. It usually eased the stress, but this morning it didn't do anything for him. He felt winded and the cigarettes he kept smoking erased any benefits of the run. He had tried to quit and almost came close, but in the end the nightmares and the guilt kept him coming back. For a while it was alcohol, but once he met Sophie he wanted to be the kind of husband that his father was and he couldn't be an alcoholic and the man that Sophie deserved. He had quit drinking and replaced it with the jogging, but the cigarettes made it a joke. The cigarettes were the only vice he had left and he just wasn't able to give them up.

As he walked into the house he could see Sophie looking out the window as if she were waiting for him. She smiled and it was the most beautiful thing he had ever seen. Her eyes lit up every time she looked at him. She was a beautiful woman, even in the early morning hour when her hair was a wreck and she was dressed in one of his old t-shirts and a pair of sweat pants.

"How was the run?" she asked, planting a kiss on his sweaty lips.

"It sucked. I may just take up walking. I feel like shit." He poured another cup of coffee and headed into the living room.

The house was a testament to how well he had done in life. It had depressed him to hear about people he had graduated high school with were still treading water and had failed to do anything with their lives. He had followed in his father's footsteps and went to law school, but found criminal law too confining, so he went into family law and became a successful divorce attorney. Seeing so many marriages crash and burn only made him more determined to make his work. Despite what he did for a living, Robert still believed in love and the ideology of happily ever after.

"So either quit smoking or jogging. You can't do both. You okay?"

"Yes, I'm fine. I'm going to see Doctor Yost this morning and I promise all will be well."

As he got ready for his morning, he wondered for just a second if everything was okay. Why were the nightmares coming back in the first place? His sessions with Yost had helped him heal and he was sort of able to shove aside the guilt. *You just shoved it aside and focused on other things. The guilt's still here, so what?* He had found that focusing on Sophie and his career was a nice pleasant distraction. It was better than dealing with his guilt. He needed it to feel alive. The guilt reminded him that he *existed*. It kept things in perspective. Everyone needed something to keep them distracted. Was it healthy? No, but everyone did it; so who was it hurting? His friend had been murdered, so maybe the guilt was necessary. It kept things in perspective.

At the age of thirteen, Robert had never once thought about death. It wasn't something he was supposed to think about because at that age death happens to other people. He truly had believed that he was immortal. It was perfectly normal, but when Nate died, he was forced to stare at Death and shake his hand. It showed him just how real death was, that he wasn't immortal after all. Death was a hungry greedy monster that didn't give a damn how old you were. If it wanted you, it would *take* you. Suddenly he was no longer afraid of it. When your friend is lying in a pool of blood you begin to see just how short your life truly is. Robert made sure that he didn't waste any of it.

Robert felt terribly for the kids now because they were faced with death all the time. Kids were walking into schools and opening fire at an alarming rate. It seemed as if the fear of death no longer existed. If you spent any time surfing the net or watching cable news, death was right there, bringing in high ratings and gore for the whole family. All you needed was Wi-Fi and a strong stomach. Life was just as precious as ever and the mystery of death was still there, but the belief in immortality was a thing of the past. It almost made him long for the simpler times. He had seen a lot of shit go down in his life and he longed for the innocence he used to have before it had been stolen from him. No one needed to deal with death at that age. It wasn't fair.

As he grew up he shied away from making any real friends. He preferred to flee from any human interaction, a direct result of the guilt he felt. He deserved to be punished for Nate's death, so he spent his time alone until he fell into a group of kids who lived only to drink and do as much drugs as humanly possible. That helped to numb the pain for a while and even kept the nightmares away, but there would be those sober moments that would remind of that night all those years ago. There was no escape from it. No amount of drugs or alcohol would take that guilt away. If anything, it just made the guilt worse because he was wasting nights in a haze of self-destruction. At some point the party had to end. He knew where all those kids were going to end up and he didn't want to end up the same way, so the only option was to come to grips with the guilt.

The therapy might not be working as well as he had hoped, but as he sat in the comfy couch, thumbing through the same out of date magazines, he felt a wave of hopelessness. Maybe it was time to stop therapy and try something else. *What else is there?* He had been seeing Doctor Yost for so long the idea of not seeing him filled him with panic. He had been going to therapists for years. It was almost a part of who he was. At first it was supposed to help with the grief, and then it just morphed into helping him deal with the guilt and the nightmares.

"Good morning, Robert. You look terrible. No offense. Bad night?" He ushered Robert into his office and he was overwhelmed by the pungent odor of his pipe. He only smoked in long stretches between patients, but apparently the doctor had been booked solid that morning. It was always busiest between fall and Christmas. People, it seemed, were more likely to kill themselves during the darkest parts of the year.

"Yeah, it was. I don't think I'm making any progress here. I think we need to try something else."

Robert sank into his usual leather recliner and put his feet up. There was no desk in this room, just a matching leather couch. The walls were adorned with knock offs of paintings by Picasso. The room was designed to instill comfort and it usually worked. At least for him it did.

"I agree, and I have an idea. What would you say to revisiting the house that Nate died in?" Doctor Yost asked indifferently. It was almost as if he were throwing out restaurants to eat dinner at.

"Are you serious? I can't do that." Just thinking about it filled him with dread. Sweat beaded on his forehead and his hands began to shake lightly.

"There's something else aside from the guilt. I truly believe that there is no guilt. You're afraid of something else. Do you remember the first thing you said to me about the night of Nate's death?"

Robert shook his head. He had been coming here for a long time. There had been a lot of words spoken about his fear that he would be a terrible husband and his strong desire against having children. There had been a multitude of conversations about the kind of person Nate was, and could have grown into. "No, I'm sorry."

"You said that you believed that someone was in the house with you all. You felt a presence, which supports everything the police came up with. Someone killed Nate. You had no idea that there was someone else in the house with you, but you have always insisted that whatever killed Nate wasn't human."

***

"I saw someone standing in the corner." He also remembered how they felt *watched*. Even Thomas had said that there was no one upstairs when he walked up the stairs. "Whatever killed Nate wasn't human."

"It was, and you going to the house is going to prove that there's no ghosts. More than anything, you're afraid. I want you to spend the night in the house, just so you can see that there's nothing to be afraid of. Once you get over the fear, the nightmares will go away."

"How can you be so sure? The house isn't an option. I'm pretty sure someone lives there now," Robert offered with a tremor of fear in his voice.

Dr. Yost smiled an eerie smile. It was the kind of smile that held many secrets. "I thought so too, but I found out over the weekend that it's up for sale again, so I arranged for you to spend the night there."

"And if I refuse?"

"Look, I can't make you do this, but I think there's something to the nightmares. Something that's in your subconscious. I think if you return to the house and see that it's not haunted, you'll be able to let go of whatever it is you're feeling."

Robert frowned and failed to see the logic behind it. "My friend was killed in there and you want me to return there to stay overnight?"

"I think this could help you." Dr Yost responded simply. Robert looked at him open-mouthed. After the appointment he had thought about not going, but Sophie just glared at him.

"Maybe he's right. Maybe if you go to the house you'll see that it's not as threatening as you remember. This is a chance for you to make peace with Nate for what happened. We all need closure," Sophie replied, wrapping her arms around his waist.

***

"You're supposed to be on my side," he replied.

135

"I think you should do this. It sounds unorthodox, but who am to say what's right? Just promise me you'll do it."

"Fine. Will it make you happy?" He lit a cigarette. Maybe he was wrong. He wanted the guilt, and most of all, he wanted the nightmares to stop. He wasn't exactly sure what a night in the house would do, but there was no way he could say no. Sophie was worried about him, and if she thought this would help him, then he would try it. He could refuse, but Sophie was a stubborn woman who always got what she wanted. She wasn't annoying about it, but when she pouted and just looked at him, his resolve would melt away. No other woman had ever had that effect on him, and it was frustrating at times, but she loved him more than any other woman had.

That was why he found himself standing in the very yard he had avoided for many years. After Nate's death, Robert's father had gotten a new job with a law firm in Cleveland and they had never looked back. Milford, it seemed, hadn't changed at all. While the world grew and changed this town had seemed to exist in a time warp. Even the house seemed unchanged. Only the siding appeared different.

"I didn't think you'd make it." They shook hands, and Robert felt as if he were twelve again.

"I almost didn't. Sophie made me come."

"She loves you. You know, this was actually her idea. She's worried about you and thinks this will help."

"I should have known." Robert lit a cigarette and thought about leaving. This was all bullshit, and surely Sophie and the Doctor knew it. "Fuck it, let's get this over with. What's the plan?"

They made their way to the house and, for just a second, he thought he saw someone staring at them through the upstairs window. He shrugged it off as they made their way to the front door. "You think I'm going to leave you here alone? We're going to stay overnight. I'm just here to observe, and if you need me I'm here to help. Pretty simple, right?"

It was, Robert had to admit. "How did you manage to get this place for the night?"

"I know the right people, I guess. I brought in some food and a couple of air mattresses earlier. You okay with sleeping in the living room?"

"What makes you think I'll be sleeping? Let me ask you something. Do you believe in ghosts?"

Doctor Yost shook his head. "Not a chance. So do you want to show me where it happened?"

They took the stairs slowly. A multitude of memories flooded his mind. He could hear Nate's voice laughing at them, urging them forward.

In the corner of the hallway he saw someone standing there, watching them. Icicles of dread formed around his heart. He wanted to stop and run back out the front door, but he was determined to prove to himself that he was brave. He had to finish this. There was no turning back now. He could see Dr Yost, but he was somehow transparent. If he reached out to touch him, his hands would go right through him.

There was something else different-the light. He hit the top of the stairs and saw that it was no longer daylight.

Where did the sun go?

Now the fear inside of him was spreading through his body like a brush fire. His feet stopped moving as he saw the hall bathed in sinister shadows that swirled around him in a mist. From the room directly in front of him he could hear the soft drip of water. He opened the door slowly and gasped.

Thomas was in the bathtub, idly spinning a razor, and looking through him as if Robert wasn't even there. Thomas was younger , through the years Robert wondered how he was doing. Thomas brought the razor against his wrist and began carving into his flesh as if his forearm was a Thanksgiving turkey. A smile spread across his face as the blood splashed onto it. He slowly sank into the water and, as quickly as the vision had come it left again, leaving only a darkened bathroom. There was nothing in the tub. He sat on the toilet heavily and tried to gather his thoughts. He needed to erase the fear, but it kept washing over him in waves.

This isn't real. It's just the stress of being in this house again. You've fainted and soon Doctor Yost is going to slap you back to reality. It all *felt* real. The sight of Thomas was as vivid as Doctor Yost had been on the stairs. He could smell the blood as it leaked from Thomas' butchered forearm. What the hell was happening? A sudden movement caught his attention and warm piss exploded in his pants. There was someone watching him, and as the figure got closer Robert felt a scream building in his throat. *He has no face!*

A shifting darkness moved across his featureless face like storm clouds. This was who he had seen that night so many years ago. There was something else he had blocked out that night. There had been laughter coming from upstairs. He had ignored it just like he had ignored the footsteps. He had just assumed it was Nate's or Thomas', but as the figure got closer it became clear why no one stayed in the house very long.

Sometimes it's better to not know why a house was haunted. It just *was*. Some people were oblivious to what existed in their houses but that night he and Nate had tapped into it. What had Thomas seen? Robert tried to get off the toilet, but it felt as if his ass had been cemented to the seat. The figure began to shimmer and the features solidified into the face of Nate.

"Nate, I'm so sorry. I didn't know!" The words were spoken among hitching sobs that made it hard to breathe. He was no longer a grown man. He was twelve again, somewhere Thomas was watching them and in his hands was a rusty razor. There were no other sounds as the Nate thing stepped closer. A smile spread across his face as he reached out for him. For just a second Robert hesitated, but he needed to be forgiven. As he reached out to Nate he felt the cold darkness embrace him and he was free. He felt a searing pain explode across his cheeks and his eyes slammed open. He was bathed in the bright blinding light of the sun. Doctor Yost was standing over him with a look of concern on his face.

"What the hell happened?" Robert tried to stand up, but a wave of dizziness washed over him and he lay back down. He was half in and half out of the very room that Nate died in.

"You passed out. Are you okay?"

"Yeah, just get me the hell out of here." Doctor Yost helped him to his feet and they made their way back down the stairs like two drunks.

"I'm sorry I brought you here. It was a bad idea." Robert freed himself from the doctor's grip and found that he could stand on his own.

"Maybe someday I'll tell you what happened." They stood on the walk for a moment and then made their way to their cars.

Robert glanced at his watch and saw that they had been in the house for over two hours. "Thanks for trying to help. I'll see you on Monday?"

The doctor nodded and Robert could see the worry in his face. "Look, I swear, doc, I'm fine." He relayed the story without the vision of Thomas and saw the doctor frown. It was obvious that he didn't believe him, but that didn't matter. He *knew* what he had seen. It was the house that had killed Nate, and if the doctor hadn't been there it would have killed him too. Whatever existed in that house was evil, and if it had suddenly burnt down, he doubted if anyone would miss it. He was now free and that was all that really mattered.

About Michael Noe

Michael Noe is a horror writer from Barberton Ohio. He is the author of Legacy and has been featured in various anthologies. When he isn't writing he can be found at home watching Netflix. You can also find him here https://m.facebook.com/splatterpunkmonkey?ref=bookmark as well.

Sepientia Suburbia
By Brian Barr

The oldies were goldies, dependable goodies, highlighting a nostalgic time and era Winston had never experienced. Well maintenanced lawns, happy faces, dependable milkmen and paperboys. Wives as domesticated as Rover, kids getting in no more trouble than lying about their homework, gangs softer than The Sharks and The Jets. Cinema movies, innocent kisses with cheerleaders at drive-ins, dad reading the paper in the den and scolding Junior near the end of the episode with a sermon before son and father laughed together right before the credits rolled. A sunny time, a happy time, hokey and clean.

Winston's neighborhood was not like this.

Winston's suburb was not in black and white. Had it really been like that in the 1950s, colorless but bright, ladies smiling in dresses and aprons over the evening pot roast? Winston's mother wasn't home anymore, strung out on meth, either dead or in jail for all he knew. Dad wouldn't say. He hadn't even brought her up in weeks, lost in a well-paying but dead end job that he hated, not coming home until late, way late, when Winston was asleep, gone before the thirteen year old even woke up.

On the old shows, the schools were clean, and the kids spoke a language just as sanitized. Kids at Winston's school swore. Many of them owned rags that proclaimed the neighborhoods they came from. Winston was glad that there wasn't a prominent gang in his neighborhood- even though there were still some knuckleheads here and there, it was still the *burbs,* just a little better than Jagmann Gardens five miles downtown, and Cedar Block, the two areas where most of the kids at Medgar's Middle School were bused in from. Winston didn't look down on those kids; he came from a neighborhood probably just as run down before he and dad moved a few states away, with dad having a higher paying job and mom promising to get clean if they could just change their environment. How much good had that gotten them?

Winston thought the suburbs would be nice. Sure, there were neatly cut lawns, and the houses all looked the same, like the houses on those old shows from TV. But there was a hell of a lot of things different, things that weren't like the show. There were the houses that dad showed to Winston on the family computer, houses marked with squares. When you clicked on the squares, it showed you the sick crimes those guys had done, and dad had warned Winston to stay away from those areas like the kid was an idiot.

Then there were the gossipy ladies that all stood on the corner, sharing all sorts of stories with one another. They always looked at Winston strange, and one time his dad told Winston that the ladies told him Winston had let one of his friends come over when he was home alone, a guy friend. What the gossipy ladies obviously were insinuating really pissed Winston off.

We were just playing fucking video games, Winston remembered with rage. *Ratguy: Austin Asylum, a superhero action adventure.* Ever since that day, Winston's dad kept asking him if he was talking to any of the girls at school, obviously praying his kid was straight.

There were more annoyances in Winston's neighborhood than loquacious, fat housewives sitting on lawns and perverts readjusting to society. There was the next door neighbor that Winston could *hear* beat the shit out of his wife almost every night, right outside of his bedroom window. One of Winston's other neighbors had a kid that he had *seen* skin a squirrel alive (Winston never knew a squirrel could sound like that) and burn toys with a lighter before stomping them out. On the weekend, another of Winston's neighbors, some lady in her forties, let strange men come over whenever her husband was out, probably at work or on business trips. In the nearby park, some weirdo wearing a fedora and flip flops with a robe often ranted on and on about aliens (kids learned quickly *not* to play there). An ex-neighbor up the street got arrested for beating up religious missionaries going door to door, killing them with a hammer, and some strange person that probably wasn't the mail man kept dropping off pamphlets in mailboxes to join the Tu Tux Tan, some crazy racist organization. There were the cops that patrolled the area and stopped Winston on the way home, wanting him to confess that he had broken into a house two streets down (dad had *the talk* with him: "Son, I know you don't sag your pants or wear hoodies, but you are a young, black male in this society, and there's just some things you'll have to accept. And don't just think that since your light skin and biracial, you're exempt from harassment. I went through it, too..."). Luckily, after one of the cops pushed Winston against his patrol car and yelled at him a bit, they were finally convinced that Winston wasn't the boy that did the crime, although they still mean mugged him whenever they rode by the kid as he walked home from school.

The suburbs. They were supposed to be *better* than the other neighborhoods- the projects, the trailer park before that. Instead, they were shit. They were hell, a silent hell, pretty on the outside, but strange on the inside, like a David Lynch film.

Winston's dad *worshipped* David Lynch. Twin Peaks, Blue Velvet, Inland Empire- his dad forced Winston to watch them all, even though Winston wondered quite loudly whether they were movies a son should watch with his parents, or whether one should watch them at his age at all.

"These are about the real world, Winston," his father would tell him. "Not those hokey bullshit old shows your mom got you hooked on. That's why she's so fucked up now. Escaping in drugs the way she escaped through those fantasy shows. How many people do you see that look like you on those shows, Winston? How many black, happy faces?"

Well, there's not many black, happy faces in David Lynch films either, dad, Winston would think with a musing smile. But, fuck it, maybe dad was right. How many faces could Winston relate to in a black and white 1950's suburban family sitcom, biracial or black? Well, there was Linda, the cleaning lady that was on that one episode of *Mother Cleans Well* for maybe five minutes? Oh, and that one time Uncle Garry was in the train station on *The Dweeber And Me,* where there was a black butler holding some fancy dressed gentleman's bags in the background. And maybe...

Hell, who cared? Winston liked those shows. They were from a different time. When he watched old black and white sitcoms, he wasn't thinking about civil rights or how fucked up things were during the time. Was there any perfect human time, any perfect moment in human civilization? People were still trying

143

to master ethics and respect for fellow human beings *now,* in a time that was supposedly socially enlightened and forward. Winston didn't look to those archaic programs for a mere *escape.* He liked those old shows for their entertainment value; they made him happy and they reminded him of mom.

Mom. A time when she wasn't getting high. Moments where he came home and she wasn't staring mindlessly at a spoon, the house looking like crap because dad had been busy, out of town for over a week looking for better places, better jobs. Situations where his mother actually showed she loved him, kissing and hugging him, calling him her *little guy.* Wondrous memories, times that didn't require a solace, no need to get out or run away. Precious times to treasure, beautiful scenes still programmed in his head like a syndicated sitcom.

That was his *Mother Cleans Well,* his *The Dweeber and Me,* his *Peppy Parents* and *Dad's The Bees Knees.* There were some differences, from life being in full color to the interactions being real. Winston, his mom, and his dad had once had those perfect moments, beyond television. A house used to feel like home. That was in the hood, the trailer parks, far from the suburbs.

Now, in the perfect neighborhood, Winston felt further away from a perfect life than ever before.

How could he find such a perfect life? A junkie mother missing in action would do nothing to help him accomplish anything, especially since she couldn't help herself. An angry, stressed out father that worked all the time and was never home when Winston was awake couldn't give the youth a satisfactory childhood or benefit his budding adolescence. The kids at school would continue to have their gang disputes and drug deals under the noses of teachers that didn't give a fuck, happy to reach tenure or itching to transfer to another public institution. Cops would continue to see a little "high yellow" boy, as his father called him, as a threat and potential nuisance that deserved dagger eyes and shoves against police vehicles.

So where did nirvana lie in the suburbs? Perhaps nowhere, unless television truly was the one tool in which one could peer into Elysium, see paradise in the form of colorless hues, neatly cut lawns with lemonade stands, happy moms in aprons and oven mitts, smart dads that could put down a newspaper long enough to deliver an awe inspiring, life changing moral like Buddha on the mountaintop. Through the screen, peering into the bright clarity of fictional worlds beyond half a century into the past- perhaps that was where the answer lied.

An escape, Winston could finally admit to himself. So dad was right, about mom, about him- they were looking for a way out of the bullshit reality they didn't believe in. But Winston didn't need the drugs, didn't need the crazy crap his mom had put into her system through injections and oral consumption. He would stick to the black and white, a gateway drug where he would remain forever at the threshold. Peering into the screen, he would just get lost right there, moving no further.

***

"You are your mother's son, Winston."

Winston came back from his evening bike ride, right on time for *Mother Cleans Well* He was surprised to see his dad standing on the front porch, hands on his hips as he shook his head with a pitying yet amused smile.

"You're home early," Winston noted, too disappointed to be welcoming.

"Don't worry. I won't invade your fantasy TV time. I got some time off of work, luckily. I'm going straight to bed."

Good, Winston thought, not wanting to talk any further. He walked past his father, moving his bike onto the bike rack in the front hallway. Then he went into the living room, grabbing the remote off the coffee table and turning on the TV.

As *Mother Cleans Well* started, Winston could hear his father's heavy shoes ascending the stairs. *Good,* Winston thought, *go away, don't ruin this for me. This is the best part of my day.*

The opening credits and scenes were rolling. The father of the show tripped over an uneven rug on the front porch before waving to the camera. *Steven Van Gooper as Mr. Howie Rogers,* the credits read on the screen.

The young son of the show hit a baseball with a bat, watching it sail before turning to the camera and waving. *Joseph Bullock as Timmy Rogers,* the bottom of the screen displayed.

A teeny-bopper daughter sat with a bunch of records with

her brunette ponytail, snapping her fingers to the pleasurable music in her headphones, completely ignoring the camera. Winston had a huge crush on her. *Cynthia Lewis as Candy Rogers.*

Candy's boyfriend, a jerk that always made fun of Timmy, faked out the camera with a football in his hand, laughing and pointing proudly as he wore his letterman jacket. *Eddie Rascal as Matty.*

What a tool, Winston thought, anger and jealously flowing for just a moment.

Then, the star of the show appeared, proud in her apron and dress as she moved through the kitchen. The kitchen was her sanctuary, not her prison. Her throne room, her Zion. *....And Kathy Jefferson as Judy Rogers, Mother.*

I wonder what episode this will be? Winston thought with excitement.

It could have been his favorite episode, where Timmy secretly bought the dog and hid it in the basement, but the mutt ended up knocking over all of father's paint cans. Dad's moral scolding was particularly lengthy on that episode, and Winston wished his dad would take that much time out of his day to talk to him.

Maybe this episode would be another of Winston's favorites, where mom secretly borrowed dad's wallet and ended up getting the scolding at the end of the episode. Or maybe this was where Timmy finally told Matty to can it. Matty was so shocked on that one! He didn't know what to do, having someone tell him to shut up, let alone an eight year old!

Whatever episode it was, Winston had seen them all, and he could usually tell in the first five seconds of the show, after the opening credits finished. But the show had been on for nearly a minute, and Winston recognized nothing. The camera went from room to room, and not a character had been seen yet. Judy's room was empty, her records more neatly stacked and organized than usual. Timmy's toys and collectible cards were all put away in his room, dad's robe and slippers were hanging in a clean den with a fireplace burning.

Mom must have cleaned up, Timmy reasoned.

Suddenly, the show moved into the kitchen, where mother's back could be seen from her hair to the bottom of her long dress.

She was standing over a stove, obviously cooking something, and boy, did it smell good.

Smell? Winston thought. *How d-*

"I hope my little guy has room for all of this pie."

Mother turned around, smiling. Her eyes, her lips, her cheekbones filled with life, her smile-

No. No.

Mother before the meth. Mother before the tears, the broken windows, the screams from attempted withdrawals in the night, the babbling, the strange men brought over while dad was away, obvious dealers whom she would do *anything* to please, just to get her smack-

She stood there, proud. Mom, as clean as the house she had squared away, the kitchen she had always kept in place.

The kitchen had always been the most well kept room on the show, Winston remembered. *But this is mom... my mom... dressed like Kathy fucking Jefferson.*

"Mind your thoughts, young man."

"Huh?" Winston asked in shock, jumping as he now stood besides the counter, inches away from mother as she held her pie over the stove. Some ghost audience clapped all around him. Color was gone. He looked at his skin. Still the same complexion, a bit darker than mother's, though his yellow brown tone was lost in the lack of hues in that classic world. He looked at the shiny oven top and could see his reflection, the hints of nubian facial features, his full lips, his proud father's nose.

The clapping of the ghost audience died down.

This can't be real.

His mother was there. She looked... she didn't look like a meth whore. Her wrinkles were gone. Skin was brilliant, smooth and soft like when he was a little boy. Her blonde hair, now just as white and bright as her face, flowed in a beautiful collection of slightly curly tresses. "Now we need to hurry and get this to the dining room table. You know I don't like you eating in the kitchen."

"Mom? How did you- what-?"

"Come on, now, let's go, before your piano practice! We don't have much time!"

A laugh track sounded, dying a few seconds after it was

born.

Piano practice? Winston's heart didn't know whether to sink or fly. He hadn't practiced piano since his mother had stopped taking him to practice, since she had gone off the deep end and left him to struggle in that project apartment, looking for cereal in a nearly empty refrigerator. Now, she was vibrant, healthy, talking as if none of those horrid years had ever happened.

He wanted to ask questions, but like a puppet on her string, Winston followed mother into the dining room. He sat at the table, looking at the plate placed before him, staring as mother cut a slice of the pie.

"You know I've been baking this all afternoon, Winston," Mother remarked.

"Mom... where's dad? How did-?"

Mother placed a finger to his lips, shushing him. "Winston. Do you really need to bring *him* into this? This is our world. It's never been *his.*" Winston had never heard male pronouns spoken with such vehement venom, such salient hatred. Even more confusingly, a laugh track played inappropriately in the background. "Now eat up. Come, come. You'll have time to get your vegetables later."

Winston found a fork waiting right there, on the edge of the plate. He took a bite. His eyes swooned, his lips nearly erupting from the taste. "Wow. Mom. This is delicious!"

"Of course, mister. I cooked it!" She smiled and winked before looking at her plate, diving into the piece she had cut for herself.

"Mom. How did you do it? You look... you look so clean. Healthy. Not like-"

"When I was your age, you know what I used to do? I used to dream. I used to dream that I could be just like Katherine Jefferson." The ghost audience briefly offered awws. "Such poise. Such grace. And old fashioned. She was the star! People probably think she was pathetic, a horrid figure setting women's lib back decades-"

"Women's lib?"

"-toiling in a kitchen, feeding a family, letting dad give the moral talks and scriptures. But let me tell you something, Winston. She was the *star.* The matriarch. The show was built around her.

She was the fabric of the family. Cleaner of the rooms. Washer of the clothes. Provider of the kitchen. The maker of the pie. Have another bite, dear, go on."

Winston took another bite, listening obediently. "So we're on the show, now? We're on *Mother Knows Best?* Where's Judy? Where's Matty, and Timmy, and their friends? Where's Father Rogers, and... and... what, are you the mom now?"

"That was *their* show, son. We all live in our own programs, don't we? We make our own sitcoms, even if we're inspired by shows that came before us." Mother chuckled. "Oh, look at me. Sounding more like Steven Van Gooper than Kathy Jefferson."

"Mom. I love you. And I missed you."

"I love you too, son."

"I don't want to lose you again. The drugs, the binges-"

The mother held a hand to her son's face as a laugh track erupted in the background. Her eyes were glowing with excitement, her lips mirthful with a smile. "Do you hear that, son? They love it. You're really funny!"

"Mom-"

"You're a good supporting actor, son."

The laughs were even louder this time, more boisterous, more entertained.

"Mom... we won't ever leave each other again, will we?"

Louder, the laughs grew, like rising tides, stirred by a mad moon. Mother's skin was becoming translucent, fading-

"Mom!"

And then she was as ghostly as the laughter, poltergeist chortles surrounding him on all ends. The kitchen faded. Existence became bright as white, contrast lost. Winston didn't know where this classic world ended and his body began. Invisible, he felt as if he were melting into an infinite light.

***

Winston knew what to expect when dad told him.

Mom had been found in Louisiana, her cadaver rotting in a trailer. If police hadn't conducted a bust, who would have known when they would have found the body? Whoever the cooks and

149

dealers were, they were gone, abandoning ships.

Sure, Winston didn't pinpoint the details in some clairvoyant precision. He just knew that she was dead. Gone. The dream was her way to reach him, her way to know that she *was* there.

Death held no separation.

Mom's parents had retrieved her corpse from Louisiana. She was to be buried at their family's cemetery, where great and great-great relatives had been laid to rest. Winston hadn't seen grandma and grandpa since he was six, so he knew the funeral would be nothing but awkward.

And dad was going to be there, too.

Winston watched feet away as his father did the final touches to his black suit in the downstairs mirror near the front door. Winston couldn't help but feel sick to the pit of his stomach. The way dad tugged on his tie and straightened his collar, staring coldly into the mirror, upset him.

"Well, let's get going," father said, staring at his polished shoes for a final moment. "We've got a long drive ahead of us. We got to cross three states just to get to the damn church."

Dad wasn't going anywhere. He didn't expect that gunshot as Winston stood behind him, aiming a pistol. His brain matter splattered quickly from one bullet, and Winston had just walked up behind him.

Winston's father was dead, the man who locked him in some forced state of 'reality', the last human closest to him, yet so distant, so lacking of understanding. He bled on the carpet, his brain leaking, life gone.

A gun was easy to get in a school filled with gangsters and gangster wannabes. Winston was just going to end his own life at first, just going to commit suicide and be done with it, but he couldn't. No, he didn't have to die. His father did.

Dad never believed in magic. Never believed in miracles, or paradise, or eternal bliss. He just believed in reality. The mundane.

Hell.

Suicide. Could it have brought Winston to heaven? A colorless paradise with drug free mommy baking apple pie, making sure he ate his veggies by dinnertime? Maybe. But now, seven years later, in a jail cell where clothing ripped before he could hang himself with it, and shanks were taken before he could use them effectively on himself, it seemed like suicide was so far away. The guards took his threats to kill himself *very* seriously, and there was hardly a time that he wasn't on watch.

The suburbs were so far away. He hadn't seen the outside world in nearly a decade. Grandma and grandpa never visited. Dad was gone forever.

But mom came. Never when he expected, but her door was always open. Past the front door, beyond the living room and into the kitchen, cooking something nicer than the meth served in those prison walls. Pie wouldn't rot his ethereal, dream formed teeth as quickly as his own physical teeth had been ruined in that state penitentiary, and mother never did anything to hurt him. She just smiled, wearing her Mother Rogers dress and apron, smiling pretty. Winston always asked about Judy, if she had grown up, too, and the laugh track would howl horrendously at him. Mother would giggle too, though lovingly, caringly. A question about dad would come up and Winston would quickly regret it, another laugh track drowning him out as mother pressed a finger to his lips.

Winston would ask about suicide. He would ask about drug overdoses, about slamming his head against the wall. Winston would ask about TV hour in the slammer. He would ask if this method of death was the answer, or this one, if that other idea was the real escape.

Mommy would smile. The audience would fade. All would become white.

About Brian Barr

Brian Barr is an American author and artist. He writes novels, short stories, and comic books both under his pen name, Aghori Shaivite, and his real name. He co-writes and co-produces for the comic series *Empress*, along with Chuck Amadori, with art done by Pencil Blue Studio. His first novel, *Carolina Daemonic*, is currently being edited for release under J. Ellington Ashton Press, and he has a second novel, *Psychological Revenge*, slated for release as well. His works have been featured in many anthologies, including *Nonbinary Review Issue 3: The Wizard of Oz* and JEA's

Inanna Rising, Autumn Burning, Cherry Nose Nightmares, Kaiju: Lords of the Earth, and many others.

Jake

By Dani Brown

"I should be paid for sitting on Facebook all day," Jake muttered to himself.

He didn't have anyone else to speak to. Everyone else had left, driven off by his obsessive need to inflict veganism on them through his regurgitated pseudo-science babble and his need for control. Not many people could get past his blob-like form - usually spread out above skinny legs on a festering mattress - enough to endure a real life conversation with him (or several hours of Jake speaking at them). Not many people wanted to. It wasn't so much the effort, more the desire to not find out if he wore pants underneath that moth eaten blanket. In the gloom of his flat, it was, thankfully, hard to tell.

Jake only saw daylight when it was his turn to stand in the dole queue and claim he been looking for actual paid employment. He hadn't, but it was easy to pretend, even for someone such as himself. In fact, he had it easier than people actually seeking employment. Sometimes he would argue about how he should be paid to troll Facebook all day and night, but most of the time he wouldn't; the people behind the counter were on his level of intellect, so it was easy to slip up and be revealed as the lazy internet troll he was. When that was the case, he would have to endure a few weeks of his vegan gravy train being watered down. He didn't care. Unlike most vegans, he wasn't a fan of healthy eating and healthy living. And unlike most people on the dole, he didn't shy away from underpaid, under-the-counter employment to sustain himself for a few weeks for those times he wasn't pestering a woman to feed and fuck him whilst he told her all the reasons she shouldn't have a job.

The online world was something else entirely for Jake. He

was popular, with thousands of friends, admirers and well-wishers. His arguments were ripped off rather well, often aided by an ancient thesaurus he'd stolen from the library. The laziness of the people at the other end of the screen was equal to Jake's, so they wouldn't trace the argument back to the source, even if they knew how. Most didn't.

Jake was the unofficial king of the slack-jawed professional slacker. If they ever met him in real life there would be an uprising, and someone less-blob like and minus the cloud of molecular faecal matter would be put on the throne --an actual throne and not a festering mattress picked off the roadside, held together with many years' worth of dried skin cells and dust mites.

Jake created what he referred to as free content for his peasants. It wasn't free, but more something he found on the peer-to-peer networks with the use of a proxy server.

He didn't want payment from his peasants with hygiene related issues in a borderless homeland of fibre optic cables and satellite signals. He wanted payment for informing the public about the way things should be, from the government of his country of (festering) residence. He was providing a service for the people.

In Jake's bloated head he worked out the way things should be – actually a rip-off of decades of research by a team of people with PhDs and personality disorders, pissed off at the proverbial man and therefore determined to take down the system with misinformation and conspiracy theories. They had PhDs, thus were rendered believable to the general idiots lurking in the dark spots in the World Wide Web. They could spout whatever bullshit they wanted and make a million dollars in the process. The Jakes of the world ruined their gravy trains.

He desired to share this and his two-room, furnished-from-a-dumpster flat with a lucky lady. Jake was choosey when it came to women. He wanted one he could claim ownership of. Then he would force her to slave over a hot stove all day with ingredients from the vegan supermarket. He didn't care that she would somehow need to pay for this food while not being allowed a job. That was what unemployment benefits were for. They'd receive more state money for each baby he made her pop out. She would have to breastfeed; while not strictly vegan, he wanted to present an air of being all-natural. His fantasies, while the rest of the time zone slept, revolved around finding a vegan way to pump himself full of hormones to lactate. That way wifey would never have to stop cooking, cleaning and wiping the shit from his arse with a sponge on a stick. Feeding a baby wasn't hard. He could wrap it up in a sling and let it suckle all day and night while he ruled the internet.

Jake was God's gift, in his mind at least, so he created profiles on every free dating site and waited for the little wide-eyed fishes with hourglass figures to come to him. And he waited. And waited some more.

Women were shallow stupid whores who required a strong man of superior intellect to show them their place. Women thought they wanted flashy cars and fancy restaurants. Jake had to show them they didn't want all that, they wanted a simple life, slaving away to his every need and whim. They would never get what they wanted. They had to settle. Only complete tossers worked. Advertising was brainwashing them to buy cars. It told them what franchised restaurants to eat in. They required deprogramming and re-educating. Franchises were a sign of the coming apocalypse. He learned that by following a series of links to the underbelly of the alternative web, to places where not even the pedos would go.

His profile only showed his face in the shadows and a Photoshopped (Pirate Bay copy) picture of his dick. They weren't taking the bait. In his daymares, Jake envisioned that the type of woman he was after - the house-wifey with no sense – only preferred men with fat wallets and numerous houses. In reality, he knew perfection was but an illusion; house-wifeys had more sense than most and sometimes they were house-husbands. Jake didn't desire a house-husband - homosexuals creeped him the fuck out. He didn't swing that way and even if he did forget the homophobia, men didn't want him either.

Jake alternated his time between social networking, dating and alternative news, history and science websites all day, every day until it was time to meet the delivery driver at the door with his deep-fried vegan fast food or relieve his bowels. His mattress never swallowed him and his computer screen never sucked him in, but the three of them merged, linked together by growths of mould and parasitic worms. He picked up these parasitic worms by sucking his fingers after scratching his arse, which was always coated in shit-flakes because toilet paper was a lie sold by advertising and public health officials.

Neighbourhood children would dare each other to throw stones at his windows, which were crusty with years of dust and nicotine. If Jake was already standing he would appear and lecture them on the virtues of not working – if he wasn't, it was too much effort to move his festering blob and drip slime everywhere. He'd tried rigging up a stone-sensored audio recording and hologram from his mattress but it kept over-heating.

As the months turned into years Jake's body morphed to the point where he was put onto permanent sickness benefits. Without his having to leave the flat for any reason, as everything he needed to could be delivered, Jake's legs shrunk as his stomach expanded, bloated on rice and chick-peas. It hung low and eventually swallowed the legs, pissed off at the years of being deprived of meat. With the women Jake desired being non-existent, his cock never saw any action, so that too was swallowed.

Eventually, his landlord received complaints about the smell that came seeping out from underneath the door to his flat. The other residents claimed it was visible, but that could have been their crystal meth talking.

Jake had clogged the door up with old towels picked out of rubbish bins by his 'freegan frenemies'. They gave Jake towels because they felt sick every time they inhaled his odour and thought he might take the hint and have a shower if he had something to dry himself off with. If they showed willingness to help him, maybe he would help himself and begin to help his fellow man, although Jake was still convinced spreading misinformation on social media was his job and great service to humanity. The neighbour's cat had climbed through Jake's open window and had attacked the towels, mistaking them for a sick rat.

The owner of the block of flats was a charitable man who took in the otherwise unhousable. He was used to bad smells, dirt and grime, and even the occasional used needle that washed up on the stairwell. If the other residents complained then it was sure to be bad. He went expecting to find a body in a puddle of puke wearing a blanket of flies. His residents were often alone in life, so no one was there to miss them, and rent was always paid direct from the government into his business account.

He knocked on Jake's door but had his key out ready. His

heart stopped beating when Jake answered the door. Or what he thought was Jake. Or something that had swallowed his tenant. He couldn't be sure which.

He took a step back and tripped over his shoelace. From the floor, this Jake appeared bigger. A giant slug-Jake, a former Jake, something that had swallowed Jake – whatever it was, slimed towards him.

The landlord didn't know that the creature before him was a vegan. He thought he was about to be eaten. Sweat broke out on his forehead and under his arms in a last-ditch survival effort to make him salty. Slugs don't like salt.

Jake didn't realise people didn't like him. He was, after all, God's gift. He provided a service of informing the public. Even when someone was very blunt with their opinion, Jake couldn't take it in – he wouldn't listen, and on the rare occasions when he did, he couldn't comprehend. Years of having the online audience of the slack-jawed meant he knew he was smarter than everyone else and held all the answers, even if they were simple regurgitations of someone else's ideas.

Jake's landlord had had the breath knocked out of him, which was a good thing considering the smell coming from Jake's flat was worse than the meth lab he'd had to sort out two weeks previously. He would need to start breathing again. He wasn't sure if it was a good idea to breathe through his mouth or not – on one hand, he wouldn't have to take in the smell of urine soaked sheets and methane-tinged, stale cigarette smoke; but on the other hand it would be entering his body through his mouth, in which were thousands of taste buds. He didn't want to taste it either.

Jake still had arms poking out from somewhere on what would once have been his torso. He remembered to hold out a hand to his landlord to help him up, based on watching it on a pirated film not so long before the knock came. Jake couldn't read the fear etched onto the man's face.

The landlord kicked himself half way down the stairs. He had plenty of flesh on his backside to protect against inconvenient things like slipped discs. His eyes had never before seen anything like the creature standing before him. Jake oozed after him, dripping slime that would need double industrial strength cleaner to wash off the stairs.

Starry-eyed neighbours, wiping the crust of sleep and drug addictions away, poked their unwashed heads out of their doors. They hadn't seen Jake in years and if they had, they would have written it off as a hallucination. They saw the landlord on the stairs, close to falling down more and probably landing on his neck. Without this saint-like man, they would all be living on the streets. A woman, down on her luck and not addicted to anything or lazy, dashed out her door to help.

The landlord was a fat man, one more sausage roll away from heart bypass surgery. The woman lived the floor above Jake's and would have to pass him on the way down. She took her chance, running, near enough flying down the stairs. She slipped on Jake's slime and knocked herself out cold.

Jake oozed downstairs. It was a slow process due to not having used them since he'd had proper legs. His blanket fell away, revealing his naked form to the watching tenants. His flesh was a pale white, glistening with moisture after years of keeping himself in the gloom. He spat as he breathed heavily, his body unused to the movement. He'd spit when he lectured the neighbourhood stone throwing children too, but on the ground they couldn't feel its burning rain.

The landlord tried to kick all the way down, a broken neck was better than being near Jake. His arse-fat was caught on the safety feature (a must have if one was housing addicts) nailed to the end of each step and painted in glow in the dark green. Jake was nearly upon him.

The rain of spit was the first to hit the landlord cowering on the stairs and wishing his heart would choose that moment to give up. The landlord could feel it burrowing through his skin and arm fat, infecting him (slowly) with a bad case of extreme laziness. (Laziness is a slow acting disease due to its lazy nature). He clenched his arsecheeks together, lest he should lose a little trickle from his bowels into his pants.

The neighbours couldn't help but stare at Jake. His image would have a permanent spot burned into their minds, returning to haunt them during withdrawal periods. The smell surrounding him was more overpowering than their flats. It caused more than one resident to faint. The landlord wasn't so lucky.

Jake smiled a toothless grin – sucking charcoal did nothing

to prevent decay. He even waved at his neighbours. He didn't own a mirror and was unaware of his appearance. He hadn't even noticed his stomach had swallowed his legs, even though he oozed instead of walked down the stairs.

He wanted to speak to the landlord. Jake felt he should be paid to live in the flat rather than the government paying the landlord. His reasoning was he was providing a service by not allowing the flat to go derelict – he'd read so on a forum.

The landlord didn't want to speak to Jake. His fingers pressed buttons on his touch screen phone. He was going to try the police first, to remove the immediate threat, but this was a case for the British equivalent of Mulder and Scully.

Jake was upon him as he stuttered something incoherent down the phone. The weight of Jake's bulge broke his feet. Jake didn't notice the landlord beneath him. His body was so desperate for nutrients it couldn't get from processed cardboard and overcooked vegetables it started to inhale the landlord's flesh through his arsehole (which had expanded when his stomach swallowed his legs). It even sucked up the bones, as it couldn't pry them apart to get at the marrow. Jake didn't realise he was eating meat. He started to argue his case with the confidence that came from being a lazy idiot.

"You should be paying me."

He allowed a pause to let the landlord try to get in a word, but if the landlord were to start speaking Jake would raise his voice to talk over him. The landlord was more concerned with the agony that came with being eaten by an arsehole.

"I keep the flat from decaying by living in it."

It was actually the slime that Jake secreted over everything that stopped it from falling into disrepair. It formed a protective layer of goo. Jake certainly did not do any cleaning. He was a man; men didn't clean.

The landlord's knees were gone. Sucked away into his tenant's bowels.

The protein gave Jake instant body hair. It didn't improve his ability to think for himself. No amount of meat could do that. As he worked up to the landlord's thighs, Jake's body began the bloating process. His pale flesh was criss-crossed with pink stretch marks ready to split open.

159

Jake didn't realise it, but for a few moments until it dissolved and was sucked through his body, he had a cock in his arse. Years of queer-bashing under a pseudonym and disguised ISP, and he had taken a cock with a brown embrace.

The landlord had finally passed out from blood loss and pain. The neighbours were too drugged up to run into their flats, bolt their doors and leave the building via balconies and fire escapes. Jake's body was hungry. He even swallowed the landlord's toupee.

The first steps into the outside world were always the hardest; he'd grown too large to re-enter his building and return to his flat. The team sent by the government to cage him had to wait in the shadows for him to fall asleep so they could drag him off.

About Dani Brown

Dani Brown is a rather boring person and spends far too much time knitting and trying to get cat fur off her clothing. Her novellas *My Lovely Wife* and *Middle Age Rae of Fucking Sunshine* are out now from Morbidbooks. You can check out her art at facebook.com/doomsdayliverpool. She dreams of moving to Iceland.

Won't You Be My Neighbour
By Kent Hill

Turkey sandwiches at midnight. Then a little Gentleman Jack in some sarsaparilla. There is a recurring sound outside the window, a light jingling of metal on metal that twinkles like the stars in the clear sky and finished with a crash. I look out through the venetian blinds and I see that it is Clancy. I realize that I don't know Clancy's Christian name. When you don't know or can't pronounce your neighbor's name you call him 'man,' or 'woman' as the situation dictates.

Clancy is my stage name for Amanda's boyfriend. He looks like a young Clancy Brown and talks in that same deep guttural voice that makes you want to buy the guy some laxatives and help him achieve the cleansing to make that tone of his effortless and decipherable. Amanda is the neighbor's half-wit daughter who washed her pet cat in kerosene because it was on the move even while at rest as it was walking with flees. Problem is, she forgot to wash the kerosene off and the cat inevitably licked itself and was later found on the front lawn like the rampart lion, stiff as the dick on a bronze statue.

Amanda was perhaps partially retarded and unaware of it. But she fucked like an Amazonian monkey at the sight of the full moon, and Clancy knew which side his bread was buttered on. Not only was this muscle-bound blockhead an easy rider, he was one with perks. 'Cause, you understand, Amanda's whole family were the kind of folks even Satan worshippers refuse to invite to barbeques.

Her father, Eric, had been on welfare since he was 18 and was now on the pension. Dirty fucker used to sexually invade the family's pet poodle on the front steps of the house for all to see and be offended. But he would cast the animal aside and pile the family into their station wagon whenever he caught wind of a highway collision on his police scanner, eat tacos and watch the blue boys mop up the carnage.

Her mother, Daphne, knew three words: FUCK, SHIT and HORSE. She would use these hard learned descriptives in varied combinations at top note throughout the day and night; sometimes in jest, but often times in rage. "Horseshit FUCK!" "Fuck Horseshit!" "Shit-Fuck Horse!" With verbal dexterity like that in play, one couldn't help stopping all action and frantically listing the combinations; half out of amusement, the rest for future reference.

Finally, there was Brother Douglas. Doug was a full blown spastic and a danger to himself for reasons known only to his imaginary friends. Motherfucker knew everybody, but none of the people he waved at, or waved down or shot a smile at knew him. He was the

kind of cat who probably, as a toddler, tried to make love to a garden gnome and never really got over the rejection. I remember writing on the porch on a sultry February afternoon as I watched him and another of his demented devotees try to start a motocross bike with no engine.

So on this night in question, all was relatively tame over the fence until a family friend by the name of Tasman Harp--a giant with tiny legs, granite arms and a spherical beer gut that doubled as a table—pulled into the drive. Atop all this sat a head that only a mother could appreciate and from the mouth there came a voice that made every dog for six blocks run and hide.

"Hey, PUSS-NUTS!" he farts and a squadron of mosquitoes bite the dust, "Hey, PUSSNUTS – you like lamb?"

Harp re-enters his utility and backs up the long drive and stops before the boat Eric built after the last flood. Next time, he'd be ready. His boat was finished and stocked with supplies, so, next time the town flooded, or, as he predicted, was completely submerged by the wrath of God, he would survive – just him.

Puss-nuts was Harp's pet name for Eric, and though he loathed it, he responded.

The sheep was still kicking when they dragged it out of the tray. It gave a last cry before death and then the smell of the slaughter filled the night as these fucking maniacs tried to make like butchers and cut the choice meats.

The sound of dripping guts on the dirt, Clancy and Amanda

162

humping, and Daphne swearing and Doug howling at the moon now made writing impossible; all this plus the sounds of police sirens roaring into the neighborhood.

Doug had always wanted to ride in a cop car, so he went quietly. Daphne chose to forgo the right to remain silent and told the pigs to, "SHIT HORSE FUCK!" but they struggled to oblige her. Eric tried quoting something he heard on TV, but it was not only out of context, but completely irrelevant.

Thirty minutes later and it was quiet again. Amanda and Clancy I saw dash from the bushes in the backyard naked, leap the fence and run giggling into the murk. Brave Clancy being led into the unknown by a girl he loved only to pump and when high, as he was now, to laugh at, even though her well-intended attempt at evasion was largely unwarranted.

The only one left at the scene was Harp, who was now approached by the neighbor who probably made the call to the authorities.

"I am fed up with those bastards," said the old woman.

"Really," said Harp.

"Them and their savage cats."

"Like that one," said Harp, pointing out a scabby feline creeping along the fence.

"Yes, that's one of them," said the woman.

"Right!"

Harp moved fast and grabbed the cat by its hind legs. It screamed and clawed and fought for freedom before Harp wrapped the pussy around the nearby water tank and made a sound like someone wringing a gong at an emperor's palace to signal the coming of the divine one or lunch, or summoning the ruler's cum-guzzling-fuck-sluts.

The cat's head quavered like a loony tune character, after being clobbered by an iron
skillet.

"That was fuckin' cruel," said the old women.

Harp tossed the cat in the bin and wiped his hands on his blood-stained singlet and replied:
"Next!"

Temple Of The Burning Moon
By Kevin Candela

They gathered two nights before the Burning Moon, meeting in a Sonora backyard that was once their holiest of grounds. The Exalted saw the last of his peers pass into the tangible realm from The Plane of Shadow and approach from the final cardinal direction.

Then he took his rightful place at the south end of the circle.

South was Fire, the Home of the Sun. Fire was Change.

So The Exalted *was* Change.

And with a nascent Burning Moon rapidly approaching, this most unusual confluence of control and opportunity was scorching within him.

"Before they came this land was ours," he said. "Before they came, my brethren, with their dividers and their hard shell nests and their great rollers, we lived in peace. And when the Little Great One is sacrificed under the Burning Moon, we will rule this land alone once again."

Most of the Council pounded the ends of their staffs against the hard soil, signifying approval.

Deirmose objected.

"We have no proof of what you say, Exalted," the lesser priest said. "You promise us an end to this long occupation, but you do not tell us how this promised change will take place."

The Exalted displayed the expected patience. Even Fire was not allowed to run amok with the other elements.

"You are young, Deirmose. You have not seen the Great Actions. Others here have. Speak to them of your concerns. And remember as well that the Little Great One has seen us. She knows."

"She is not trusted by the Great Ones. None of the Little Great Ones are," Miglak said.

165

"What of the Beast?" Deirmose said.

"The Beast will not interfere. We have wards for it now."

"Tell that to Shawklan, Exalted," Deirmose said. "With all respect."

"The ward was not properly executed," The Exalted said. "And Shawklan is nearly healed."

"I shall execute it properly this time, Exalted," Shawklan said.

Norgo chuckled.

"This is not an occasion for mirth, Norgo," The Exalted said. "We meet in the Land of the Enemy to discuss his end."

"The Burning Moon is but two suns away," Kolok said. "Will we be ready?"

"We must," The Exalted said. "The Darkening of the Burning Moon will not occur again for a great many cycles."

The circle of eighteen-inch-tall priests paused as one as the cloud cover momentarily parted and allowed the nearly full moon to bathe the Stantons' backyard with silvery light.

Nena Stanton watched through her venetian blinds. She could only see the tiny white-clad figures, not hear them, yet that was fascinating enough. And they were really only visible when the moonlight hit them; every time a cloud shielded the nearly full orb, they vanished back into the shadows and left her staring at the pale chain link fencing.

"She watches us even now," The Exalted said. "Can you not sense it, my brothers and sisters?" He didn't wait for a response. "Listen my comrades," he said, "we shall *use* her interest. We shall usurp her will via her fascination. We shall lure her here and two nights from now we shall perform the ceremonies. We shall drink her blood and reveal her still-beating heart to the Burning Moon. And when her eyes go dull, the Earth shall rise in gratitude and swallow these abominations about us."

He looked around. A couple were smiling, most seemed uncertain; Deirmose was frowning.

"Did we not remove their predecessors?" he said. "Did we not bring on The Shadow Walkers to ravage their communities? Did their blood not run in the streams and did they not run weakened into a fellow tribe that finished them off?"

The Exalted's confidence was brimming.

"You mean *this* tribe, Exalted?" Deirmose said. He waved his staff at the swing set, garage, storage shed, the ubiquitous chain link fencing and the back of the Stantons' house. "They are far more deadly, you realize? They destroy everything that stands in their way. They even destroy the land beneath their feet! In fact they…"

KRRRAAAAZZZZZAAAAATTTT!!!

The Exalted's staff bore a noticeable red-hot afterglow. Deirmose was a pile of dust three inches in diameter.

"Objection noted, Deirmose." The Exalted glanced around. "Any other objections?"

The rest of the priests didn't object, at least not to the point of risking disintegration. In the next moment a new Northeast Druid stepped forth from the shadows where Deirmose had manifested only a few minutes earlier. This new priest – a female – moved up to the circle. A completely out of place breeze swept away Deirmose's ashes and, as it quickly subsided, the new priestess stepped into their place. She bowed.

"Welcome, Deirlahn," The Exalted said, and the others echoed him. "Hopefully you will not prove as unreasonable and inflexible as your predecessor."

She raised her head but most of her angular, bone-white face was still covered by her cowl.

"I live to serve, Exalted," she said, and she watched him nod. "I would appreciate a gracious recap, if possible."

As The Exalted quite patiently complied with the request, Nena Stanton continued to pay such rapt attention to the distant proceedings – the zapping had actually made her jump – that she was completely oblivious to her older sister's deliberately stealthy entrance.

"What are you looking at?" Lorrene said.

She suppressed a smile as her sister popped out of her crouch and momentarily tangled herself in the window blind.

"Sorry," she said with minimal sincerity, crossing the room and moving to help her little sis get free of the blind…if only to get a look at what was so fascinating. "What are you doing anyway? There must be something pretty interesting out there to keep you staring like that for half an hour."

"You've been watching me that long?" Nena said. Clear of the blind now, she lunged out, grabbed Lorrene's wrist and pulled her away from the window. "Why?"

"You're fascinating, of course," Lorrene deadpanned. She tried to tug herself free and get back to the window but Nena was being tenacious. "Let go!" Lorrene finally said, prying herself loose. "What is it you don't want me to see?" She pulled the shutters back but her sister grabbed the other wrist and drew her away again. "What are you doing, Nena?"

"It's not Nena," her sister said.

The room was growing dark again as the moon was being eaten by yet another thick cloud.

"Yeah, I know. You're Princess Siddona…"

"It's Sitala."

"You are so weird."

She jerked herself free so hard that she nearly wrenched Nena's shoulder. The girl yelped but Lorrene ignored her and went for the window.

Nothing. Just the same old shadowy backyard. She watched for a few seconds but nothing moved, or at least if something did, it would have taken superhuman vision to notice it. Nena was still whimpering, so Lorrene relented and withdrew to see if the noise was legit.

"You okay?"

"You hurt my arm," Nena said. "But yeah, I'm okay."

"Sorry," Lorrene said without meaning it for the second time in this brief conversation alone. "Enjoy staring out the window. I'm gonna go watch CSI."

The moment Lorrene cleared the door Nena hastened on over to it, shut it, regretted once again that it didn't have a lock on it, and then sped back over to the window. Her timing was excellent since the moon was coming back out of the clouds.

But the show was over for the night.

There appeared to be no meeting the next night as the threatening cloud cover of the past couple of days finally produced a fairly prolonged thunderstorm. Nena watched in vain for about an hour, hoping each lightning flash would reveal that odd little cluster of "white clothespin priests" again. When she finally realized her vigil's futility she went back to the computer.

She stayed on it until she was made to go to bed and then got up later and was on it some more.

The skies cleared for the Night of the Burning Moon. At a little past ten that night, the ghostly white moon would burn twice: once because this moon was in fact the Burning Moon – the hottest full moon of the year – and again as a full lunar eclipse would also turn it fiery red.

The priests arrived prepared at a little after nine. Stakes were driven, ropes attached. Knives were sanctified and set on pristine cloth. Sacred powders were scattered. The stars and moon were so intense that the ground was milky white. Despite the late hour, the temperature was still around ninety and the rain of the previous day had created a rare mugginess across town that wrapped its victims in an invisible wet blanket so stifling that it made all but the most rugged scream "AC!" and run right back indoors.

Nena strode naked out into the steamy night, which condensed on her slender form as she closed the back door – very quietly – and padded out barefoot into the mossy-damp lawn. The priests were stunned by her approach.

"What is this?" The Exalted said as she calmly made her way toward them, all silvery in the painfully bright moonlight. "Which of you has done this? She was not to be brought here until the darkening began!" He looked around at the others. "Miglak? Kolok? Deirlahn?"

"No, Exalted," each of the three replied in turn.

The Exalted scanned his council. They all seemed genuinely surprised.

Nena approached to within twenty feet of Shawklan, who held his ground (albeit a little uncertainly, knowing the proportionately huge human now drew near behind his back.)

"Halt!" The Exalted said in perfect English. "This is a holy circle within which we are protected and into which no outsider may enter!"

Nena stopped. If she felt odd with seven little cloaked and hooded figures staring at her nude form she wasn't showing it.

"You wish to sacrifice me to the Burning Moon," she said. "Isn't that right?"

The Exalted allowed Shawklan permission to turn and view the intruder as well.

"How can you know this?"

"Does it matter? I am here and this body is yours to do with as you wish. I freely consent."

The council was actually dumbfounded. Even The Exalted had no immediate response.

He finally came up with one after the eyes of his brethren had all come to train upon him.

"Very well," he said. "We shall begin early. Prepare her."

As the moon began to redden, Nena lay spread-eagled, her slim wrists and ankles roped and the ropes pulled so tight that they tore and chafed even though she wasn't moving against them. The Exalted climbed atop her stiffened midriff and stood with his boots on either side of her navel. He looked down into her eyes.

"I do not know why you made this so much more simple for us," he said, "but know that we are thankful and shall beseech the Burning Moon that your passage be as painless as this process allows."

Nena seemed to be completely relaxed. She wasn't tugging at the ropes. She hadn't resisted their attachment or even squeaked as they were subsequently pulled painfully taut. She appeared to be absolutely accepting of her fate.

The Exalted threw back his cowl, revealing a narrow and angular almond-like head with huge round black eyes that bulged and reflected the pale orange moon almost perfectly.

He held aloft his holy blade.

"I pledge this blood to The Burning Moon, that as I drink of it I may ignite the Fire that will cleanse our lands of this scourge known as humans. And as my brothers and sisters join me in drink, may our combined wills turn her spirit into an immortal titan of rage and retribution. In return we pledge a return of the Cult of the Moon and a restoration of respect for the lands beneath it. In your name, O Great One!" He strode up Nena's belly, stepped onto her rib cage and paused there. "Deirlahn!" he said, snapping his head toward the newest council member.

"Yes, Exalted!" she said sharply and stepped forward, drawing her own blade.

"You must serve me," The Exalted said. "And remember that not one drop may touch the sacred land until I have tasted it."

"Yes Exalted!" Deirlahn said.

She moved up to the right side of Nena's face. Nena barely looked her way before returning her focus to the now fully orange moon. Deirlahn threw back her hood, revealing a smaller and less articulated visage that was otherwise identical to The Exalted's. She thrust out her left arm and pushed Nena's right jaw. The girl didn't resist, allowing the diminutive priestess to turn her head fully to the side. Deirlahn knelt down, still holding Nena's chin in place at a tilt with her odd little three-fingered hand. She raised her blade to the moon.

"For the glory of the Burning Moon and the benefit of our lands!" she said.

She brought the blade down just under Nena's chin. Slicing carefully, gently, she opened the skin until a crimson seam appeared.

"Careful!" The Exalted said.

Deirlahn tilted the blade and caught the blood on its breadth. She rose and handed her blade up to The Exalted, then quickly returned to her crouch beside Nena's neck to smear and otherwise detain the continuing trickle before it formed a potentially disastrous falling droplet.

The Exalted licked the blood off the blade, allowing a few drops to splash onto Nena's ghostly pale sternum. Smiling as the blood rolled down his weirdly smooth white chin and too-thin neck he looked around.

"Give thanks my brothers and sisters," he said. "And join me now in partaking of the Feast of the Blood Moon."

Deirlahn ceased curtailing the blood flow and began lapping it up off Nena's pulsing neck. The other six priests and priestesses strode forward to claim their own spot for bloodletting. They raised their blades to the orange-red moon as one.

"To the Burning Moon!" they cried in unison.

"To the Burning Moon!" The Exalted cried, and he dropped and plunged his dagger into Nena's chest an inch or so above her solar plexus.

The others followed suit, ramming their two inch weapons into Nena's sides, outer thighs and upper arms and twisting until blood flowed freely.

Not only did she not scream, the girl didn't flinch.

The priests and priestesses gorged themselves on her blood. Fed by the bloodlust all around him The Exalted pushed down harder until the bone cracked and his weapon plunged into Nena's chest up to the hilt. He pried it back out with considerable effort- and more crunching noises- and was rewarded as blood spurted up like a fountain. He fell on it and drank from it as such. Deirlahn opened Nena's neck wound wider by plunging her blade in and relished the free flow of sticky, salty elixir.

The ground began to rumble.

The moon was as red as Nena's free-flowing bodily fluids.

"It has begun, my brothers and sisters!" The Exalted said, rising from his glutton's crouch to stretch up exultantly at the moon. "Hail the Temple of the Burning…"

"Now, now, we'll have none of that."

Nena had spoken, somehow belying even the trickle of blood that had oozed out of a corner of her mouth. Her eyes opened, balls of black fire now. She smiled wickedly up at the absolutely stunned council chief.

She sat up, effortlessly ripping the long stakes out of the ground and sending The Exalted flying. He hit the ground and was tumbling helplessly as Nena rose to her feet. She reached up and pulled Deirlahn's blade out of her neck.

The wound healed instantly.

Only Kolok had managed to hold on. Nena looked down at him even as she pulled Norgo's blade out of her left side and added it to Deirlahn's.

"I'd let go," she said, but he seemed determined not to comply. He eyed her defiantly. "Okay then," she said.

Her black eyes flashed. Kolok and his blade turned to dust and fell in a mist on Nena's right ankle and foot.

"He gets replaced, right?" she said to the awestruck priests and priestesses, who were now backing up even as they huddled into a cluster.

Behind them the disheveled and mildly disoriented Exalted was struggling to his feet. Seeing his council backing his way before the devilishly smiling Little Great One – whose wounds had all now healed – addled him even more.

"What kind of trick is this?" The Exalted said as his senses slowly returned.

"A pretty good one, really," Nena said. She focused her gaze on The Exalted as she strode forward, her body red now only because of the warped moonlight. The others parted before her.

"You don't remember me, do you?" she said. "You were there last time. You were the new one then. You drew first blood from me under a Burning Moon and sentenced my people to extinction."

The Exalted was still a bit hazy from the unexpected cannonball onto unforgiving California turf. Nena stopped several feet before him and stood unabashed and oozing with confidence.

"This is my new body," she said, looking over herself. "Not too impressive looking yet, I know, but now that you've so kindly made it immortal that can wait."

"What madness do you speak?" The Exalted said, his senses close enough to back now.

Nena giggled. "You know a lot," she said, "but you don't know everything."

"Who *are* you?"

Nena's laughter faded. "Nena Stanton," she said. "But you also knew me as Sitala."

The Exalted fell back, staggered and weak. He dropped both his staff and his now spotless blade and seemed about to collapse.

"What is it, Exalted?" Nethla beseeched her leader.

"You already sacrificed me once," Nena said. "When you tried to do it again, you gave me all your power."

"Impossible!" The Exalted cried.

He glanced around, desperately seeking his staff. Finding it, he lunged, picked it up and aimed it at her. Nothing happened; The Exalted could no longer channel and release the power of the world beneath his feet.

Neither could the rest.

Only Nena could. She had it all. And she really had no further use for the bizarre little council of ancient druids at that point, although she really did want some sort of memento of the occasion on which she became a supremely powerful child druid. That only happens once, after all.

She turned her dark gaze on the now terrified druids.

A few minutes later she returned to the house. She went to her room, striding past her drugged family and their spilled after dinner coffee mugs, and put her clothes back on over her once again flawless young skin.

And so the residents of a good portion of central California narrowly escaped disaster thanks to the efforts of a sacrificed and

173

reincarnated Native American girl whose name – Sitala – means "of good memory" in Miwok.

Of good memory indeed.

The next afternoon found Nena quietly straightening her room when her sister finally got home from cheerleading practice. Lorrene couldn't catch her sibling off guard this time and thus make her jump again because Nena's door was uncharacteristically open and she was nearby organizing her shelves.

"Hey, squirtlet," Lorrene said. "How's tricks?"

"Fine," Nena said, not looking up from her work. "How was practice?"

Lorrene shrugged. "Girls are bitches," she said. She noticed the oddly tall figures that Nena was currently arranging and grabbed one to look at it more closely. "Where'd you get these guys?"

"Put it back," Nena said calmly.

"What?" Lorrene said, bringing the little cloaked head up to her face and pulling back the cowl. "Ew...aliens!"

Nena turned and looked up at her.

"Put it back," she said with deadly cool menace.

Lorrene set it carefully back down.

"Thank you."

Lorrene stared at the seven cloaked figures.

"What are they, alien Jedi?"

"Sure," Nena said. "Now get out of my room."

Lorrene didn't say a word. She just obeyed, leaving Nena smiling at her back. Once her sister was out of sight – muttering to herself about why on Earth she had just let her little sister push her around – Nena went back to straightening and admiring her new collection.

She studied The Exalted's face, frozen into a perpetual expressionless state (not that he and his council had faces capable of much expression in the first place.)

"Don't worry," she said, "I'll keep you guys nice and clean and dust you every week."

She pulled his little cloth cowl back up over his head and finished setting him just right. Then she rose and headed over to the door. She cast one more glance at her new figurine collection before going off to greet her mom coming home from work - and to persuade her to buy a locking doorknob.

"I know you don't appreciate this culture I live in now," she said to the petrified priests and priestesses. "But you have to admit they have some great phrases. Like 'Payback's a Bitch.'"

Apocalypse in Sunnyside Acres
By Dixie Pinoit

It all started with Sunnnyside Acre's famous Memorial Day Parade and Freedom Jamboree. Or, rather, Ellie Gifford's desire to have the best dessert *ever* at the Jamboree that year. *Ever.* "Ever, Chet. Do I make myself clear?"

Sunnyside Acres was a retro community that prided itself on its joyous attention to getting every detail of fifties and sixties suburban living exactly right, down to the traditional neighborhood get-togethers and events – like the dessert competition Ellie had her heart set on winning – and the horseshoe tournament all the husbands would compete in later.

Her husband, Chet, eyed her nervously from his Barcalounger and reassured himself that he knew nothing about desserts, cooking, or the kitchen in general, as Ellie was forever reminding him. Or her cherished green Jello salad recipe, which she was waving around right now. Most of the great catastrophes of Chet's life could be traced back to Ellie in one way or another. More than one to her green Jello salad.

"Now, for the last time, Chet, should I use the mandarin crème layer, or the cherry? Oh, wait, I know!" Ellie crooned, inspired. "I'll do a double layer and use both. Let's see what that stuck up Pamela Poundwit thinks of that! Ha!"

***

It was Tuesday when Ellie received the fateful phone call from her older sister, Phoebe. A woman, if possible, who Chet found even more intimidating than Ellie. Together with their mother, they were the triumvirate of the female irresistible force. He

177

was powerless against them.

"Ell? It's Mom. I mean, it's Phoebe, but I'm calling about mom. She's driving me crazy. I can't do anything right. I'm giving the plants too much water, and not putting enough salt in the oatmeal. The toast is too brown and the coffee's too light. If I don't get some help here, I'm going to kill her, and the whole hip surgery thing won't be a problem anymore, because she'll have a butcher knife sticking out of one of her eyeballs. Except she'll probably tell me I should have used a carving knife instead!"

By this point, Phoebe's voice had scaled the desperate nasal heights of a middle-aged woman driven nearly to homicide by post-surgical stress. Chet was eavesdropping for all he was worth – not hard, since Phoebe's nails-on-a-chalkboard voice came through clearly. She laughed hysterically and then said with chilling sincerity. "So, which is it, do you come down here and fill in for a while, or do I kill her?"

Ellie felt a twinge of guilt. Or, at least, a pang of calculation. Mom dead would equal inheritance, but would also equal funeral planning, putting the house on the market and cleaning out Mom's attic and garage. So far, except for putting in an appearance at the hospital, bringing flowers and chocolate and a cute plush bear that read, "Get well *BEARY* soon!" embroidered across his stomach, Ellie had done very little to contribute to her mother's successful recovery.

"Well," she began tentatively. "I could probably come down for a few days. I'd need to talk to Chet first, and wrap up some things here, but . . ." Green Jello salad weighed heavily on her mind. She gave Chet a speculative look. There was a written recipe, after all. And she could call him and walk him through it when the time came. They could even Skype. "... I guess I could figure something out..."

Phoebe cut her off before she could get out another syllable.

"Thanks a mil, baby sister! I'll tell Mom you'll be here tomorrow! Oh, my God, I appreciate this so much. Can you make it tomorrow by lunchtime? I'll start packing up my stuff so that you can move right into Mom's guest bedroom. Thanks, thanks, thanks! I'm going to tell Mom, now. She'll be so glad that you're finally going to come see her! Bye!"

Phoebe slammed the phone down before Ellie could protest.

Ellie sighed. Between Phoebe's near psychotic desperation, manic gratitude and the heaping dose of guilt that she had tossed into the mix, Ellie hadn't stood a chance. Ellie really admired her big sister for that.

***

Despite his Barcalounger timidity, Chet Gifford was a different man at work. As a matter of fact, he was the director of the Federal Department of Future Science Peacetime Research and Development. His interests had diversified since his early days at the University of Michigan, when he had specialized in Nuclear Irradiation applications, but it was still his first love. Ellie frequently remarked at cocktail parties that Chet had a remarkably even temper for someone who worked in such a volatile field, to which Chet inevitably replied, "and it's a good thing!" Their friends always laughed. She'd been making that joke since his first management position. She and Chet never got tired of it.

When Ellie got off the phone, she informed Chet that she was leaving in the morning for a stay with her mother. He accepted the news with the equanimity which she had come to expect from him. His calm was due in part to the fact that he couldn't quite picture himself arguing with Ellie about anything she'd decided to do, regardless of the circumstance. Also contributing to his easy acquiescence was the fact that the only viable alternative his fine intellect could discern was to have Ellie fetch her mother back to recuperate in Ellie and Chet's home. And that would definitely be a disaster of cataclysmic proportions.

The only small disturbance in the force occurred when Ellie explained she still planned to win the upcoming dessert competition – and how she was going to do it.

"What do you mean, you don't want to help me?" Ellie patted Chet's shoulder amiably as she walked by, like he'd momentarily lost his senses, but would regain them any second. "Of course, you do." Ellie began pulling out the ingredients Chet would need for her special Jello salad.

"If you do, I'll make my special meatloaf for you before you leave," she coaxed.

Chet wavered. Ellie's meatloaf was nothing to sneeze at.

"Well, I do have a new gadget from work to test out ..."

"Oh?" Ellie said. She knew she had him. "What's that, Chet?"

"It's a personal irradiator," Chet replied, oozing shy pride. "Kind of like a microwave, but without the box. Made it look like one of those old fashioned TV remotes. Just don't point it at the dog, eh?" He pulled it out of his pocket and hopped up on the counter, pointing it at a cup of coffee Ellie had let go cold. In seconds, the cup had begun to steam. "It's a little slow, though. If you made me meatloaf, I could use it to work out the kinks on this thing." He gave the gadget a shake.

Ellie fixed him with *the look*. "If I made you a meatloaf, would you make my green Jello salad and enter it in the competition for me? Under *my* name?"

Chet sighed. "Yes."

Ellie enthusiastically supported Chet's career – and the lavish salary which it produced – in every way possible, was a strong proponent of better living through science.

The bread crumbs Ellie used in her meatloaf were the product of a loaf of rye from which the ergot virus had been blasted with targeted nuclear particles. The water that moistened them was heavy. The tomato paste came from genetically enhanced tomatoes, the meat plumped with steroids and rendered tasty through the infusion of flavor enhancers and red dye #43.

The three eggs had been grown in a chemical bath that completely eliminated the need for actual chickens. The onions were nearly five years old, rendered bacteria-free and perfectly preserved through the use of narrow spectrum bacterial agents, guaranteed to prevent decay and enzyme conversion for a minimum of . . . well, of a little over five years now.

On top, she sprinkled a nutritious cheese substitute created entirely from synthetics. The molecules were bound together with a sticky proton "glue" that one of Chet's junior researchers had come up with in his spare time.

While the meatloaf was bubbling merrily away in the microvection oven, Ellie and Chet enjoyed garlic roasted chicken breast which had been harvested from vats instead of actual chickens. They dined by candlelight and toasted each other with a nice white wine made from blight and frost impervious grapes, the contribution of one of Chet's most prominent designer geneticists, Aubrey Winford. If there had been a Nobel Prize for the creation of the finest new white of the 21st Century, Aubrey would have won hands down.

After dinner, Ellie sliced a commercially prepared triple-chocolate flavored torte, made entirely from artificial sweeteners and imitation chocolate. Even the fat that made the layers so lusciously moist was a fake – a celluloid-based derivative guaranteed to pass unabsorbed through the human digestive system. The wrapper proudly proclaimed "Irradiated Before Packaging - Refrigeration Not Needed!" and "The Amazing Diet Cake! The More You Eat, the More You Lose!" No one seemed to consider the potential for irony in that claim.

Chet measured out a scoop of freeze-dried coffee into each of their cups, used his new gadget to heat the water, and added hazelnut non-dairy creamer made entirely from recycled motor oils through the use of split-neutron reconfiguration technology. Ellie pulled the meatloaf out of the oven and set it in the macrowave to extract the excess heat energy.

By the time Ellie had licked the last of the whipped chocolate-flavored artificial topping off her fork, and Chet was sighing contentedly and patting his stomach, the meatloaf was cool enough to slice and pack into plastic containers and store in the chiller, which ran silently on an atomic power pack that would not need to be recharged for several lifetimes. Over another glass of wine, Chet actually teared up at the thought of doing without Ellie for several weeks. But the thought was immediately quelled when he considered the alternative – Ellie's mom, up front and personal, sitting in his favorite chair, clutching his remote greedily with her crimson coated talons, barking out orders and opinions with no appreciation whatsoever for the man who paid the direct feed satellite bill. The picture made him shudder, and immediately quelled his sentimentality.

So Chet stood up and stacked the dinner dishes in the waterless UV cleaning cabinet. When he was done, he turned to Ellie and gave her a loving smile. "Honey," he said, "let me help you finish packing."

Sailing along on the smooth sea of protracted matrimonial complacency, Chet and Ellie retired for the night.

***

For the first two nights, things went well for Chet, and between his hectic work week and Ellie's numerous phone calls, it hardly felt as if she were gone. He had mixed feelings about the weekend, though. It would give him a chance to work on the hand-held irradiator, on the one hand. On the other, it was time to make the dreaded green Jello salad.

Saturday morning, Chet decided to fuel himself with an Irish coffee before calling Ellie to get started on the Jello. It tasted so good, he decided to have another. Then he decided to have a meatloaf sandwich for breakfast – he'd been waiting to break into the meatloaf for when he really needed it, and if he didn't need it today, when would he? He grabbed one of the neat little containers out of the chiller, grabbed his personal irradiator, made the first adjustment he'd decided to try on it, and pointed it at the container, pressed the button.

Nothing.

He touched a finger to the meatloaf. Still frozen. The phone cam trilled. Ellie. Damn it!

He diverted the call and tweaked the hand-held. Pressed the button. The phone rang again and he dropped the controller into the meatloaf.

"Damn it, Ellie, hold on to your pants," he said, but this time he took a quick gulp straight out of the whiskey bottle, then answered the phone.

"Ellie, hi, hon, how you doing? How's Mom?" Gingerly, he picked the hand-held – hot, hot, hot! – out of the meatloaf and dropped it on the counter. Working!

"Chet! Why didn't you answer the first time I called?"

In the background, her mother screeched, "Tell him not to call me that!"

Chet pasted a smile on his face. "In the bathroom, darling. Look, I think I fixed the irradiator!"

"Chet, have you been drinking?"

Chet groaned, silently. *How did she know these things?* "Just an Irish to start the day, love. I miss you." *But not enough for you to bring your mother here,* he finished silently. *Please God, anything but that.*

Ellie appeared somewhat mollified.

Her mother, on the other hand, was not. "So he's a drunk, now? I warned you about him, Ellie, girl. Oh well, at least you'll get a good settlement in the divorce." She let out a cackle that left no question about who she thought Ellie should spend the money on.

It was just then that Chet noticed the green peppers in the meatloaf were glowing green.

Ellie sighed. "Okay, you two. Just stop. Chet, it's time to make the Jello. Get out the big red bowl ..."

***

Finally, a full pint of the best pseudo-Irish whiskey later, and Ellie's finest green Jello double layer cherry and mandarin crème salad shimmered in all its glory under the kitchen island light, waiting for transport to the Sunnyside Acres Annual Memorial Day Parade and Freedom Jam Dessert Competition.

Halfheartedly, Chet poked the slice of meatloaf he'd never had time to eat. It was still juicy. He perked up and went to check the fridge for imitation horseradish and guaranteed ergot-free rye bread. The glowing green pepper bits didn't bother him at all – to his mind, they looked rather festive. As a matter of fact, Chet thought, taking a bite of his sandwich and looking at Ellie's Jello salad, a little bit of green glow might just be the thing that put Ellie's dessert right over the top and made it the winner. If he set the heat to 'zero' and the radiation to ten, could he accomplish the same effect without changing the temp on the salad?

Chet glanced at the clock and cracked the seal on the second pint of whiskey. He'd need to summon the cab to get him to the Jamboree in about thirty minutes.

Plenty of time.

***

By the time the cab got there, Ellie's green Jello salad was glowing proudly, although it did show a decided lean to one side. However, so did Chet, so it all seemed to work out okay. His tummy felt a little sour, but then he belched sourly, a mix of

183

glowing meatloaf, horseradish and old whiskey, and felt better immediately.

Chet picked up the leaning tower of Jello in its pretty container and pointed over the cabdriver's shoulder. "Lay on, Macduff," he said, hardly slurring at all.

When Chet arrived at the dessert table, he quickly registered Ellie's green Jello salad, then called her and showed her the registration tag, so that she could see he'd done it correctly. "She's home taking care of her mother," he explained clearly, to make sure Ellie could hear. "She asked me to come up and drop this off." That way, there was no question about Ellie having made it. She'd been drumming to his head all week. It would have taken ten times the whiskey to make him forget *that* script.

At Ellie's insistence, Chet carried the phone the rest of the way down the table so that she could poo-poo the other desserts. Soon enough, the judging started, and judges made their rounds, tasting and whispering and making little tally marks on their sheets.

Chet's stomach felt worse and worse. He began to silently urge the judges to hurry, hurry, hurry. He wasn't sure how much longer he could wait before something really, really horrible happened. Finally, the judges retired to a corner to make their decision and then returned, smiling, and made a beeline for Chet and his phone.

"Chet? Ellie? On behalf of the 98th Annual Sunnyside Acres Memorial Day Parade and Freedom Jamboree Dessert Competition, we'd like to Award you the First Place Prize for Dessert of the Year!" said Head Judge Thorton Mesque.

"Oh, my goodness," said Ellie. "I'm so thrilled and delighted to accept this honor! I just can't believe it! Tell me, Judge Mesque – was it the cherry crème? The mandarin? Or the little tiny bits of pineapple? Be honest."

"Actually," said Judge Mesque, "It was that lovely green glow. We adored it. The flavor was fantastic, but you had us at the glow."

Chet's stomach rumbled. Loudly.

"The green *glow*?" said Ellie. "That's … well … I'm glad you liked it," she forced out, giving Chet a what-did-you-do-now kind of look.

"I don't think I feel too well," said Chet. "Do you mind if I sit down?" he asked, and promptly sat in Pamela Poundwit's lemon meringue pie.

Before Judge Mesque could say, "Oh, boy," Chet slid to the ground. There was a ripping sound, and a large chunk of meatloaf, complete with a lumpy face, forced its way out of his abdomen. It quickly gobbled up a small child. The green pepper bits were still glowing.

Chet lifted his head to regard it woozily.

"Oops," said Chet. Then he died.

With a chortle, the living meatloaf doubled in size and spit out the child's bones, high, high into the air, then gobbled up Pamela Poundwit, she of the lemon meringue pie. Her bones, too, were quickly spit high up into the air, and the meatloaf again doubled in size.

The Jello began to quake, and a smile split it from one side to the other. "Hey, hey, hey," it boomed. "Who's ready to be lunch?"

Amid screams of panic, the little park was quickly deserted.

"Now is that any way to be?" said the meatloaf.

"Tsk, tsk, tsk," agreed the Jello salad, as they lumbered out together in search of a meal.

***

Fortunately, more than one of the escaped Jamboree guests also worked with Chet at the Federal Department of Future Science Peacetime Research and Development, and had the number to the OSHA Department of Experiments Gone Wrong Emergency Clean-Up Division on speed dial – they all did, the same way they all knew the location of all the fire exits and Experimental Subjects Break Schedules.

Within two minutes, the WECUP truck was screeching to a halt in front of the park, where a small crowd was now contemplating the meatloaf and Jello that had now eaten at least half a dozen people. The WECUP responders wasted no time.

"That the killer foodstuffs we were called about?"

"Yes."

"Kitchen experiment gone wrong?"

"As far as we know. The fellow that brought them is dead."

185

"Here's his wife," Judge Mesque said, stepping forward to hand Chet's phone to the responder.

"Excellent thinking, Sir." With a surprising touch of humanity, the WECUP agent laid a comforting hand on Mesque's shoulder.

"Ma'am? You're married to the man who brought the meatloaf and the … ah … Jello salad to the party?"

Ellie nodded miserably. "But I'm out of town, taking care of my mother," she said. "I had nothing to do with whatever happened. He did that on his own. He has some gadget from work he was experimenting with – some kind of hand held food warmer. It's probably still at our house."

The agent nodded "It's hard to resist the vision of a nice hot meatloaf, when the wife's away, ma'am. I can't condone it, but we've seen worse."

Ellie looked up, hope dawning in her eyes, but the sympathetic WECUP Agent had already turned away to confer with one of his colleagues.

"It's a 207 situation, Bob."

"Is that the meatloaf, or the pot roast?"

"Meatloaf, big guy, with a side of Jello. You know what that means."

The other agent nodded his head solemnly. "Time to bring out the atomic cockroaches?"

"Atomic cockroaches?" said Ellie.

The friendly agent nodded. "Mutated. They really saved our cookies in the Great Irradiated Jello Salad Incident of '94. They'll eat anything. After it's all over, we pick up 'em back up with vacuum hoses that have a built-in Geiger counter. Nice thing about the radiation trail. We can always track 'em back down. Only thing on the planet that can stop an irradiated meatloaf and green Jello salad combo once it's on the move."

About Dixie Pinoit

Dixie reports: "I'm out, I'm out, they let me out! Nine months in the Little Lolita Creampie Correctional Center for Debauched Degenerates was more than I could take. I need a bottle of Jack, a couple of bois and a laptop. Anybody know where I could find a couple of subbie nuns?"

The God Below
By Richard Ramsey

Trevor slowed his caddy down to a crawl and pointed out of the passenger side window. "That's the one. That's the one right there."

Sean didn't have to ask, there was no doubt. The house was a huge two-story building with columns out front that held up a large balcony. A circle drive made its way from the street on either side of the block and came right to the front door, except on the side where it diverted to a large three-car garage. "That one? You want to go into that one?"

Trevor pinched his nose and rubbed his moustache the way he did when he was anxious. "Yea, that's the one."

Sean shifted in his seat. "Man, I don't know. That's a big ass house. People like that have *got to* have alarms and security systems and all kinds of stuff."

"Dude, I'm telling you, my cousin already scoped it. He works for the city and they keep records of all that stuff. There's no system or nothing! All we have to do is walk in, take some jewelry and walk out. It'll be the easiest job we've ever done."

"Get us out of here, people like us in this neighborhood draw attention." Sean turned his head to make sure no one was walking their dog down the sidewalk or something like that.

Trevor sped back up slowly and snaked through the roads of Madrigal Hills Estates, eyeballing the homes as he went. "Look at these places, man. Just *look* at them. All these rich sons of bitches eating caviar every day and drinking champagne while the rest of us have to struggle. It ain't right, man, it just ain't right."

Sean shook his head in agreement. There was no need for some people to have so much when others had so little. Sometimes people *deserved* to be robbed. He had gone after jewelry before plenty of times, but this looked like a big haul. He knew he was ready for it, but he worried about Trevor. His counterpart just didn't know how to think. He always wanted to just rush in and go, but these things had to be planned out.

"Look at these houses, man. They're old."

Sean peered out the window, "How do you know they're old?"

Trevor grinned with the side of his mouth, exposing his rotten yellow teeth. "Just look them. There's ivy climbing up just about every brick wall in this neighborhood."

Sean peered around. He was right.

"Every one except the house we're going to hit. There ain't one plant around that house, much less ivy growing up the side. That means those people are the worst of the worst. They got it and they got it good, I'm telling you."

The old yellow Cadillac pulled out onto the highway and merged with traffic. The oak trees in the neighborhood had cast a certain shadow on the street and the men had to squint in the fresh sunlight. All along the side of the road, the entire neighborhood was cut off from the rest of town by a fence that was higher than any man was tall. All that peeked out from behind it was oak leaves and the occasional terracotta roof.

"And you're sure they don't have security?"

Trevor pinched his nose again. "They don't have it!"

For three weeks Sean and Trevor watched the house. There were lawn maintenance people that came by and mowed on Wednesday, but no maid service. As far as they could tell, there were two women that lived there by themselves, one white and one Indian. Trevor kept saying "Maybe we should go in when they're home! I'll be the meat in their sandwich!"

"Shut up, Trevor." It was a phrase that rolled off Sean's lips easily enough because he had to say it so much. The man just couldn't keep his mind on the task at hand. The only reason he kept him around was because he knew people and could get information pretty quickly.

On Tuesday and Friday nights they would leave together around dusk and not get back until almost midnight. Aside from their individual day jobs, that seemed the only routine they kept.

When Sean finally decided they would go in, he knew he was going to have to get Trevor in line. The man was way too unstable for such a high stakes game and they were going to have to go in smart, security or no security.

"You're going to have to calm yourself."

Trevor drummed on the steering wheel of his car with his fingers. "Man, get off that, I'm fine."

"No, this isn't like a house on Baker Street. One wrong step here and you go back to county." He had said the right thing. His counterpart had found himself in lockup way too many times over the last couple of years and every single time it was because of a stupid, hotheaded mistake.

"Okay, okay. I'm good." He held his palm up to Sean as he spoke. "When do we do this?"

"Thursday morning."

Trevor shook his head. "Thursday morning? Are you out of your mind?"

"No!" Sean turned his body in the seat of the Cadillac, making the old vinyl squeak. "Look at this place. These people here all work bankers hours and the only people here during the day are domestics. Look at me, I'm a six-four bald and sleeved out badass. You look like a meth junkie. We come strolling into this neighborhood on a Friday night and the cops *will* be called. We come around here on a Thursday morning and we blend in with landscapers and plumbers. We'll walk right in there in broad daylight and walk out with enough stone to keep us for years. Think, man, think."

Trevor finally agreed and they made plans to park the Caddy well out of the neighborhood and walk to the house. It was around a quarter mile walk and the entire area was heavily shaded under squat oak trees, so it was nice and cool.

Their timing couldn't have been better; the two women's cars pulled out of the garage almost simultaneously and drove into opposite directions. As soon as they disappeared around the corner, the two men advanced on the home. A swath of sunlight covered the immaculate front lawn; it was the only yard in the neighborhood not shaded out by the arboreal canvas.

Dressed in similar overalls and carrying oversized toolboxes (they were mostly empty now, but bound to be filled on the way out), the men walked through the gate that separated the house's secluded backyard from the street and shut it behind them. Sean felt himself grin. "You see, a little planning goes a long way!"

The backyard was just as immaculately cut as the front, except there was a patio with heavy, cast iron furniture. It almost looked out of place against the perfect house, but Sean expected to see stuff that didn't always make sense. The richer people got, the weirder they became.

After surveying the yard to make sure they were truly alone, he pulled his bump key from his toolbox and went to work. The back door was French style and the lock gave way easily, allowing the men to open one door and sneak in.

Inside, the house was as immaculate as the lawn out front. They had entered into a kitchen that was larger than Sean's entire apartment, with stainless steel appliances and a wine rack in one corner half full with corked bottles.

Trevor took off around the corner and walked away from his partner. Sean ran after him. "Will you wait up? We don't need to separate!"

When he finely caught up with the other, he had found a living room that was beyond anything they had imagined and Trevor was spinning around in it with his arms outstretched. "Hey, Sean, will you look at this place? We hit the motherload! We're going to be rich as hell and they're never going to know what hit them!" He danced around furniture that probably cost more than a brand new Caddy.

Sean whispered through clenched teeth. "Will you stop it? Get your head on straight! We've got work to do. The sooner we're out of here, the better."

"Yea, but isn't this place awesome?"

Sean couldn't help but be taken aback by the majesty of the house. "Yea, it's perfect. It's too perfect. Quite frankly, it's creeping me out. Let's just get what we came for and get out."

They walked throughout the home, admiring the interior until they found the staircase. Trevor pointed up the stairs. "I bet that's where the bedroom is, and I bet that's where they keep the pearls. Man, I want to see the bed where those two eat each other out."

He started up the stairs when Sean held his arm out and whispered, "Stop!"

Trevor was bouncing from foot to foot and grinning. "What is it?"

Sean put one finger to his lips. "Shhhh."

Silence.

"I thought I heard something."

"What did you hear?"

"People talking."

Trevor started up the stairs. "There's no one here. We did our homework, I'm ready to cash in, let's go!" Reluctantly, Sean followed him towards the second story.

The stairs let out into a long hallway with every door shut. The only light was what came from the windows downstairs and it made long shadows across the wall. Sean flipped the light switch, but nothing happened. He toggled it a few times. "It's good to see that rich folks lights burn out, too."

Trevor groaned. "Here you wanted to come in the morning. Man, if we would have come at night like I wanted to, we would have brought flashlights. But, no. You had to come during the day."

"Shut up, Trevor." Sean stormed down the hall into the dark, went to the furthest door and opened it.

The room was completely empty. A single window let in bright sunlight that reflected off of bare walls and bright white carpet. "What kind of people get a big ass house and leave it empty?" Sean mumbled.

He went to the next door and found it in a similar state. Nothing. Trevor was opening doors on the far end of the hall one by one. "They're all empty, man. They're all empty!"

"This place is creeping me out. I bet the bedroom is downstairs. Let's just get what we need and get out." Feeling sweat form at his temples, Sean marched over to the top of staircase and stopped.

Standing down at the base of the stairs was a group of around twenty children, all girls and all dressed in similar white robes with their hair tied back. They all looked up at Sean and he noticed that their eyes were completely whited out, no pupils or even blood vessels. "The fuck is this?"

Trevor stepped up behind him and stopped. Sean glanced at him just in time to see him pinch his nose and rub his moustache. "Man, I think we got the wrong house."

Sean turned back towards the crowd as one of them spoke. He didn't see which one it was, but he heard her well enough. "Two for the god below." It was a soft and monotone declaration.

The rest of them repeated in unison, "two for the god

below."

When things went sideways, they tended to go sideways fast. Sean started walking down the stairs. He made a plan for him and his counterpart to just bypass these weird kids and walk away. "Now, girls, just let us go and I promise none of you will get hurt."

The group of children started climbing the staircase.

"Sean, come back." Trevor's voice had started to waver.

Sean wasn't going to listen to a nervous coward and he sure wasn't going to be intimidated by a group of children. Slowly, he took another few steps down and the girls kept advancing.

"Sean, I don't like this!"

"Shut up, Trevor!" He came within an arm's length of the first girl. "Get out of my way!"

The child didn't move. He reached out his hand to push the child to one side. She blinked and her eyes went from stark white to pitch black. The rest quickly followed suit and they all began to run towards the men, yelling as they went.

Sean tried to push them away, but there were just too many. He knocked one down and the others started to climb over the fallen one to get to him. He swung at a few and knocked them back, but they got up and advanced on him again.

Not wanting to take his eyes off of the mob, Sean back-stepped up the stairs. He managed to repel a few more of the girls before one of them swung her hand at him. Her fingernails were long and filed to sharp points that tore into the skin of his forearm. Runners of crimson coursed across his skin and dripped off of his hand as he continued to try and fight them off.

More rushed him with outstretched claws, swiping at his muscular arms as he pushed them down the staircase one by one. They would tumble a few feet, right themselves and come back for more.

Sean cast a glance at his friend and yelled "Run, Trevor! Run! Get out of here!" His partner in crime had already bolted into one of the empty rooms and was locking the door before Sean could even finish his sentence. He ran to the other end of the hallway, through a door and locked it behind himself.

The window was small, but he was confident he could fit through it. Second story or no, it was worth the jump. Both of his arms were bleeding from multiple scratch marks and he could feel some on his face, too. Those little bastards had scratched him up pretty good. He would come back later and burn this damn house down, but first he had to get out. Sean took off his shirt, wrapped it around his right hand and punched the glass. Nothing happened.

The doorknob started to rattle as the children tried to open it, but the lock held. He punched the glass again and again, nothing. That was impossible! He'd knocked grown men out with a single punch before and now he couldn't break glass? He looked closer and realized that it must have been at least an inch thick.

The children started banging on the door. Outside, he could hear Trevor start to yell and then escalate to a scream. It wasn't a scream of pain or fear, it was sheer terror. Sean had never heard anything like it before, but he immediately knew what it was.

"Sean! Sean, help me! They're killing me!" The screams faded as Sean heard his friend dragged down the stairs and then finally stopped. The empty room door rattled with the effort of the children banging against the thick wood. The window was the only way out. He took the shirt off of his hand and punched the glass again. It splintered, but just barely. His knuckles split open and his hand was on fire, but he had to keep trying.

"One for the god below." The children were chanting now. He had to get out.

He punched again. Slivers and fissures spider-webbed out from the point of impact, but the pane was still intact. Suddenly, the door splintered and a mass of little arms pushed through the wood. One of them reached for the doorknob, trying to unlock it.

Sean stepped back to the middle of the room and ran towards the window, slamming his fist into the thick glass. The entire house seemed to shake with the impact. Waves of pain shot through his arm and up into this shoulder as the window shattered in a shower of broken glass. One of the children managed to open the door and the mob poured through. Sean could see the sunlight and well-manicured grass just a jump away as they grabbed his legs and pulled him back into the room. He turned just in time to see one with a heavy lead pipe that connected with his head and sent him into a dark spiral.

Sean awoke to his head pounding and throbbing. There was a tender spot on the top. He touched it with one hand and winced; something had hit him and hit him hard. Memories came flooding back and he suddenly recalled what had happened. He stood up quickly and banged his head on a low ceiling. Fresh bolts of agony shot through his head and neck, forcing him to the ground again.

When he was finally able to open his eyes, he stayed down and surveyed his surroundings. He was in a room with small windows high in the air. *A basement*, he thought, *I'm in a basement.*

"Somebody's awake."

Sean looked around for the source of the voice but was startled to see that he was in a cage. The bars were made of heavy iron and the top had only enough space for him to sit up in. He grabbed the bars and tried to move it, but it didn't budge. He tried to push it up off of him, but it wasn't going anywhere that way, either.

"Oh, stop. You're not getting out." The owner of the voice approached his cage from a dark corner. It was the blonde, the one who they had seen leaving the house every day. She was wearing a pantsuit and had on a pearl necklace that looked very real to Sean's criminal eye.

"Let me out of this damn thing!" He banged a fist against the roof of his enclosure, making a deep ring.

His captor leaned over, stretched her neck and took him in. "I swear, you guys just make this easier and easier. You and your friend are the first ones we didn't have to go out and get."

"I don't even know what you're talking about. Listen, I have some money, a good amount of money. If you let me out, I'll pay you whatever you want."

The woman laughed. "Really? Really. Do you honestly think I want your money? I know you saw the furniture when you came in. There's no amount of money that I want from you."

"Then what do you want from me?" He controlled his tone this time, trying to reason with the woman.

"Oh, you'll see soon enough." She stood and walked away from the cage. There was an old wooden staircase at one end of the basement. She paused, waved at Sean with just her fingers and climbed the steps.

"What do you want from me?" He yelled as loud as he could this time, but she gave no answer.

Not too far on the other side of the room came a long moan. Sean scurried to the side of his enclosure, grabbed the bars and peered out. He surprised himself at how quickly he grew accustomed to being in a cage. He had never been in jail before, Trevor was the jailbird.

Trevor! It was him. As his eyes adjusted in the fading rays of sunlight he could see another enclosure with the outline of a man lying down inside of it. "Trevor. Trevor, wake up!"

Trevor groaned and rolled over to expose a face that was only intact on one side. The other had been reduced to scraps of flesh caked in dirt where the children had clawed him and then dropped him off in this dirty basement. "What? What happened? Sean?"

"Trevor, Trevor, it's me!"

"Sean? I can't see you! Where are you?"

"I'm here. Don't talk, just listen. Those two ladies? You remember, the ones you thought were lesbians?"

Trevor tried to stand up and banged his head on the top of the cage. "Ow!"

"Don't try to stand up, we're in a cage."

Trevor sat down and looked around. "A cage? Why am I in a cage? I can't see anything. Sean, I can't see anything!"

"Trevor, shut up! Just listen! Those kids. Those kids knocked us out and now those ladies have us locked in cages. I don't know what they plan on doing with us, but I don't like it. We have to find a way to get out of here."

Sean could see his counterpart moving around the cage, feeling every bar. He felt sorry for him. He didn't know if the man had enough sense to really understand the danger they were in.

"Oh, God, what's that smell?"

Instinctively, Sean inhaled deep and got a good whiff of what his partner had already noticed. This place smelled like death. When he was a boy, his parents had had an old German Shepherd named Molly. Molly had disappeared but his mother had found her four days later. A pungent odor had crept up from under their porch where Molly had crawled up under there and died. Their neighbor came over and pulled Molly's corpse out and she was bloated with her legs sprawled. Just as he got her out, her body cavity ruptured; spreading rotten tissues and fluid all over Sean and his mother. The smell that had been bad before was much, much worse.

Sean thought the basement smelled worse than that even. A wave of nausea flooded up, but he managed to keep from vomiting.

Trevor was not so lucky. He retched and cried and cried and retched for what seemed like hours. The sunlight coming through the small windows dimmed and finally faded out all together. The basement faded into a pitch black that was so dark that it seemed to swallow up even sound.

Sean couldn't tell if he slept or not, but seconds and minutes and hours passed by as he lay in his cage, listening to Trevor whimper. The ground was hard compacted dirt and it was cold. They hadn't bothered to put his shirt back on him and his skin readily gave up his body heat.

It might have been minutes, it might have been hours, he couldn't tell, but he finally heard voices. They were far away and indistinguishable, but they were voices, female voices. Somewhere out in the dark they grew closer, but stopped before Sean could make out what they were saying. Then there were footsteps. One pair and then another, clacking down wooden stairs. They muffled as they walked onto the dirt floor of the basement, but Sean could tell they were getting closer.

"Now, let's put some light on the subject, shall we?" It was the blonde woman's voice, there was no mistaking it.

Sean closed his eyes as the room was filled with a bright white light. His headache rushed back with a vengeance and he covered his face with one hand. Slowly, his eyes adjusted and he could see the blonde along with the Indian woman approaching his cage. They were dressed in the same fashion the children had been in. "I'm so glad you came to join us! Welcome to my dungeon!" She spread her arms and turned her head, surveying their surroundings.

In the light, Sean could see the entire basement. There were eight cages all together, but his and Trevor's were the only ones not empty. A couple were open in the front, but others were closed. In one far to the other side, Sean could make out a human skeleton with bits of dry tissue still clinging to the bones. From the ceiling, chains in various lengths hung down from wooden rafters. Some had ended in meat hooks, some in large carabiners.

"Sean? Sean are you there? It's so dark in here." Trevor was sitting up again. Both of his eyes had been gouged out and only empty, dirty sockets remained.

"I'm here. It's very dark, just listen to the voices."

The blonde woman leaned down again. "So, your name must be Sean? I'm glad to meet you, Sean. I'm not telling you my name, it's so much more fun that way, don't ya think?"

"What have you done to us? What have you done?" Their captors didn't seem very inclined to answer Trevor's questions.

The Indian woman strolled over to the cages and she spoke in a soft voice. "There, there. Just be calm and we'll let you out very soon."

Sean knew she was lying, he could smell a liar from a mile away. "Eat shit and die."

She seemed honestly surprised at his response. "Excuse me?"

"You heard me, lady. I said 'eat shit and die.'" He pulled his knees back and kicked the cage with both feet. The basement filled with a loud scraping sound as the cage moved. It was only an inch, but it moved. *That means they're not fastened to the ground.*

The blonde woman stood and dropped her shoulders. She looked at her partner and said, "he's getting pretty agitated, we'd better get on with it."

The other nodded. "Agreed." She turned towards the staircase and yelled out "Children! It's time!"

A deep worry swept over Sean as the girls who had attacked him earlier stumbled down the stairs in a mob. Each one's eyes had gone back to white. Their faces were expressionless. Without a sound, they filed in and stood behind Trevor's cage.

The Indian woman walked towards the center of the basement and leaned over. There was a hatch on the floor there that Sean hadn't seen. It was flat and flush with the ground. The material was cast iron just like the other equipment in the dungeon. She grabbed onto a lock that was recessed into the iron and pulled on it a few times before it came loose. "I swear, that keeps getting harder and harder."

"Yea, I know. We really should grease it up one day." Her partner responded. She then turned to the children and spoke to them. "Come on, girls, you don't want to keep him waiting!"

The group of children all placed their hands on Trevor's cage and began to push. Slowly, the heavy iron scraped across the ground towards the door. Trevor began to crawl around frantically. "Hey. Hey! What's going on?"

"Trevor! Trevor! No! Stop!"

Trevor reached out with both hands and blindly grabbed at the cage bars. He had no choice but to scoot in the same direction they were pushing him. "Where are you taking me? Where are you taking me?" He rushed around his enclosure on his hands and knees, clawing at the ground around him.

The cage slid over the iron door and scraped with a loud scream as metal grated against metal and reverberated deep into the ground. "What's that? What are you doing to me?"

"That's good, girls, that's good." The blonde walked over and nodded her approval. The children stopped pushing and stood back to watch the spectacle unfold. Together, the women padlocked the cage to some hooks in the ground and double-checked the fastenings.

Sean waited in silence, not knowing what would happen next. When he saw it, he was grateful that his friend had gone blind and was saved the terror.

The iron hatch in the floor bumped once, then again, then it crept slowly open and a waft of stale air rushed out. Trevor screamed. "Oh my God! It's that smell again! What is that smell?"

A tentacle, almost like an octopus, reached up out of the door and felt around its perimeter. It was covered in veins and wrinkles, muscles contracting just below the skin. It slithered through the dirt, searching out its prey. Another one emerged shortly behind it, looking for its next victim.

Sean gripped the bars of his cage and took in a deep breath. "Trevor! Trevor!"

"Sean! I can hear you but I can't see you! It's dark! What's going on?"

Sean didn't know what the thing was, but he knew what was about to happen to his friend. "Trevor! Hey, Trevor! You're my boy! You're my boy, Trevor!"

"Why are you saying that? Sean? Why are you saying that?" The tentacle finally touched his foot and found its victim. It moved very quickly after that. It slithered further into the cage and wrapped around Trevor's ankle. It started to pull and drag him towards the door.

"No! No! Let go of me! Let go!" Trevor pawed at the ground, trying to keep from being pulled closer to the hole. The

200

second tentacle wrapped around his other leg and added to the tension. Trevor grabbed the bars of his cage with both hands and pulled against the beast. He made a little progress before the tip of each tentacle rose into the air and extended something that looked like teeth. There were eight of them on each appendage and none of them were less than four inches.

The monster buried the fangs in Trevor's thighs and pulled him closer towards the door. Sean watched with horror as his friend screamed in agony and his fingertips slowly lost their grips on the bars.

Yelling like a wild animal, Trevor clawed at the ground again, leaving finger marks in the hard ground as he was pulled, inch by painful inch. Just as his body neared the door, more tentacles, much thicker and stronger, pushed out and wrapped themselves around his waist. It pulled down on his body until his back snapped. His trunk bent backwards the wrong way and he stopped screaming as the rest of his body was pulled into the hole. The iron lid slammed shut and echoed like thunder.

The two women applauded at the spectacle but the children didn't respond. They merely unlocked the cage, pulled it back and put it in its previous place.

"It looks like you're next!" Sean didn't notice which one said it, but he heard it loud and clear. The children all gathered around the back of his cage and began to push. The heavy iron scraped against the ground, pushing up a small mound of dirt as it went.

"No! No, you can't do this!" The caged inched closer and closer to the iron doorway. Sean pushed back against the children, but together they were too strong for him. He slammed his body against the side of the cage, trying to scoot it in another direction. Every time it slid the way he wanted, the girls went to that side and countered his efforts.

The edge of his prison was sliding over the iron door now and starting to make that deep grating sound. "Why? Why are you doing this? Why are you doing this to me?"

The blonde lowered her head in order to look Sean in the eyes. "Does the *why* really matter? What matters is that the god below is hungry and you were just in the right place at the right time, kay?"

The cage slid all the way over the iron door. Sean scrambled like mad to push against the bars, but it was no use. His enclosure stopped just above the door and the two women started locking it down.

The iron door started to open and the tip of a tentacle snuck out of the crack. Sean jumped on the door and pushed against the roof of the cage, pinning the appendage. A painful squeal erupted from deep under the ground as it wiggled, trying to get loose. The iron slammed shut and the tip was severed from the rest of the beast. It flopped on the ground for a second and then stopped.

The Indian woman was livid. "What did you do? What did you *do*?" She ran to the side of the cage and reached in for the severed member. Sean caught her wrist and pulled her arm into the prison. She tried to pull back, but she was just no match for the hardened criminal.

The door to the pit bounced open and Sean scurried over to it, bracing his body once again between the door and the roof of his cage. The woman screamed and jerked frantically, trying to free herself from her captor.

The door bounced and threatened to push Sean off balance as the god below pounded against the heavy iron. His muscles ached and strained, but he was unable to keep the gate closed. Multiple tentacles snaked out of the crack and felt about the area, searching for prey. Sean yanked the woman's arm and placed it directly in the path of one of them. It quickly wrapped itself around her extremity like a boa constrictor, extruded its fangs and buried them deep into her tender flesh.

Sean watched as her shoulder dislocated and started to tear away. More members wrapped themselves around her body and tried to yank her in. She cried out and screamed as her body contorted to the space between the bars and she was pulled through. Her neck snapped against the partially open iron door and all that remained of her was sucked down into the hole.

The blonde was crying and screaming. "You killed her! You killed her! I can't believe you killed her!"

Sean banged his fists against the cage and yelled back. "That's right and I'll kill you too if I ever get out of here, you sadistic bitch!"

Just then, the door to the pit opened again and a swath of

warped appendages reached out into the cage with their fangs out, flailing at anything that would come in contact with them. Sean jumped back on the door and pressed down again. One of the members caught his ankle and slithered around his lower leg. Before it could bury its fangs in him, he grabbed the tip and forced them into the monster's own tender flesh. Another scream followed by hot breath issued from the hole and the appendage tried to pull him in.

He managed to wedge his foot against the ground to keep it from being pulled in and he stabbed the beast repeatedly with its own fangs. A yellow ooze that burned his flesh poured from the wounds, but he kept on until the tentacle was completely severed. It pulled back into the pit and the hatch once again slammed shut.

Sean reached out towards the blonde woman, but she was standing back far enough out of his reach. "Come here! Come here, to me!" She was crying and shaking her head in disbelief. Out of the corner of his eye, he saw some movement and he knew what he had to do.

One of the children was just close enough on the other side of his cage. In a crouching position, he spun around and grabbed one of the little girls by the dress and pulled her against the cage. Her white eyes blinked and were suddenly black as night. Her head thudded against the heavy iron and a large gash formed there. She didn't react or bleed.

The blonde went into hysterics. "Stop it! Stop it! I can't make any more of them by myself!"

Sean yanked on her dress again, slamming her little body into the cage. "Your god below is about to come back for more and I intend to feed this thing to it unless you set me free! Let me go and I promise I won't hurt you or any more of your things!" He banged her head against the cage one more time just in case she thought he wasn't serious.

"Okay! Okay! Just don't hurt my children anymore!"

The blonde quickly undid the lock on the end and opened the front of the cage, releasing her prisoner. Sean let go of the demon-child and scurried out of his prison. She punched him in the chest and yelled, "Get out! Get out of my house."

Sean wrapped both of his hands around her throat, lifted her into the air and held her there for a second before shoving her into the cage and locking the front gate. The blonde wrapped her hands around the bars and pushed her face against them. "You lied to me! You lied! You said you wouldn't hurt me!"

Sean kicked the bars and laughed. "I'm a thief, bitch. What? Did you think I was going to tell you the truth?"

He turned and walked away, up the stairs, listening to her scream as the god below pulled her into the pit.

About Richard D. Ramsey

Richard D Ramsey is a middle-aged father, husband and restless spirit. He lives in Deep East Texas with his wife Cheryl and his three children Caitlyn, Chase and Destiny. He's an Emergency Room RN by trade and a writer/actor/musician in his spare time. Richard D Ramsey has recently been published by Tyler Rose City Comic Con and J Ellington Ashton Press. His fantasy novel *Order of the Firewalker* is scheduled for release in 2015 and is guaranteed to leave a lasting impression on you. He writes about his true-life experiences for the TV show "Untold Stories of the ER" and has starred in one episode with another to be filmed later in 2015. Richard D Ramsey is a classically trained musician who plays and sings classic rock, blues and country in music venues all over Texas. He has opened up for such acts as Tracy Bird and Sherwin Linton. For more, please visit RichardDRamsey.com!

Underground Beast Bloodsports
By Jim Goforth

Between the three of them they managed to pull everything they needed together to set the wheels in motion. It was no walk in the park, it required hours of painstaking investigation and legwork aplenty, but once they'd gotten wind of the heinous enterprise that initiated their inexorable pursuit, failing to locate when and where it would take place was not an option.

Sonia was the research specialist, tasked with the grimy, difficult chore of trawling through the world of cyberspace, delving into dark recesses on a hunt for any information to aid them. Endless mind-boggling parades of porn, incessant pop-ups, virus alerts and dead links lurched up to thwart her along the way, but steeling herself against the bombardment of Trojans, enticing cam girls and advertisements for products and sites she had no use for or inclination to explore, with the scant information she had to go on, she located a specific chat room site dedicated to the operation they sought.

The hands on work was the responsibility of Kane, a responsibility he took upon himself as the instigator of this necessary hunt. Down into the underbelly of the sordid metropolis he went, rubbing shoulders and running with dangerous unhinged elements, infiltrating and involving himself in dark circles few of the ordinary everyday folk going about their daily business would have a clue even existed.

Based on the leads conjured up through Sonia's dalliance with the vile website characters frequenting the chat room, Kane found himself up to his neck in hoods, thugs, wheelers, dealers, drug peddlers, gangsters and degenerate souls who happily boasted of unapprehended rapes and murders they wore like badges of honour, relaying abhorrent information as nonchalantly as if they were discussing weekend sports results. Like Sonia, he relentlessly pushed through the mire, the scum and the casual depravity until he acquired what he required.

As for Glenn, it was up to him to obtain the financial backing they needed, the funds they knew an enterprise of this magnitude, with this many shrouds and shields up to keep it veiled from the eyes and the knowledge of those who couldn't be trusted to be any part of it, would require for them to even consider gaining entry.

It was a long hard slog comprised of countless hours poring through dead ends and running into brick walls at every turn, staring hopelessly at the glow of a computer monitor in the dark, surrounded by a haze of drifting cigarette smoke, of endless phone calls finagling money for ventures that technically didn't exist, and ploughing through a seedy underworld of scary individuals with even scarier stories to brag of, but in the end their efforts reaped rewards.

Between the three of them, they had the right information and the tools they needed to gain access to the illicit sanguinary world that was Underground Beast Bloodsports.

***

"Man versus man, beast versus beast, man versus beast," Glenn mused, almost to himself, from the back seat of the vehicle as Sonia piloted it through city streets lined with a rainbow cornucopia of neon lights, billboards, shop fronts and a perpetual deluge of humanity streaming along either side.

It wasn't the first time the big man uttered the words in a murmured mantra as he hunched back there, watching the sights of the metropolis pass by in flickers of multi-coloured illumination and activity from the night crawlers.

With his tattooed frame, medium length hair tied back in a short ponytail, and a plethora of earrings festooning both ears, the chain-smoking behemoth of the trio didn't look like he was a corporate soul, but a shrewd business mind lurked behind the imposing features.

Up in the front, the statuesque brunette beauty Sonia attended to the directions of her satellite navigation system, eyes on the road, hands on the wheel. She saw the lights and the throngs of nocturnal folk out in their element, but only in her peripheral vision; her mind was already ahead, on their destination.

In the front passenger seat, alongside her, was Kane, the spearhead of this expedition, buried in a profound silence, deep in thought as the vehicle rolled through moderate traffic. It might have been alive with pedestrians and foot traffic out on the sidewalks and the pavements, but the amount of automobiles on the street itself was remarkably minimal, meaning none of the peak hour stop and starts were in play, and for the most part, the run of the traffic lights was with them.

"Time check," Sonia broke the quiet that descended after Glenn's quiet ruminations, asking because she wore no wristwatch.

"Quarter to eight," Glenn responded, a wispy trail of cigarette smoke accompanying the words from his mouth as he relentlessly puffed on another stick, lighting it with the smoldering butt of one he'd just finished, extinguishing the predecessor in the dregs of a drink can.

"Plenty of time," Sonia nodded, her green eyes catching those of Glenn in the back "Provided the luck of the traffic lights stays on our side, my sat nav doesn't fail me, and we don't suddenly run into some bottle neck elsewhere. Place goes on lockdown at eight thirty sharp, nobody gets in, nobody gets out until its closing time. And if we miss that boat, it's back to the drawing board for this…"

She glanced over at her front seat companion and Kane returned her gaze with an impassive stare, finally speaking himself, the low even tone coming from him sounding calm and steady.

"We'll make it. We're not missing this. No chance in hell. Not this one, not this time."

He slipped back into his quiet ponderings, his face half hidden by long shrouds of black hair. Sonia returned her attention to the driving, steering the vehicle through the neon blast of the city, aiming for less illuminated climes, less populous outskirts where industrial estates and warehouse complexes replaced the gaudy trappings of the centre of town.

Of course they wouldn't miss it, they *couldn't* miss it. They'd all invested too much time and energy into this to let a late arrival jettison all the hard work, the dodgy dealings, the many things Kane had done--which he was far from proud of--all to maintain the façade and ingratiate himself with those who wielded the power in the Underground Beast Bloodsports.

Sonia imagined her taciturn partner was either mulling over these events which had him mired in an underground murk of vicious criminal elements with scant regard for life, or was also projecting his mind forward into the world they were about to embroil themselves in.

She knew Glenn was. His oft murmured phrase was a direct result of investigations into the seedy underbelly of dreadful activity, where copious blood was spilled and pain, violence and gruesome death was king, all in the name of entertainment, sold to those willing to part with top dollar to sate their palate for destruction.

The tagline of the enterprise, the selling point of the UBB.

Man versus man, beast versus beast, man versus beast.

***

The satellite navigation issued a directive that their destination was five hundred metres ahead to the right.

With the lights of the city behind them, they were now deeply ensconced in the dark and morbid industrial warehouse district, a place of grim appearance and old towering buildings, hunched in the manner of giant silent monstrous entities waiting to swallow up souls foolhardy enough to be wandering into this austere landscape of steel, brick, concrete and chain-link fences.

The light around here was dim, forbidding, the brightest aspect of anything in the whole region the yellow diamond security signs warning of dangerous possibilities, or politely worded threats. Most of these referred to high voltage in certain areas or unsafe regions, hazardous chemicals or lockout tagouts, but some seemed more ominous, as if they were there for another reason. Not just because those who'd placed the signs were in some way concerned for the welfare of unwary wandering souls. No, these signs were beacons bluntly advising trespassers to stay well the fuck away.

They put Sonia in mind of some of the old joke signs she'd witnessed before, which, though potentially meant in a jocular manner, hummed with a tension of genuine threat.

Trespassers will be shot, survivors will be shot again.

This area guarded by shotgun three nights a week. You guess which three.

Trespassers will be handed over to the authorities. One body part at a time.

Except there was nothing joke-like here in this complex of concrete and portent. The whole atmosphere was thick with threat and fraught with grim tidings, everything about it bleak, dark and unnervingly quiet.

"Do we pull right up there?" Sonia indicated where the sat nav determined their final destination lay. Kane shook his head adamantly.

"Doesn't really matter, but no. We'll walk the rest of the way."

With that decided, they did so, leaving the car locked and parked in a bed of shadows within a warehouse car park not gated off by the wire tipped fences, chain link boundaries and other preventative devices that marched around the perimeter of some of the more security conscious establishments here in this dusky, dim enclave.

Though the evening was a pleasantly warm one, tempered by a gentle breeze that kicked lightweight pieces of rubbish and refuse along the concrete, Sonia felt a chill steal over her, prickling her skin with gooseflesh, raising her nipples erect, and not in a good way.

"Hope you know where you're going from here, hun," she murmured to Kane, and the lynchpin of the trio nodded assent brusquely and then began to walk, his long legs carrying him swiftly out of the shadows and through patches of moonlight that appeared brighter than they might have actually been, striking the dull concrete and steel where no thick gangs of shadows lurked and loitered, like the sinister folk of the night they were heading in a rough trajectory for, somewhere in this massive congregation of huge, silent, ominous buildings.

Indeed the trio's leader seemed to know precisely where he was going, his path unerring as he led both Sonia and Glenn right into the belly of the warehouse complex beast, snaking through busted sections of wall, locating weak spots on fence perimeters or low dips where they could gain access, not with complete ease, but certainly not with any extreme difficulty.

Sonia didn't question Kane's motives in approaching the UBB in this manner, he clearly had reasons for not electing to drive right up to whatever point would gain them access to the hellish spectacle she knew would be unleashed within, and Glenn didn't either.

Soon they were traversing an underground skeleton of what was obviously a disused warehouse shell, its roof still held aloft by multiple rows of steel structures, but large parts of its walls absent. Whether this was intentional or due to abandonment and neglect Sonia wasn't sure, but she was certain of one thing.

She was becoming more and more uneasy with each ensuing step through this seemingly deserted industrial wasteland, apprehension chewing on her with the insistency of a dog gnawing on a particularly rank favorite bone.

Ahead, Kane didn't seem to share this apprehension. He strode with long purposeful strides, almost as if he were tracking, trailing a scent that was leading him right where he needed to go. He appeared unconcerned by the myriad spaces where dark shadows were breeding, where any number of potential assailants could be secreted in hiding places, waiting to launch an assault on intruders of any nature. Though he was tall and well built, his physique was well shrouded under his jeans and leather jacket, and any possible aggressor probably wouldn't think twice about blindsiding him.

They might have reconsidered that notion encountering somebody with the formidable intimidation of Glenn's size, but Glenn and Sonia were a distance behind the fast moving Kane, and if there were only eyes on the leader of the group, the lagging duo might not even come into consideration.

Glenn must have been of the same mindset as her, for he was paying closer attention to their surroundings and the potential perils they presented, along with the figure of Kane making a beeline for a destination only he seemed fully aware of, seemingly more so than he was the refuse strewn concrete floor beneath his feet.

The toe of the big man's boot punted a random beer bottle lying out on the concrete and it skittered away like a startled animal, clattering with an ensuing noise that, though not exceptionally loud, rang out crescendo-like to Sonia. It went largely unnoticed by Kane, or in any case he paid it no mind, but it made Sonia lurch with startled fright, the sound of the glass clinking along the concrete ringing resoundingly in her ears.

"Fuck," Glenn hissed in a hushed undertone, cursing his negligent attention to detail as Sonia's heart hurled its way up into her mouth, thumping erratically.

Off to the right, some distance up ahead of where Kane was aiming for, a large section of shadow detached itself from the main body of dark hanging all around the internal perimeters of the construction and moved out into Kane's path. A man-shaped piece of shadow.

On instinct, Sonia immediately wanted to hide, to duck for cover somewhere in the abundant darkness she'd only just been fearing concealed potential ambushers, but there was little chance of that. She and Glenn weren't so far back behind Kane that the shadowed human figure wouldn't be able to see them approaching as well, regardless of the dim lighting. And besides, they weren't in a position where somebody Glenn's size could hide himself away quickly.

What was more, the emerging individual planting himself squarely in Kane's path hadn't launched any attack on him, but merely stood before him, in the way. Maybe that was a precursor to an assault, Sonia thought, but even she knew better; it was merely someone affiliated with the UBB bailing up interlopers on the premises.

The faceless man-shape moved forward out of the darker regions and enough radiance fell over the visage to display a hard faced individual with bushy brows, malevolent dark eyes and an unruly shock of curls. This fellow wasn't too much smaller than Glenn in width and physique, just a handful of inches shorter.

The butt of a handgun protruded prominently from above a snakeskin belt, the firearm casually jammed into the man's pants; he evidently wanted them all to see it, though he made no sudden attempt to draw. A half smoked cigarette with a long drooping ash hung precariously from the corner of his thin downturned lips.

"What's your business here?" His voice grated in a low sludgy rumble, the words coming out the corner of his mouth not hampered by the cigarette. That chunk of dangling ash dropped off as he spoke, but he paid it no mind, his eyes lancing into Kane before slipping away to observe the two newcomers trailing in the former's wake. Lecherous interest flared almost instantaneously in his charcoal optical orbs as he took notice of Sonia, and the dark expression on his countenance morphed into one of unmitigated lust.

"Beast fights," Kane replied, not so rapidly he sounded overeager, but prompt enough so it didn't seem as though he was searching for a genuine reason to be on these premises unauthorized.

Gunman nodded his shaggy head once, clamping his lips around the cigarette butt and inhaling deeply, the end of the stick glowing bright orange for a second, and then he ran his eyes over the trio once more, letting a momentary, but uncomfortable silence cloak the scene.

"What y'all doing out here? Entrance be round the other side, this here's the back. Y'all trying to sneak your asses in without parting with dollars or some shit?"

"Not at all," Sonia was quick to interject, feeling compelled to do so, even though Kane obviously had designs on responding in a similar fashion. "We have the money for the entrance fees."

"Good to know. Still don't tell me shit about why you're wandering around all furtive-like and shit out here, round the wrong side," the Gunman grunted, skepticism still lurking in his tone.

"We don't know the area," Kane said. "Got a little lost out there, figured we'd park and just try to find it on foot."

"Lucky y'all got old Dirk on watch out here then, someone else will be liable to knock your ass out or put a coupla slugs in all y'all asses and drag y'all inside for bait meat."

"Bait meat?" Sonia echoed, not enjoying those connotations.

"Yup." Dirk nodded emphatically and another portion of ash fell from his smoke, breaking up into dusty particles and dispersing as it dropped. "Bait meat. Reckon they'd keep you for somethin' else beforehand though."

This in particular was addressed to Sonia, accompanied by a more sleaze-ridden stare, with unconcealed lust plain in the charcoal eyes.

"Let's get down to business," Kane spoke up, his tone sharp.

The corridor Dirk lead them down was as dimly lit and cloistered in shadows as the warehouse entity he'd bailed them up in outside, lined by rows and rows of grimy little cages, each one containing a host of random animals like chickens and rodents, giving vent to a panicked assortment of sounds as the entourage passed. The air was thick with a fetid odor, a rancid combination of blood, shit and undetermined foulness, and though Sonia felt dirty enough from the lecherous gropings Dirk had been sure to give her while frisking each prospective customer before taking their entrance fees and allowing them access, just being in here made her feel filthier still, as if the abhorrent stench was seeping into the pores of her skin.

"Bait meat," Dirk told them unprompted, malevolent glee in his voice. "This is where y'all mighta ended up. Locked up in some damn shit stinkin' cages waitin' to get tossed into the ring to stir up some hungry fuckin' critters. Y'mighta gotten a few chunks taken out of ya before ya get your ass pulled out, but ya might still be alive. Depends how hungry or quick whichever breed of beasts are set to duke it out y'know. Can't let them get too much otherwise it'll take the edge offa that hunger, and a fed beast is a lazy beast. Ain't worth shit for fightin' and well, the punters don't pay good coin to see no 'gator or no tiger or fuckin' what-have-you sleepin' on the job."

Involuntarily, Sonia shuddered, the words slithering from Dirk's mouth only enhancing that horrific grimy feel, splattering gruesome images across the screen of her mind.

It was darker still where he next led them, trooping in silence broken only by his infrequent commentary, which was relayed with sick relish. Sonia tried not to look visibly ill, while Glenn bought into it for the purposes of keeping up appearances, and Kane added monosyllabic responses, remaining mostly taciturn.

Here there were no cages, the walls were lined with undefined enclosures and shrouded in darkness it was impossible to gauge what lay within. As they trailed down the center of a narrow walkway, a soundtrack of fearsome growling noises could be heard reverberating around the place, hideous snarls, grunts and other animalistic sounds which further set Sonia's nerves on edge and chilled her blood.

"Some of the combatants," Dirk grinned, tossing a glance at his companions, looking like some freakish corpse painted clown with the shadows crawling around his visage. "They all sound mighty fired up, dontcha reckon? Ready to rip and tear, crush bones, fuckin' bite chunks outta one another. And any fucker thinking he's got the stones to match it with them."

Abruptly, they ran out of the hall, the unidentified beasts in their well-covered compounds left back behind them, and Sonia realised Dirk's journey ended at a simple door, the smoking lecher with a thirst for bloody tales coming to a halt.

"Here's where I love ya and leave ya, folks. Get my ass back to make sure ain't no other motherfuckers trying to catch the show without shellin' out. Hope you are goin' to toss your hat into the ring in there," he directed at Glenn. "I might be inclined to put a coupla bucks on you takin' out a bear, maybe puttin' up a fight against a big cat or somethin'. Be too easy, you takin' the soft route so many do and pickin' another fella to tangle with, so I'm hopin' you go the man versus beast choice."

Then he turned his attention to Sonia, offering up his sleaziest grin yet.

"As for you, sweetcheeks, well, if blood n' guts n' wild animals tearing the fuckin' shit outta one another or wild men doing the same shit, or men takin' it to the beasts or getting' themselves ripped to hamburger meat, any of that shit gets your sexy panties all wet, you be sure to bring your hot snatch out and look up old Dirk. I'll be fixin' to scratch your itch, no sweat."

Fighting the urge not to vomit, Sonia mustered up a curt nod.

"I'll keep that in mind."

"Make sure ya do, I'll be sure to keep myself hard for ya," Dirk sniggered and then swung open the door. Then his voice was all business again as he added a final statement. "Once you're in there, ain't no getting' out until the show is over. Shit all goes on lockdown at hal' past eight on the nose. Ain't no motherfucker getting in or out. So, y'all got any last minute change of heart, speak now or forever hold your dicks. Or your snatch, darlin'. But any refund will only be fifty per cent of what you paid, best remember that."

"No. We're good," Kane said succinctly. Sonia said nothing, not in a rush to be inside this house of horrors Dirk spoke of so gleefully, but desperate to be away from the degenerate eye-fucking her.

"We're here for the…blood, guts and fucking mayhem," Glenn put in and Dirk nodded once more, his cigarette now a defunct butt hanging on his lip. He spat it out and then pushed the door open wider, a rush of crowd noise blasting out as he did.

"That's what I figured. Nice doin' business with ya. Listen up to what the boss has ta say in there. Enjoy the fuckin' show."

***

If Sonia was expecting some dingy, filth-encrusted, blood-stained, dark cesspit for the beast battles to take place, with standing room only as sweating, swearing drunken hoodlums circled and shouted obscene encouragement, she was dead wrong.

Instead, she and her companions walked into an enormous viewing arena which almost defied description.

It was as if the MMA Octagon and the Thunderdome from *Mad Max* had engaged in a ménage à trois with a baseball stadium, the sporty fuckfest resulting in one of them being impregnated with some conjoined triplet offspring that was a bastard hybrid of all three participants.

An enormous dome-shaped cage structure separated the arena below, around which rows of seats marched, ascending from ringside front row to the top tier many levels up, and though there were a scattering of available seats in various places, for the most part, the stadium--Sonia could dredge up no better word for it--was almost full to capacity.

Rather than the sorts of leering thugs and criminal brutes she suspected would be in the majority in attendance, a massive cross-section of folks assembled in loud, jabbering, hooting, cat-calling hordes. Sonia was appalled to see how many women were present. A large number of girls, either topless with just thong bottoms or other forms of lingerie floated around serving drinks to the seated punters, or those that stood around in throngs down near the giant structure over the ring. But it wasn't these women which left Sonia aghast, it was those who formed part of the paying crowd.

They weren't trashy females, rough looking broads, or gangsters molls, redneck loudmouths or overly made up trampy sorts, but what one might have considered upper class society folk or business women, clad for the most part in conservative suits or demure outfits, yet their carrying on and loud abrasive voices put them on par with the rest of their spectator companions.

There were indeed plenty of the rougher folks Sonia expected to see, but what astounded her was the number of everyday ordinary looking people she'd pass by on the street and think nothing more of, who wouldn't warrant a second glance.

Almost directly opposite where Kane led her and Glenn to available seats, albeit positioned a little higher up, was something she supposed was a private viewing booth, a corporate box of sorts, segregated from the remainder of the seats. In it were a small knot of people, most of them seated.

One, however, was standing up, staring out over the arena and the large crowd, a smug smile of satisfaction adorning his visage. He was a towering individual, broad-shouldered and physically impressive; with his clean cut appearance, strangely boyish good looks and neat attire, he might have been incredibly handsome, except Sonia knew without a doubt that this man was the compère of the heinous event which was to take place here, the master of ceremonies, the emperor of exotic animal death matches, overseeing his kingdom with smarmy pride.

Those in the box with him were the typical thuggish henchmen folk on a par with dirty Dirk outside the back door, but this smiling sociopath considered himself a deity elevated above all of them, and all those he held in thrall in the stadium below. His hands were not visible, perhaps clasped behind his back.

Dirk must have delayed them outside, almost to the point of cut off and lock down time, whilst searching them for weapons, for it seemed like no sooner had Kane found them seats he considered suitable and the three of them were seated when the Compère of Cruelty brought his hands out from behind his back, revealing a microphone.

"Welcome!" His voice resonated throughout the arena in a deep boom, and a crescendo of applause populated by loud cheers and whistles greeted it. He politely waited it out, then resumed speaking as the expectant crowd let the rapturous noise subside.

"I am your host, Enrique Hovato. Welcome to the Underground Beast Bloodsports--the premier event in showcasing exotic wildlife dueling to the death-and, of course, the bloodiest, which is what all you good folk out there are here for! Naturally, we aren't the only players in the world of such niche entertainment. Any fool with a mind to make money can round up a bunch of knuckleheads with more greed than fear. Any idiot can figure out ways to attain exotic dangerous animals from all around the globe, throw them together and have other sanguinary sickos lay down dollars or place bets on the outcome. But here, we go above and beyond those rudimentary means."

Enrique paused again, as once more the assemblage erupted in a stentorian roar of approval. Clearly, plenty of these gathered souls were either frequent visitors or highly eager onlookers, keen for the bloodshed and violence to begin. He then held up a hand for silence, his thug posse milling behind him.

"Yes, we do command a high entry fee. We expect that entertainment of this quality is to be paid for accordingly--after all, we risk life and limb to bring it to you. Yes, there are bets involved, but, of course, that is where you too, can walk out of here far more affluent than you walked in. It's true you've made me wealthy, but aside from enjoying the finest in the world's deadliest creatures at their most aggressive and lethal, you as well can make yourselves wealthy with some smart decisions and choices here. And, of course, what else sets us apart from your run of the mill 'smurfing' venture is the fact that we cater to fantasies.

"Yes, that's right. We fulfill fantasies. For those who may be first timers here, let me explain. Not only will you witness animal upon animal brawls to the death- and to the victor the spoils- you will see man upon man trying to do likewise to one another. Meat for the winning beast, and a pot of gold to the winning man. And now, the fantasy part. All you lot out there who fancy yourselves as pretty rough and tumble sorts, ever entertained thoughts of wrestling a bear, fancied tangling with some breed of big cat? Ever thought, well shit, I'm a big man, I reckon I would like to punch the fuck out of a silverback gorilla? Well, here...here is the place you can do it. And before you start clamouring to get a piece of some beast and trying to collect a fat wallet, just hold your horses until a little later, there's plenty of time. We've already got a few standard events to kick off proceedings. So, without further ado, let the Bloodsports commence!"

**

What Hovato referred to as 'standard events' were anything but to Sonia.

Despite the crowd baying for the expected exotic beast clashes, the first scheduled exhibition featured two human combatants.

As the pair of them emerged one by one out of a tunnel that led out into the arena from below the towering corporate box, accompanied by entourages, from another entrance a scantily clad blonde woman perched on blood red high heels wheeled out a tarpaulin draped trolley which she pushed to the very centre of the arena before whipping the shroud off with a flourish. Sonia realised it was some revolving dumbwaiter, a lazy susan which contained a frightening array of bladed weapons and bludgeoning implements, devices to maim, inflict serious injury, and kill.

Taking the discarded tarpaulin away with her, the undressed blonde women exited the scene, leaving the strange weapons carrier spinning in the centre while the two prospective combatants stalked in their opposing corners, shucking off outer garments and flexing muscles. These two were exactly the type Sonia thought would have been outnumbering the rest of the audience; big brawny brutes with massive impressive physiques comprised of sheer muscle.

Being an old action movie tragic, she automatically likened both of them to actors. One of them, a dark skinned fellow with a closely trimmed shave of hair, was Carl Weathers; the other, a bristle-faced, unruly looking slugger, reminded her of Randall "Tex" Cobb.

Dancing around on the balls of his feet, his skin dusky and packed with muscular promised violence, Carl adopted a martial arts stance. Randall shuffled like a barroom brawler, arms swinging loosely at his sides, the pair of them trash talking and staring daggers at each other. Then all entrance gates were slammed shut, sealing them both in, and though there was no official word that this was the start of the bout, both men wasted no time in launching at one another.

Neither immediately went for the deadly dumbwaiter doing remarkably fast revolutions in the arenas middle; soon enough, Sonia figured out why. The weapon-laden creation was controlled via remote by Hovato in his armchair corporate box, who at his whim could alter the speed, change the direction it travelled, or any number of things to mess with the fighters whenever they might attempt to snatch something hazardous to their opponent's health.

The duo traded blows to begin with, keeping things as if it were just some standard MMA free for all, grappling, punching, throwing in kicks, but then it all descended into true bloodsport with escalated violence supreme. Despite the best efforts of Hovato, amusing himself with the remote control, Randall got his meaty fingers to a cleaver handle and snatched it off the spinning implement holder.

Though both men were bloodied, with swollen eye sockets, claret dripping noses and gouges out of their faces from bruising knuckles and boots, Carl looked the worst, his martial arts stance surprisingly proving unsuccessful against Randall's backwoods brawling. Until Randall saw his ability to seize a weapon from the dumbwaiter first as his ride home to the jackpot.

He struck with the bladed tool, but sloppily, over-confident, not priming for a killer blow. Carl, wavering on his feet, blinking through a blood haze, still managed to deflect the thrust with an arm, and the blade sheared into a giant bicep, cutting off a hunk of meat that didn't quite come free, but hung, flapping like a raw steak as blood gouted.

By then, Carl was armed with his own weapon, an Arkansas toothpick dagger, grabbed in desperation with the hand he wasn't trying to fend off Randall with. He didn't squander the window of opportunity presented, but stabbed Randall dead in the throat with it. The bearded brawler took a handful of erratic stabs in a backwards direction, one sideways and then sprawled in a bleeding collapse.

While the triumphant figure of Carl grandstanded, celebrating his victory in a bizarre dance, holding one hand high while the other flopped at his side, seemingly oblivious to the ragged meat slice flopping off it, a throng of Hovato's lackeys were quick to re-enter the blood-spattered ground and drag Randall's carcass away…

'To become bait meat,' Sonia shuddered, feeling physically sick, nausea and sheer horror threatening to take total control of her.

It didn't get any better after that.

***

"Anybody ready for Chimp Norris?" Hovato boomed into his microphone, malicious glee evident in his voice and the ensuing deafening response indicated to Sonia that whoever-or whatever-the smarmy death-dealing UBB kingpin spoke of was well renowned.

As more of Enrique's goon squad materialised, almost even before others had escorted the battered but triumphant Carl from the arena to parts unknown, they brought forth a large cage situated on wheels. Inside hunched a massive hairy black shape which Sonia at first couldn't identify, until those bringing it out began to antagonise it by jabbing it with cruel spiked implements, banging the bars, intending to rile it up and make it supremely aggressive.

She soon saw it was a large male chimpanzee, a fully grown adult male, intensely battle scarred and marked with old healed wounds, missing patches of hair here and there. One eye drooped as if some severe bite from another beast had rendered muscles around it useless and the ear on the opposing side of the ape's head had an ugly chunk taken from it. Quite evidently, Chimp Norris, along with being an actual chimp, was a veteran of the Underground Beast Bloodsports, and from the looks of him, one who'd survived some horrible battles.

Once they had the cage clear of the entrance, the host of tormentors enraging Norris inside beat a hasty retreat as the huge misshapen beast growled and screeched angry incantations, skittering from side to side, engaging in threatening displays that promised great violence to those antagonists. A couple remained with the cage in order to get the door open, but they had the foresight to get on top of the cage, which consisted of a plain steel roof with no bars Norris could reach through to snatch at them.

Norris wasn't tardy in escaping from the cage; once the two lackeys left atop it had his door opened, and they, in return, were prompt to get the hell out of there, back behind the cage.

As Norris emerged, in a highly agitated state, the crowd noise hit the roof in volume and before the chimp could be left alone in the arena too long, more of the entrances around the rough circular shape of the arena disgorged occupants. Not one, not two or three, but four opponents were unleashed into the dome with the capering aggressive Norris. They came in almost simultaneously in equally belligerent states.

"Jesus Christ!" Glenn hissed in a sharp intake of breath from the other side of Kane.

The combatants released into the ring were all massive dogs, but none of them ordinary canines, they were all animals largely banned in their respective countries for a number of reasons.

There was a Gull Dong--an off white coloured beast as equally scarred and scored with old ragged wounds from numerous previous scraps, a snarling ferocious animal with lips peeled back from its teeth--coming in alongside another white entity, this one a Dogo Argentino stalking in on stiff legs.

From the other side of the ring came a Presa Canario, the tan brute looking like a tank on legs, its massive head atop a giant neck and barrel chest a weapon within itself and with it was another banned breed, a Filo Brasileiro, towering above the other canines.

"Oh my god..." Sonia murmured, not entirely sure what sort of other opponents Norris had been forced to tangle with in the past, but pretty certain that this time was going to be the war-torn chimp's final stand in the UBB.

Then she acknowledged that the lazy susan of weaponry, brought out for the bout between Carl and Randall, had not been removed from the ring. And as all four of the snarling fearsome dogs began to stalk in towards Norris, the chimp proved that he'd learned plenty of skills during his tenure in this bloody battlefield of sick entertainment.

Rather than exert any superior strength his compact body of muscles might have possessed, the wily ape went straight for the dumbwaiter. As the two white dogs broke rank and launched their attack first, the feral Gull Dong led the assault, fangs bared to rip the chimp asunder.

As Sonia watched in disbelief, Norris snatched up a gleaming machete in one paw and a straight metal spike that looked like a shortened javelin. The Gull Dong came in a snarling, slavering onslaught, lunging with big paws outstretched. Norris thrust the spike straight into the beasts' chest, piercing deep and spraying blood. In the same chain of movement, Norris hacked at the Dogo with his machete, the razor sharp steel edge of the blade causing maximum damage, meaty pieces sliced right off.

By then the bloodscent was thick in the air and the two brindled canines behind sprang into the fray, huge muscular bodies and crushing jaws driving into both Norris and the bloodied forms of their supposed team mates, spraying crimson gore like a hideous fountain high.

Sonia could barely tell what was occurring; the whole scene was painted in gore red, as if the death tangle of combatants were being drenched in a horrible rain of blood and illogically, Slayer's "Raining Blood" looped inanely in her brain. When the red mist cleared to some extent, pattering all across an already comprehensively bloodslick arena courtesy of Carl and Randall's brutal slugging and bladed assaults on one another, all four canines were deceased and partially dismembered. The battered and bitten Norris was looking the worse for wear, having been mauled by the brindle canines before he managed to gain an upper hand, but he was alive, still the reigning king of his domain.

As the sanguinary sickos, the thugs, the demurely dressed business women, the nondescript souls with forgettable faces all roared demented approval, Norris picked through the entrails and remains of the bodies left strewn across the ground, selecting delicacies for himself.

Hunching forward so her head was virtually between her knees, Sonia valiantly struggled not to heave up every content of her stomach, while beside her, Kane stared straight at the scene, his face impassive, the only sign of his escalating fury and horror a pulsing vein on the side of his head.

More atrocities followed in a grotesque torrent of brutal images that seared their way into Sonia's brain with such indelible horror she doubted she would ever sleep properly again.

More animals pitched against animals, the types of exotic beast that should be roaming free in wild environments, not enslaved and forced to duel to bloody death with unnatural enemies. Crocodiles matched against big cats, snakes against snakes, more money-hungry men bashing one another senseless before one seized the opportunity to end the life of the other. And more optimistic, foolhardy men who chose to confront the lethal animals in Hovato's twisted menagerie.

Sonia witnessed a giant of a man die, his skull crushed by a leopard he was certain he could nullify with a pick axe. Another narrowly escaped a feral boar, managing to snare a bloodslick discarded weapon from one of the previous bouts long enough to kill the antagonistic pig.

Finally, Hovato's voice boomed again, tearing through the lull in violence that happened after the porcine slayer, his legs ripped to ribbons by massive tusks, was taken from the slaughtergrounds of the arena.

"And now is the time I present the opportunity for some game souls out there in the audience to stick up their hand for a chance at fame and fortune. As most of these bouts here have been prearranged sometime beforehand with those fortunate--or perhaps unfortunate--fellows getting in early for the chance to bring you prime entertainment, and yes, occasionally die in the process, now I provide a chance for you too to be immortalised in the UBB."

Before it was even ascertained whether Hovato was finished speaking or not, Kane stood up so quickly his motion left a rush of air swirling around Sonia. She'd been clutching Kane's left hand so tightly throughout each violent display, begging him to do something to halt the brutality, that crescent moons of indentations were left on the skin of his extremity and as he straightened rapidly, her nails inadvertently dragged lines of fiery pain along his skin.

A whole bunch of others also stood, fat, sweaty, beer-bellied slobs who fancied their chances, undeterred by the lopsided results for humans down there in the ring, against creatures or other humans, but Hovato overlooked all of them, his attention captivated by the blur of motion from Kane.

"Get that man a mic," Hovato ordered, gesturing directly at Kane, and Sonia felt her heart leapfrog once more. It was coming, the climax of their harrowing expedition here to this underworld of violent brutality and exotic animal exploitation.

One of the goon squad materialised alongside them, thrusting a microphone over Glenn's bulky shoulder and into Kane's hand, and as he raised it to speak, Hovato's voice sounded again, tinged with a mocking tone.

"So, you were up in the blink of an eye there, sir. Even after witnessing what sort of carnage and chaos can ensue down there in the ring, you fancy yourself a chance at snatching fame and fortune from the jaws of death?"

"Absolutely," Kane snapped out brusquely, anger rolling off him so tangibly Sonia could almost feel it coming in waves. "And I want to compete against the most dangerous, bestial, brutal creature inside these walls."

"Well, you sure as hell do have tickets on yourself, my good man. Seeing all of this bloody destruction and trail of broken bodies, man and beast alike, has done nothing to temper your desire to take on one of my magnificent animal warriors?"

"Not a chance. But I'm not talking about any of your poor abused animals, you sick fuck, I'm talking about *you*. The biggest beast right here, that heinous fiend I refer to is none other than you, Hovato. And yes, I'm aware that your appropriated surname means 'Brute'. It's a most apt one. You, and no other man, no helpless animal pushed to the limit and made to attack, are the only soul I seek to face in the ring."

***

They stood facing off in the blood-stained ring, sanguinary splatter spreading right from the centre where the lazy susan of weaponry still revolved out to every edge.

Seeing Hovato standing out in full view, Sonia could see now how much he dwarfed Kane in stature, virtually the same size as her monstrous companion Glenn. He shucked off his neat shirt and tie and revealed a physique so packed with rippling muscles it looked hard enough to repel bullets.

Scars adorned him, just as they had many of the animals and the men who'd battled tonight, and while initially he'd been taken aback by Kane's brazen request, it was evident that he too had seen many a man or creature die by his hand in this very arena and he wore the war wounds proudly. He was no stranger to bloody victory and the challenge by the audacious upstart was too tempting to pass up. Slaughtering a man and spilling his blood with that of countless others would be a fitting culmination to a most brutal evening of entertainment.

He didn't waste time though, perhaps impatient to be done with this pesky intrusion on his grand show, and unlike the other men who sought to pummel each other before attaining blades or bludgeoning implements to destroy each other, Hovato went straight for the weapons. After all, with him in the ring, nobody was changing directions or fucking around with it to foil the combatants.

And as Sonia and Glenn watched, morbidly mesmerised by what they knew was coming, Kane changed.

It wasn't any subtle or gradual transformation, it was a virtual explosion of flesh, a gory blast of skin bursting and blood fountaining and then pouring down in a reverential rain over the source of it. From the shattered flesh shell of Kane came a monstrous bristling beast that defied real description, all curved black claws, gaping red maw lined with wicked razor fangs, coal black eyes with an eerie red slit of a pupil, and a massive shovel shaped head that made the canine craniums of Chimp Norris' dog opponents look miniscule.

For all their bravado and chest thumping as they watched the slaughter of previous fights unfold, the cowardly crowd erupted in a soundtrack of piercing screams, shocked exclamations and utter terror as they witnessed this most shocking moment occur.

"A fucking werewolf!" A panicked voice screamed alongside Glenn and Sonia, and Sonia turned her head, unable to keep the smug pride from her voice. She picked up the microphone, discarded by Kane before he travelled down to the ring and raised it to her lips, her voice ringing out over the pandemonium in the crowd.

"No. He's not a werewolf, fools. He's a skinwalker. With the ability to morph into any beast of his choosing, including some that don't even exist in your simple little worlds. This isn't the first underground ring of animal brutality we've eradicated and it probably won't be the last. And sometimes, it takes a beast to bring down a beast. So, for all of you smart enough to run before he comes for you all, go ahead and try, but remember, nobody gets out until the show is over. Doors don't unlock until that ring is raised and that remote control Mister Hovato has been using there is the only device which can raise it. When, inevitably, the authorities come to clean up this mess, they'll suspect things went a little awry. Perhaps Hovato bit off more than he could chew, tangling with too many exotic animals...things went bad, really bad...animals got lose, into the audience. Terrible business indeed."

"So," Glenn chimed in. "While you're all here, why don't you sit back and enjoy the rest of the show. I promise you there isn't much left of it."

Down in the ring Kane ignored the desperate stabs of Hovato's useless bladed weapons, wearing them like nothing more than pieces of silver jewellery as his claws and teeth ripped the UBB boss apart in a bloody welter of raw flesh, flayed skin and cracking bone matter.

Then he left the scattered meat of Hovato's remains strewn across the arena and ascended into the screaming crowd.

About Jim Goforth

Jim Goforth is a horror author currently based in Holbrook, Australia. Happily married with two kids and a cat he has been writing tales of horror since the early nineties.

After years of detouring into working with the worldwide extreme metal community and writing reviews for hundreds of bands across the globe with Black Belle Music, he returned to his biggest writing love with his first book, *Plebs*, published by J. Ellington Ashton Press. His most recent release is a collection of short stories/novellas, With Tooth and Claw

He has also appeared in *Axes of Evil* and *Axes of Evil 2*, *Terror Train, Rejected For Content: Splattergore, Rejected for Content 2: Aberrant Menagerie, Autumn Burning: Dreadtime Stories For the Wicked Soul, Floppy Shoes Apocalypse*, the collaborative novel *Feral Hearts*, and will be seen next in the likes of *Teeming Terrors, Ghosts: An Anthology of Horror From the Beyond*, and another full length novel, *Undead Fleshcrave: The Zombie Trigger*.

He is currently writing the follow-up to *Plebs*.

Daughters in White
By Justin Hunter

Chapter – 1 The Encircling Forest

The fair haired youth ran along the dusky woodland, careful not to tread too close to the dense poplar trees that encircled the town like a ramparts. She wasn't aware of anyone who'd been snatched away unless they actually went into the woods, but she was bright enough to be aware of the nagging pull of curiosity, that singular handicap she shared with all children her age, and stayed away. Nobody she knew had ever gone through those surrounding trees, but there were stories of those that did, and they always ended the same; long screams, cracking sounds, low laughter and then silence. The person was never to be seen again. These were the types of stories that the village elders told the children before they lay down to sleep. She heard nothing of happily ever after. There was only the warning: Stay away from the forest.

The woods would have been frightening enough even without those stories. The tree line was so dense that even the perfect light of day would only allow the viewer a few feet of view into the forest. Screams there were, maybe only in her mind, but she thought she could hear voices coming from far off, tormented and long; souls lost from ages past who dwelt there, waiting for someone daft enough to venture away from the safety of the warm, simple village homes. Cindy didn't know that there was anything beyond her small village. Only a few thousand strong, hearty people called it home and didn't even bother to give it a name. There didn't seem to be a reason to.

A roiling rose in Cindy's belly, not of hunger, but unease. She wasn't supposed to be out at night. Nobody was. But she felt a need to go out to the barn. There were several barns in the village, and all were used to store up food for the winter- save one. If she had told anyone that she was going to 'the barn' they would know exactly the one she was talking about. It was the one that held the girls, including her sister Joan, whom she was wanting to see. She missed her sister dearly, but had kept most of her grief to herself, nobody would be very empathetic to her woe. It was the way of things in the village for young girls, and many had lost family along the way. The way of life in the town was almost a religion and to speak against it, even with very real feelings from loss, would make the elders shut her up and fast. Joan had been dead now for almost two years. Cindy couldn't believe it had been that long since her sister's choosing.

Joan had been only fourteen years old when she was chosen. It was a rare thing, but most people understood why. Joan was an exceptional beauty and many believed that she would make the perfect daughter-in-white. Cindy had turned fourteen this year and tomorrow would be her first Maypole ceremony. All the young girls ages fourteen to twenty had to take their place among the choosing. After that they could live out the rest of their lives in the small village in relative peace. They could find a husband, raise children, and do work that was delegated to them by the high elders. Life was simple, yet good.

Cindy, lost in her reverie, bumped into the current daughter-of-white, and fell on her rump. The girl was only a couple of years older than she was, but it was like running into a petrified tree. Cindy brushed off her clothing, hoping against hope that she hadn't stained anything lest it give away her night wanderings to her parents.

"Please, forgive me," Cindy said, her voice trembling due to her surprise at seeing someone out when she was. "I wasn't watching where I was going." The current daughter-in-white said nothing. That didn't surprise her, for they never did. She just looked at Cindy, or rather through Cindy, with deeply sunken eyes the color of the clear sky. "Sarah?" Cindy ventured, for that was the daughter-in-white's name. She had been friends with Sarah before her choosing, but you couldn't be friends with a girl after they were selected. It wasn't that you couldn't try, but talking to the daughter-in-white was frowned upon beyond very basic small talk, which was never returned. Cindy wasn't surprised at seeing the daughter-in-white walking about at night, because they walked about all the time. They wandered around the village the whole year long, never eating or drinking anything, at least not that Cindy had ever seen. They moved about like ghosts until the next choosing. Then the last daughter-in-white would end up in the barn like her sister, Joan. Then the next girl was chosen and the whole process repeated itself. It always had been this way and always would be. It was just the way it was.

Cindy clasped her hands respectfully behind her back and waited for Sarah to stop staring at her and move on. A part of Cindy wanted to follow her and see what happened to the daughter-in-white on the last day of her chosen year. She wanted to know who put them in the barn and how they could stay so still. She wanted to know why they looked so very much alive even though they most assuredly were dead. A person cannot stand somewhere, day in and day out, with no sustenance, in complete silence and not be dead, at least this is what Cindy told herself. It was only logical.

In the end, she let Sarah wander off on her own way. Cindy was of a mind to see her sister before her first choosing ceremony and she usually kept to her task, even if there were a few tangents that stole her interests along the way. She was nervous about the morrow and maybe just seeing her sister would make her feel better. Cindy quickened her pace and got to the barn when the moon was at its height. The barn was two stories tall and had no windows. The building was one of the oldest in the village. Every few years a select group of men would mend and paint the structure, which was then roped off in every direction to keep nosey people from peeking in at the barn's contents. It was said that nobody had ever seen inside the barn, but that wasn't true. Everyone had seen inside the barn. It was a rite of passage of childhood to look inside the barn. There was a board on the Southeast corner of the barn that was loose on one end. All a person had to do was pull back slightly on that board at the corner and it would pop out on one side and move easily up or down like the big hand on the clock.

Cindy was at this board now. The wood was well-worn and two deep scrapes marred the wood above and below the plank where it had been lifted or lowered by generations of curious children, and even some adults. It would have been quick work to secure the board so that nobody could look in, but the unspoken consensus was that allowing people to take a peek, even though outwardly forbidden, was a natural thing for curious humans and would keep others from breaking into the building in more damaging ways.

Cindy pulled the corner of the plank out from the wall. It came loose without a sound, but was so heavy in her hands that she almost dropped it. What the board did was make a loud scraping noise as the uneven sides scraped together. She lowered the board end as gently as possible and waited for a full minute in the silence, listening for anyone who would come up on her and ask her what she was doing at the barn after dark. The thought of being caught by an adult was scary, but not as scary as Cindy's thoughts about her noise awakening one of the daughters-in-white in the barn. She couldn't decide which was worse, but the thought soon wandered away. There was no noise in the night. She leaned in to take a peek. A fire burned in a large pit in the center of the barn, which was always kept burning by Sven the mongoloid.

The walls of the barn were lined with wooden shelves that ran every five feet, all the way around the barn, and continued up to the edge of the roofline. Harnessed to these walls, standing ram-rob straight, side-by-side, were the daughters-in-white. They filled the barn halfway. They all wore the same frilly white dress that looked too girlish for the chosen ones who were just in the beginning stages of adulthood. The old seamstress, Agnes Ray, was in charge of the daughter-in-white's clothes. Her mother sewed them before her and it was certain that the job would be passed down to her own daughter, Scarlet, who was nearing fifty years old herself.

The queer thing about the girls was that they never aged. Each had a porcelain doll appearance to them. Their skin didn't have the healthy ruddy glow that a young girl's should. It was nearly white, almost matching their dresses. Their eyes didn't seem right to Cindy either. They were sunken deep into the sockets, almost matching the very old or mongoloid members of the village. They would have been pretty, if it weren't for their mouths. Cindy wished that someone would close them. They hung open and taught at the corners as if in an unending scream.

Cindy knew her sister Joan right off. She was three rows up and dead center on the short side of the barn across from her. She was easy to spot because she was the last one to be placed in the barn. Her eyes were open and her mouth held the same terror as the other girls. Cindy even thought that she might be staring at her. She waved a little, but, of course, her sister didn't return the gesture. Many thoughts ran though Cindy's head as she stared at the chosen ones. She wondered if they felt any pain. She wondered what they had thought when they were chosen at the Maypole ceremony. She wondered if they could still see. She wondered why they didn't age. She had all these questions about what might happen to her, but she never dared to ask an elder these things. She never spoke to any of the other girls about them either, although she knew they must be wondering about the same things she was.

She picked up the heavy board and put the end back into place on the barn wall. She pushed with all her strength so that the board would look level with the rest and as untampered with as it always looked. She wiped away traces of dirt on the edge of the board and, satisfied with her efforts, decided it was time to go home. The last thing she wanted was to be caught out of bed.

"I miss you, Joan," Cindy whispered. She put her hand against the barn wall as if trying to comfort the body of her sister inside. She dropped her hand and wiped her bangs away from her forehead.

Just as she was about to turn, a heavy hand clamped down upon her shoulder, sending rivets of pain up her arm and into her neck. Another hand covered her face. It was so big that it covered her chin up to her forehead. The palm was warm and wet with sweat. She tried to scream, but only tasted salt from the palm of the hand that assaulted her. She panicked. She kicked her legs back, trying to strike her attacker, but it only seemed to amuse him. He laughed and picked her off her feet as easily as one would pluck a dandelion from the ground. He carried her away. Into the night.

Chapter 2 – At Home

Cindy hung limp in the man's iron grip as she was hauled at a limping gait through the village. She couldn't see or smell anything other than the man's musky skin scent, but by the way she moved quickly, she felt it was safe to assume that he wasn't taking her into the forest. When the man jostled her about as he kicked hardily at a door, she assumed the second worst place he could take her; back to her house. When she heard her mother scream as she opened the door, Cindy knew that she was in big trouble.

She felt the hands of her mother, thin with long scratchy nails, tear her away from the huge, hairy hands that gripped her. Her mother was shaking her so hard that Cindy could feel her brain banging back and forth inside her skull. Stars whirled around her vision when her mother finally stopped, dropping her carelessly to the ground. Cindy took a few deep breaths and held back the tears that wanted to run down her face. She didn't want to give her mother the satisfaction. Cindy looked behind her to see the mongoloid standing there, looking sheepish and baby-like although she knew he was at least double her own age.

The mongoloid wore nothing but a simple canvas shift that was belted around the waist by a thick leather belt. His face always wore a look of astonishment. His mouth hung open, and he breathed with thick wet breaths. His forehead was broad with ample bone structure that made his eyebrows stick out a full two inches farther than his eyes, making the lower half of his face always shaded. She found his face unimposing, but his size definitely was. The man stood over seven feet tall and Cindy realized, after taking a glimpse at his ham-sized hands, that she should have known right away who it was that grabbed her at the barn.

The mongoloid had been in charge of the bodies of the daughters-in-white since Cindy could remember. The elders told the children that it was always a mongoloid that watched over them. They were supposedly simple people, who could be taught the simple tasks of keeping the fire burning inside the barn and making sure nobody did any mischief to the girls inside. The elders once took a leather strap to Cindy's backside when she was four years old and asked if the mongoloid dusted the girls. Barns were a dusty place and the girls never seemed to move, although they looked so clean and neat. She quickly learned to keep innocent questions to herself, but even at the age of fourteen she still wondered if she had been right. The daughters-in-whites' mouths being open all the time bothered her as well. She was sure that spiders and other creepy crawlies would go inside the girls' mouths and that was just gross. She hoped that if she was chosen, that the mongoloid would make sure her mouth was closed. Some of Cindy's friends told her that they had seen them with their mouths closed, but she didn't believe them.

"Put her down, Marge," Her father had woken up and entered the room wearing nothing but the sheet he'd wrapped himself up in. "You're going to shake the brains right out of her head."

"I can't believe that she would go out in the middle of the night, to the barn, to gawk at the daughters! What if someone found her? She has her first ceremony tomorrow." Her mother was furious. Cindy thought that if she was so worried about her being found out, she might want to quiet down a bit or she'd wake up the whole village.

"Someone did find her," Her father said, gesturing to the mongoloid with a smile. "You won't tell anyone about this, will you?" The mongoloid shook his head and smiled back at Cindy's father. Cindy stared at the mongoloid's huge, straight white teeth. They looked strong enough to bite a tree trunk in half.

"See?" Her father said. "No harm done. I would expect that someone about to partake in their first choosing ceremony would have a hard time sleeping."

"What if she went in the woods?" Her mother seethed, she was unwilling to quickly forgive the close family scandal. "She could have been taken by *them*."

"Cindy's smart enough to stay away from the woods. Just not smart enough to stay inside at night. Now I'm going back to bed, you're coming with me, and Cindy is going to her room and won't leave this house again tonight. Clear?" Cindy's mother shot her husband an angry look, as if to tell him that this conversation wasn't over by a long shot. Cindy hurried past them both and went to her room. She heard the pantry door open and knew her mother was getting some food and drink to give to the mongoloid as a thank you for bringing her daughter home, as well as making sure to buy his silence.

Cindy lay awake in her bed long after she heard her mother and father settle down. She looked at the frilly white dress, a little young looking to be worn by a girl her age, which was hung against the back of her door. Tomorrow she would wear the dress and go to her first choosing, a thought that both excited and terrified her.

She rolled over on her side and looked out her open window.

Her home was close to the encircling trees and they loomed dark and heavy before her. The wind was picking up outside, she thought there might even be a storm. Through the wind Cindy thought she heard the unmistakable sound of little girls screaming.

"It's only the wind," She told herself and hugged the covers closer.

Chapter – 3 The Mongoloid

Sarah, the current daughter-in-white, walked along the tree line near the barn. Her clothing clung to her body from the palpable mist. The fog was becoming denser, until it was like walking through a cloud. Sarah was barefoot, her shoes had worn away several months ago. The skin of her feet was calloused and tough as leather. The night air was cold and the dew cast an even deeper chill, but Sarah didn't shiver. She didn't seem to feel at all. She reached out her hand and ran it along the line of trees and circled the town. Her hand made a dull slap on each wet trunk, the rough bark leaving small scratches on her palm.

The soundless woods came alive with the pattering of feet along the foot deep bed of leaves within the forest. The steps came closer to the girl as she tread her same simple pace, slapping each tree as if she were signaling that she was ready for something. The footsteps from within the woods were very loud now. They were gathered close together like a mass of people were coming together just beyond the tree line. Sarah stopped and turned to face the trees. The footsteps stopped as well.

The forest was so peculiar because of its soundlessness. Night is when the woods come alive with nocturnal hunters, scuttling small mammals, and millions of insects braying their singular songs. There was no noise here. These woods were cursed and no living creature other than the ones who dwelt there took refuge under the looming trees.

Sarah let out a high-pitched scream into the noiseless darkness. It was the first and only sound she had made in the last year since she had become a daughter-in-white. The sound resonated haltingly from her ill-used vocal chords. She sounded like a rabbit just bitten by a rattlesnake; shrill and chilling, but quickly surrendering to its fate.

Hands reached out from between the trees. Pale skinned hands, with dirty and cracked fingernails, groped and swiped in the darkness. So many hands, hundreds of them, searching for the newest member to dwell among them. They stretched along the tree line for fifty yards. Sarah looked small and vulnerable among the grabbing mass of flesh that reflected perfectly white off the light of the full moon. From near the top of the tree line came two impossibly long multi-jointed limbs. They were grey, with silvery long hair and covered with a hard exoskeleton flesh that glistened like it was sweating. At the end of those limbs were curved claws with serrated edges that clacked as they opened and closed as if of their own free will. These arms extended out of the woods and down around Sarah. The claws closed gently around her, slicing her dress but not tearing into her flesh.

Sarah went willingly as the giant spider-like arms picked her up thirty feet in the air and brought her above the trees, holding her image against the sky before it tore her quickly down and out of sight into the woods. The multitude of arms vanished. The only sounds were Sarah's screams, but these too were silenced before long. The sound of something like wet tearing came from behind the tree-line and then sucking, slurping sounds like someone greedily drinking the last bit of chocolate shake through a straw. Then all again was silence.

Hours later the hunched figure of the mongoloid walked to the entrance of the barn and opened the door to find what he was expecting. Sarah's body, looking just as perfect as she did a year ago when she was chosen, was lying on the ground. He gently picked up her body and walked toward the barn wall where the line of the daughters-in-white ended. He climbed up a stepladder, the girl held easily as if she weighed nothing, and he placed her next to Cindy's sister. He strapped white leather cords around her waist, ankles, neck and shoulders and nailed them to the wall to hold her in her place among the daughters from that time forth. If Cindy had been there watching him place the daughter-in-white among the others, she would have noticed that her mouth was closed. In fact, all of their mouths were closed.

The mongoloid, his task done, descended the ladder and went to the task of adding more wood to the fire.

It was a day of celebration. No work would be done that day that didn't have to do with the ceremony and most of those considerations had been taken care of in the weeks leading up to the yearly event. The Maypole was in place in the center of the village. It stood twenty feet in the air and was made from the wood of a tree that must have been long extinct. At least nobody knew what it was. The stark white color of the wood stood out against the sunlight so much that it almost hurt the eyes to look at. Long strands of cloth hung out from the pole and were staked to the ground to be used by the girls as they performed the dance of the choosing. These strands were of every color of the rainbow and chosen by the girls' mothers. The girls who would partake in the choosing had their names embroidered in gold on the cloth strands. Many of the older women would take these cloths and hang them up in their homes after they had become too old for the choosing. It was a matter of some shame to families who never had one of their girls chosen, but considering that there didn't seem to be any rhyme or reason for which girl was chosen except for beauty, this was considered shallow. Although, those families with multiple family members having been daughters-in-white held their heads up a little too high. Nothing indeed.

The girls had to go by themselves. All others were to remain in their homes. Their doors and window shut and locked. Stories of death persisted about those who ventured a peek during the choosing. The death was supposed to come instantly; sucking the soul of the curious and leaving nothing but a dried out hull of a body. The adults laughed at these stories, thinking them nothing but tales to frighten children, but they never peeked and were quick to strike any of their children who ventured too close to the window shutters.

The time for choosing had come. The girls left their homes. They moved by themselves at first, but then clung together in a protective clump as soon as they found each other. They went to the center of town, talking in hushed voices. Some girls giggled nervously. All fell silent when they saw the white tree trunk with its myriad of ribbons before them. They found their ribbons and curled them around their small hands. They pressed their dresses down and smoothed their hair. They waited until each girl had taken their strand of cloth. Like every year, there were no absences. As if on silent cue the girls began to walk in a circle.

The girls began to fall one by one. The fallen ones lay on the damp grass. Their eyes open but unseeing. Cindy tried not to look at them. She saw several of the others stutter step over the fallen ones. The air around them felt oppressive. It was as if fear itself lowered from the sky and clutched their shoulders. Cindy told herself that the fallen girls weren't dead. She knew that they would wake up when the choosing was over. She didn't look at them, the forest or the sky above. Although early, the sunlight was dying. The life giving globe of flame was becoming shrouded by another figure. A looming orb of blackness that sprouted with multi-jointed legs eclipsed the sun. Blackness flowed from its body, seeming to kill the sky wherever it touched. Cindy kept her eyes forward as she watched the other girls fall. She walked, stepping on the bodies of the other girls as she did. There were so many of them. She wondered how long she would have to walk with the demon above her. She wondered when blessed sleep would take her away like the others.

Cindy felt many limbs gently lift her up into the air. She looked down, wondering if there were any other girl that still walked to take her place. She saw them all on the ground and knew she had been chosen. Soon she would walk the village as a living dead reminder of the promise which saved and damned them all. Soon she would line the walls of the barn like the other chosen. The appendages that held her deftly turned her around. She faced the demon in the sky. Its maw was open, dripping and longing. Cindy kept her eyes open wanting every last glimpse of life as she had it. Her eyes never closed again.

About Justin Hunter

Justin Hunter has five published novels. JWK fiction has published his dark fiction novel, Nostalgia. Severed Press has published the black horror comedy series *Chet & Floyd vs. the*

Apocalypse: Volumes 1 and 2, and *Takaashigani: a Deep Sea Thriller*. J Ellington Ashton Press will be releasing Justin's novel, The Book of Titus, in 2015. MorbidbookS released the novel *What's Eating Keegan the Vegan* in 2015. Justin Hunter has also been published in several anthologies. Anthology publishing houses include Emby Press, Strangehouse Books, JWK Fiction, NoodleDoodle Publications, and Great Old Ones Publishing. Mr. Hunter is also an ongoing contributing author to the flash horror anthology *Demonic Visions* series.